THE HONOURABLE

COLONIAL

POLICEMAN

John P. F. LYNCH

Published by John P F Lynch
Copyright © John P F Lynch 2025

Lynch, John
The Honourable Colonial Policeman

ISBN 978-0-6489446-6-9 (pbk)
ISBN 978-0-6489446-7-6 (e-book)

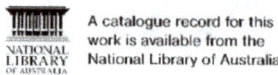

A catalogue record for this
work is available from the
National Library of Australia

Typeset Bookman Old Style 12pt

Produced by **TB Books**
      P.O. Box 8138
      Seymour South Victoria 3660
      Email: tbbooks@collings.id.au

Cover design by Betty Maher

Contents

FOREWORD v

INTRODUCTION.. vii

CHAPTER ONE
An Expatriate 9

CHAPTER TWO
The New Inspector 33

CHAPTER THREE
The New Arrivals.. 79

CHAPTER FOUR
Another Emigrant 113

CHAPTER FIVE
The Highwaymen 125

CHAPTER SIX
Quick Justice 145

CHAPTER SEVEN
The Assassin 158

CHAPTER EIGHT
Testing Times 168

CHAPTER NINE
The Prodigals Return 182

CHAPTER TEN
The Final Chase.. 225

EPILOGUE 261

NOTES 263

THE AUTHOR 265

OTHER BOOKS.. 267

FOREWORD

Over several decades of a working life as a wordsmith in a variety of roles ranging from government scribe to diarist to one who writes for relaxation and the pleasure of recording family history for a future reader, I have crossed paths with many people who have shared my passion and enjoyed an interesting life as a part-time author.

John Lynch is one such person but, unlike me, he has created stories and a readership of a discerning young audience that hopefully will influence some to become the next generation of writers. This latest nove, in a series of rollicking good yarns will be enjoyed by all who read it.

Writing, particularly in the form of storytelling, requires an imagination that is capable of capturing the attention of those who read for relaxation. John has shown that he has the talent to cast a wide net of appeal and to exploit a life of varied experiences that should see him writing on for many years.

With that in mind it has given me great pleasure to write this foreword to his latest novel, which is bound to bring pleasure to those who have travelled with him by way of his earlier stories.

Darrell S. Horton
Political Scribe

INTRODUCTION

The early days of settlement in the Australian colonies were greatly influenced by the calibre of the pioneers who emigrated from England, Scotland and Ireland. Indeed, even the convicts contributed to the expansion of agriculture, mining industries, exploration and subsequent development of this country.

The immigrants came from all walks of life, farming mainly, but other skills were needed. This story mainly concerns a person involved in upholding the law in this wild and raw land and how he performed his chosen career.

A young Scotchman, the Hon. Charles Cornelius Bartholmew Stuart is the son of an earl. His father sends him to Australia because of a serious threat to his life by an unpredictable friend. He joins the Victorian Police Force and becomes successful. However, his methods of dispensing justice were not appreciated in some quarters but were quite effective. Fugitives were killed and not arrested. Unfortunately, one person causes trouble with letters to the newspapers.

The story is set, mainly in the Australian countryside and describes what life was like in those early days. Charles marries a girl from his home village, who immigrated with her parents. He has considerable success in apprehending culprits and is justly rewarded.

Several scenarios are based loosely on actual events that occurred in the colony's history.

CHAPTER ONE

An Expatriate

The morning mist was slowly rising over the loch. It created a feeling of complete isolation for the lone fisherman in the small dinghy. He often came here. It allowed him to dream of days gone by and the pleasure he enjoyed during those lawless days in the Highlands. The only noise was from a few birds tweeting and chirping in the distance and the water lapping at the side of the dinghy.

The loch was twenty miles long and over half a mile across at its widest point. On both sides, it had steep mountain walls, covered with verdant and lush trees and shrubs.

Along the entire shoreline of the eastern mountain was a narrow section of flat green grazing land. The mountains were typical of the Scottish Highlands. If a person looked north and then south, he or she would see rugged mountains in either direction.

The north end had several streams flowing into the loch. The south end opened to a river which eventually reached the North Sea, some fifty miles distant. The only time the river really flowed was when the snow in the northern mountains melted, and the excess water flowed for a few months. Mainly, the river just slowly meandered to the coast.

The loch appeared to be timeless. In living memory, it had not been given a name, it had always just been called 'The Loch'. Even on old maps it was written as 'The Loch'.

As the mist rose, in the distance a large grey manor house appeared to the south, close to where The Loch water flowed into the river. Nearby nestled the small village of Glencairn, home to some five hundred people.

The villagers were a varied lot – from weavers to fishermen and farmers. Some even worked at the manor.

The light wind had the fisherman's dinghy drifting south. After an hour or so he had caught six good sized fish. He rowed back to a small jetty and moored the dinghy, where he cleaned the fish at the river's bank, before taking them to the kitchen and handing them to the cook. She smiled a "thank you" and kissed him lightly on the cheek.

The fisherman was Shamus McLeod, the gamekeeper for the manor's owner – the Earl of Belcannon. The McLeod family had lived in the area for hundreds of years. Shamus had a McLeod family record of his ancestors dating back to the year 900 A.D. Previous family members had etched their names on a large wooden door. It had been removed from an ancient castle destroyed in some forgotten war, between the warring Highland clans.

Shamus lived in a large multi-roomed hut provided by the earl's great-grandfather to Shamus's great-grandfather. Over the years, the McLeod families had collected artifacts dating back hundreds of years – swords, shields, kilts, even pottery. The hut was full of them and were his pride and joy.

A drum roll echoed down The Loch, immediately followed by the stirring sound of two bagpipers. It was ten o'clock. Each morning, at ten o'clock, the villagers would use the pipers to set their timepieces, if they owned one. It reminded those less fortunate of the time of day.

The current earl of the manor had started this daily event as a young man, when he realised why some of his employees were sometimes late or early for work. Their valid excuse at the time was that of having no access to a timepiece. He noted very few villagers knew the time. In summer they had long hours of daylight and in winter they had the extra dark hours. They had no idea how many hours they had worked.

The townsfolk appreciated this innovation and spoke highly of the earl's foresight.

The Loch was famous for its seemingly endless supply of quality fish.

In good weather, for around three months of the year, The Loch was visited by keen fishermen from the southern districts. These fishermen were generally wealthy and injected welcomed cash into the local businesses. Some even paid to stay in the manor.

The local people were an active community. Dances were organised to bring locals together after the long cold winter months. Group leaders encouraged a variety of activities, ranging from highland sports to art classes. If you wanted to be involved all you had to do was follow the instructions on the Community Notice

Board – "Please write your name on the list in the village hall".

Today was the local Festival Day. Each year the earl invited the local community to a get-together at the manor. Apart from food and drink, Highland games were played, such as tug-o-war and caber tossing. Not to forget highland dancing accompanied by the bagpipes and drums. Singers and fiddlers competed in the ballroom. The variety of the design and colour of the clans' kilts added to the spectacle of the occasion.

The cooking had commenced at daylight. The earl's son had commenced arranging staff their duties soon after dawn. Apart from the fiddlers and singers using the ballroom, all the other events and food serving would be held on the lawns by the river. The organising was not an onerous task; most of the staff were old hands at it.

The earl's son – the Honourable Charles Cornelis Bartholomew Stuart – was next in line for the title of The Earl of Belcannon. Charles was twenty-two years of age. He was a tall, athletic, well-educated highlander and highly thought of in the community. At university he had studied common law and excelled at swimming and fencing. He was considering, for his future career, either a legal career, which he practised locally to a small clientele, or livestock breeding. His father owned the eastern mountain pasture strip which was twenty miles long. Although it was only two hundred to four hundred yards wide, it was good grazing land.

The local persons of note and the ordinary folk began arriving before noon. They were dressed in their best clothes, which had been encouraged by the warm and sunny day, now the mist had lifted. The noonday sun cast shadows down through The Loch's trees. It was a beautiful sight, together with the colourful tartans and stalls on the green lawn and the surrounding gardens in front of the impressive manor house.

The bagpipes started tuning and soon began to play popular Scottish airs. Young children began dancing and laughing in the spirit of the occasion.

Charles had a younger sister, Nicola, a typical highland bonny lassie. She was two years younger than Charles and popular with the young men, although, she had no special male friend. She managed a workshop, weaving tartan fabrics, owned by her father, the earl, Sir Keith Stuart.

A university friend of Charles, who was a fellow fencer, often called by to say hello and pass the time of day. Ian Flint was the son of a wealthy businessman. His company manufactured various tartan kilts throughout the entire northern county. Nicola supplied the tartan fabrics for his kilts. His father employed twenty villagers and was regarded as a tough but fair boss.

At school, Ian had acquired a reputation for being a hothead. Without being provoked, he would king hit a fellow student.

Often, he was thrashed by the student he assaulted. He just couldn't help himself. He king hit Charles once and Charles taught him a lesson with his fists. Surprisingly they became friends.

During their school holidays, the two of them, with some friends, built a lookout on one of the nearby hills. They chopped down trees in the vicinity. Dug some holes for the corner posts and interlocked the floor poles. They then chiselled one thick side pole with steps. The scene was spectacular. They could see the entire l och.

The games were about to begin. Scotchmen came from near and far to test their skills and strength. First the caber tossing. This required the caber (pole) to be lifted by one end by a competitor, and when balanced, he walked forward and endeavoured to toss the caber end over end to fall forward. If successful, the distance was measured from where the caber first touched the ground.

Another popular event was the hammer throw. A large iron ball, approximately sixteen pounds in weight, was attached to a wire with a stirrup hand grip at the other end. The thrower stood in a circle and spun around as fast as he possibly could and then released the hand grip. The distance to where the ball landed was measured. The longest distance thrown was the winner. The competitors were generally big strong men, six feet plus tall and over sixteen stone. Charles and Ian were both a few stone lighter and were observers only.

Charles decided to join the indoor dancing with jigs and reels. The group dancing was most popular. He could not stop his toe from tapping and his kilt swirled with the beat of the tunes. The hills were resonating with the shrill of the bagpipes and drums. It was great to be alive in Scotland.

Charles was a keen and very good dancer of the sword dance. A sword and its sheath were placed on the floor, forming a cross and the dancer 'toed' into and out of the cross with arms held high forming a circle, to the tune of a bagpipe. It was both demanding and impressive. Charles enjoyed his dance and then joined some friends for a well-earned drink.

Nicola was dancing in a group. Ian walked in and sat down and kept looking at her. He made her feel uncomfortable. She tried to ignore him.

When she decided to leave the group, Ian stood up and approached her. 'Hello,' he said.

She realised he had been drinking and became wary. She quickly looked for Charles, who was at the far end of the ballroom and began to walk slowly towards him.

Ian grabbed her by the shoulder and spun her around, shouting, 'I'm talking to you.' He then kissed her and fondled her breast. The ballroom was crowded and only a few people saw what happened.

As Nicola struggled, a hammer thrower competitor pulled Ian from her. 'That's enough; let her be.'

As he turned away, Ian king hit him in the neck. The hammer thrower was unaffected by the punch. He turned and punched Ian hard in the face, breaking his nose and several of his front teeth. Ian collapsed to the floor, blood everywhere.

Charles heard the commotion and went to ask Nicola what had happened, but she wouldn't answer him. Charles helped Ian to a chair, but he wouldn't talk either. He put Ian on his horse and sent him home. The dancing continued. Charles would ask Nicola the reason for the incident tomorrow.

The dinner gong was welcomed by all. The cook and her team, as always, had done themselves proud providing village vegetables, fish, venison, beef, fruit and roly–poly pudding. The diners were entertained by ballad singers for the next hour as they feasted.

After lunch, several games were organised for the children – three legged races, sack races and the popular egg and spoon races for both children and adults. Often the children beat their parents.

The final event of the day was a horse race along the foreshore. Most of the horses entered were hunters used by the wealthy, so called upper-class, for fox hunting and gymkhanas. The race was about two miles. The earl would award a cup to the winner. Ten horses lined up. Charles was a keen horseman and entered each year without success. He finished fourth one year.

This year, two lassies were entered. One was a former college friend, Mary Webster. She was a well-known gymkhana competitor. Her father owned and operated the local farrier-blacksmith business at the edge of Glencairn. He also bred hunter horses for the aristocracy, wealthy farmers and businessmen. She lived with her parents on their forty-acre property.

Apart from the horse stables and paddocks, her father had formed a small gymkhana oval for her to practise her skills. Charles and Mary nodded a "hello" to each other. They wished each other good luck and then lined up for the start of the race. After the horn sounded, they galloped away.

Charles and Mary were behind the two leaders for most of the race. When the manor came into sight, they both urged their horses to greater efforts, and both were soon out in front. It was only in the last hundred yards that Mary's horse proved faster and won by a length.

After the earl presented her with the cup, she kissed Charles lightly on the cheek, which was a pleasant surprise. It was the first time he had viewed her as an attractive young woman. She stepped back and smiled.

Charles invited her to join him for a drink, after tending their horses. Mary followed Charles to the stables. They removed the saddles and bridles and stowed them away before wiping the horses down. The stables had several rows of horse stalls. Both horses were soon munching on a chaff mixture.

Charles looked at her as she left her stall. She was dressed in her gymkhana dressage attire. It accentuated her femininity. She smiled and they walked to the manor hall and sat down.

He commented, 'I haven't seen you for over four years. You look great.'

She laughed. 'Yes, it's been a few years since we've seen each other.'

Charles nodded. 'Time moves quickly. Let's have tea or something stronger sometime.' After chatting for an hour or so she left, promising to meet him again.

After the various presentations, the earl gave a short speech thanking the attendees, trusting they had enjoyed the day and wishing them a safe trip home. The middle of the afternoon saw a mass exit from both the ballroom and the lawns as the visitors began returning home. The day was enjoyed by most and was a day to be remembered by all.

At breakfast the next day, Nicola was missing. Charles asked his father if he had seen her.

His father told him she had gone to see a friend in Glasgow. 'She seemed upset about something that happened yesterday. When I asked her if she was she alright, Nicola just shrugged her shoulders and replied she would get over it.'

Charles finally heard what happened from Shamus, when they were out fishing on The Loch.

Shamus asked, 'How is Nicola?' He was unaware that Charles did not know of the incident with Ian.

Charles was furious when Shamus told him what had happened and immediately visited Ian's home for an explanation from him and an apology.

When Ian answered the door, Charles saw he had a broken nose and three missing front teeth. Ian invited Charles into his home and offered him a drink.

He realised Charles was angry. Ian quickly started to explain what happened and apologised.

Charles said, 'You are no longer welcome at the manor. You deserved to be thrashed for abusing my sister. You are a coward.'

Ian was now also angry and replied, 'Of course you would want to fight me. You're two stone heavier. I'm not a coward.'

Charles laughed at him again. 'You are a coward, always were and always will be.' He turned and left. Returning home still angry.

Charles decided to get away for a few days and with his cattle dog, he went to check on the herd. Calving was due and he wanted to bring the cows in calf back to the manor home paddock for the head stockman to monitor their progress.

The head stockman was very experienced and had handled previous difficult births, as well as most veterinarians. Charles spent two nights at a fisherman's hut at the far end of The Loch.

He enjoyed sitting around the fire with his dog by his side. The night's stillness was as if the world had stopped. After rounding up the cows in calf, he leisurely drove them home.

The head stockman saw Charles returning and greeted him. After a quick inspection, he commented, 'They all look in good condition. I'll put them in the main stable pens and check them thoroughly tomorrow.'

The earl was sitting in his study and after greeting him, he handed Charles several letters. He commented that he had received one from his brother, Stephen, near a town called Kahuna in the Colony of Victoria. He was managing a sheep station on three thousand acres for a large English company.

Charles' letters comprised one from his sister, one from his bank and surprisingly, one from Ian. He read the bank letter first. It was just a statement.

Next, he read the letter from Nicola, who was still at her friend's home in Glasgow. She explained about the incident. *I'm sorry I didn't tell you about it. It's all right. Really. Please leave it be. I just want to forget about it.*

But it was too late. The letter from Ian was an insane rant. He wanted a duel with Charles using epee swords. He wanted to prove he was not a coward. Charles ignored the letter.

However, two weeks later a friend of Ian's visited Charles telling him he was Ian's "second" for the duel and for Charles to select the date. Ian's second said he was obsessed with a duel and being labelled a coward. He said, 'He will label you coward in the village, if you refuse the challenge.'

Charles replied, 'I accept and will let you know the date.'

Charles had not fenced since leaving university and had to search for his fencing gear. It took him three hours to find them.

He had two epee swords, and they had been wrapped in greaseproof paper. After washing the grease from the blades, they were as good as new. He decided to practise using a full length mirror as a target of his image. He performed his thrust and parry exercises against his image in the mirror. Fortunately, he was fit from tasks he performed around the manor. For the last month he had been felling trees and chopping wood for the manor house's internal fires.

Charles delayed the duel, hoping Ian would simmer down. But it was not to be. He sent his second around after a week.

Charles agreed to meet Ian's challenge in seven days at dawn at the local fair ground. He took Shamus as his second and did not tell his family.

The morning was dark, cloud cover overhead. It was agreed that the person who drew blood first would be the winner. Both wore dark clothes. It was perceived light colours were an advantage to an opponent.

Their coaches arrived within a minute of each other with their second and a medical person. The medical persons were not doctors, but each had served in the military and had seen war service. They had both attended and treated war wounds. Hopefully, their knowledge would be sufficient to treat injuries incurred in the duel.

Neither combatant spoke to each other. Ian appeared agitated, whereas Charles felt calm but somewhat apprehensive.

He knew Ian had been a good fencer years ago but had no current knowledge of his abilities.

The combatants stepped forward and the duel began. They were evenly matched and attacked and counted again and again with neither gaining an advantage. Ian began to tire. Charles sensed this and lunged forward, at the same time Ian lunged.

Ian's blade struck Charles, entering the flesh just above his hip bone. At the same time Charles' blade struck Ian's sword arm, inside his elbow and severed a tendon, a ligament and damaged a muscle.

Both Ian and Charles stepped back in surprise and shock at their injuries. The seconds stepped in and stopped the duel and called in the medical attendants.

When Ian stepped back, he pulled his sword from Charles' hip wound, even with his injured elbow. His sword arm was now hanging down and bleeding profusely. The medical attendee quickly bound Ian's injury to curb the bleeding and with his second on board their coach, the three immediately left the fair ground.

Charles was in pain, but the injury was not serious. The sword had penetrated the fleshy area an inch above the hip and exited cleanly. The bleeding was soon controlled with some compression pads over his injuries and a bandage bound around his waist.

Over the next few weeks, Charles' wounds were washed clean each day with warm soapy water and coated with pre-boiled animal fat and then wrapped in a fresh bandage. They eventually healed leaving only two small scars as a memento of the combat.

Ian did not fare so well. Charles' final thrust, although misdirected, caused significant damage to his elbow area. The blade movement had been slightly downward and had severed a tendon and ligament, damaged the top of a muscle and chipped a bone. The bleeding had been stopped but the injury required a qualified doctor to repair the damage. This required a trip to Glasgow.

When Ian's father became aware of his injury and how, he was proud that his son fought a duel and had "scored a hit". He quickly organised a coach and driver to take him to Glasgow for treatment. Ian had gained considerable respect from his father. Previously his father had regarded him as a weakling.

The doctor in Glasgow had been a military surgeon and was not fazed by the injury. The chipped bone was not a problem, it would heal itself. The muscle and tendon would need stitching.

The tendon had retracted and needed to be pulled back into position and sewn to its other end, and the muscle sides also had to be sewn together.

The surgery was completed without major problems. However, Ian was advised that the elbow would never have the same movement as before, as the tendon was now slightly shorter than previous, and the muscle scar tissue would make the muscle less flexible. It would take a few months for the injury to heal. For his stupidity having an unnecessary duel, he would be left with a less flexible arm. It would be permanently bent.

The story of the duel soon became known in the village and throughout the local countryside, becoming a topic of general conversation. Life soon returned to normal, or so it seemed.

Ian's father, Alan Flint, was unaware why the duel occurred. He hadn't even thought about it. One Friday night he was standing in the local pub waiting for his floor manager to arrive and share a lager or two, when he heard a conversation between two drinkers, concerning Ian's set-to with Nicola at the dance. One of the drinkers saw Ian's father looking at them and immediately changed the subject. But the damage had been done.

Ian's father arrived home in a rage. He felt highly embarrassed and let down by Ian. He continued drinking, getting angrier as he dined with his wife. When Ian arrived home for dinner, his father immediately challenged him. 'Is it true that you accosted Nicola?'

Ian could see his father's fury and cautiously answered. 'We had words; nothing more.'

His father began to shout. 'I know what the villagers believe happened and it was more than that. You're a coward. Women are to be respected, not assaulted by the likes of you. You have defamed the family name. Shame on you.'

Ian began to get angry and agitated. He slowly walked up to his father, who was still seated and had turned away to eat. Without warning he punched his father in the neck. He collapsed face down onto the table. When he tried to stand up, his knees buckled.

He slowly slid to the stone floor, his head hitting first with a heavy thud. His wife sat there shocked at what she had just witnessed. Gathering her wits. She went to her husband, who was bleeding from his ears and mouth. She knelt beside him and could see he was not breathing. She screamed, calling for help.

Two servants came running. One helped her to the table and poured her a drink. The other servant was the ex-medical army orderly who was at the duel. He knew immediately that Alan was dead.

He looked at Ian, expecting an explanation from him. Ian was standing, staring down at his father's body. He suddenly turned and left the room without saying a word to his mother. He went to his room, packed some clothes and then visited the kitchen store and packed some food. His next stop was the gun room, where he collected a rifle together with powder, wads, caps and balls and then he left the house.

The ex–army medic went to the stables and collected a horse blanket. He returned to the dining room and wrapped Alan's body in it. With another servant, who had heard the scream and ran to the dining room, they carried the body to an outside storeroom used to store food in the winter months. By this time, a maid had arrived and helped Ian's mother to her bedroom, staying to comfort her.

Ian stood in the shadows and watched as the ex-medic took the blanket inside the house. He knew he was in trouble, so he went to the stables and saddled one horse for himself and placed saddle bags containing the food and ammunition on a second horse. Without looking back, he headed into the thick forest.

He rode for several hours until he came to the family's fishing hut. The Loch was dotted with them – small one room shelters for anglers who wanted to stay overnight. Ownership was not an issue. The shelters were there for everyone and anyone.

After he unloaded his equipment, he lay down on a bed, but he had a very restless night's sleep. This restlessness was to continue for a long time.

The next morning Ian began to realize fully what he had done. He had killed his father! Panic started to set in as he tried to decide what he should do or where he should go.

The ex–medic informed the local Justice of the Peace of the death of Mr Alan Flint.

When the Justice of the Peace questioned Mrs Flint she said it was an accident but did not elaborate.

As Ian was not available, the JP ruled it was an accidental death. 'Mr Flint was inebriated and fell, striking his head on the stone floor, causing an internal bleeding of the brain and his subsequent death.' The funeral was attended by almost the entire village, including his employees who were concerned for their future.

However, Mrs Flint assured the employees the business would continue as usual. The manager was quite capable, and Mrs Flint decided to become involved herself. The village moved on.

The death of Mr Alan Flint was the talk of the town. When it was realized Ian was absent, most thought he was too shattered to attend. Others wondered. Mrs Flint did not speak of his death, even to her close friends. She suffered at night, unable to sleep. She had lost both a husband and a son in one night's tragedy. Ian had vanished into the night.

Her involvement in the business was a very good decision. Mrs Flint carried out the office work at the factory in the morning and in the afternoon, she went for long walks along the riverbank and began to feel at peace again.

The water of The Loch had a calming effect. The fact that she was a witness to the killing, weighed heavily on her. She felt she should confide her secret to someone. By doing that, it might give her a sense of relief. Finding someone was the problem.

Strangely, she thought of Charles but by the time she was able to discuss it with him, he had left the manor. However, she decided to record the happening and wrote the details in a letter. The letter was sealed and marked 'Not to be opened prior to my death'. She felt the truth needed to be told eventually, to ensure her husband's death was not just a memory and that Ian would be held accountable. She forwarded the letter to her solicitor for safekeeping.

Slowly Mrs Flint began to accept the reality of the killing and managed to meet with her past friends. Once a month she hosted an afternoon tea with them. Some reciprocated and life began to be almost normal again. She never referred to her husband or Ian again.

* * *

Charles wondered where Ian had gone. Had he lost his mind and killed himself, or was he hiding in the forests along The Loch?

He went to visit Mrs Flint a few weeks after the funeral, but the ex-army medic saw him coming and blocked his path. He told Charles that Ian had taken a long rifle from the gun cupboard. 'You also need to know, when I travelled back with Ian, he said, "One day, I will kill Charles Stuart if it's the last thing I do." Also, I think he had something to do with his father's death. But I have no proof. I suggest you leave now.' Charles nodded and turned and rode back home.

That evening at the dinner table he told his father Ian had vanished. He also told him of the threat to his life. His father sat quietly thinking as he ate.

When they finished dining, his father took him to his study and closed the door. 'I think it's about time you started to travel,' he said. 'I don't want my son and future Earl of Belcannon killed by a known violent man with a mental condition. I suggest you go to the colonies and visit my brother, Stephen, until Ian is no longer a threat. No doubt Stephen can find a suitable occupation for you in such a vast land, perhaps in the legal profession or even with livestock. I will give you some cash and a bank cheque and forward you a monthly stipend to the Bank of New South Wales in Melbourne.' He looked at Charles and stated firmly, 'You are going, regardless of what you want.'

Charles sat thinking and then nodded. 'Yes, I agree. It's time I spread my wings. I'll arrange my travel tomorrow. I'll take three hunters with me. I'd like to breed horses as an interest.'

The only people who knew he was leaving were his mother, sister and Shamus.

He had seen Mary several times after the horse race and had enjoyed her company. He decided to tell her of his father's edict. He didn't tell her what caused the edict. It shocked her. She had grown very fond of Charles with his relaxed attitude to life. He said he would write to her and one day he would return to Scotland. He was not sure what would happen then. They would have to wait and see.

Their last meeting was dinner at the manor with his family. Charles' imminent departure was not mentioned. Afterwards he escorted her home. 'We will meet again. I promise,' he said, giving her a farewell kiss that was intimate and that left Mary in tears as he rode away.

He would write to her and use the Melbourne Bank as his address. He knew they would meet again. Unknowingly they had formed a bond that would last forever.

Early the next morning, Shamus drove Charles, leading the three horses, to the river. There he and the horses boarded a fishing barge, heading down to the port at the river's end. Shamus, and indeed most of the village, had heard a rumour regarding Ian's death threat and could understand why it would be prudent to leave. Hopefully not forever, but Ian was a dangerous man. Shamus waved farewell to Charles, and wondered if he would ever see him again.

The trip down river to the port was uneventful. The only sounds were the creaking of the sail booms and the water lapping the boat sides. It was a serene setting. Charles wondered what the future had in store for him.

Ian had been missing for two months, before he was sighted by a fishman. Ian had his head down and was gutting a fish and did not see him. The fisherman slowly and quietly moved his boat downstream. He told of his sighting in the local pub and soon the entire village knew.

After leaving home on that fateful night, Ian had headed north into the forest bordering Charles' grazing land. When he reached the family fishing hut where the streams entered The Loch, he decided to stay there. The weather was cold and damp, with snow threatening.

After hobbling the horses, he chopped some firewood and lit a fire. He then began to relax and settle his nerves. Gazing into the fire he looked back on his past life, but he had trouble finding any achievements. He kept recalling the trouble in which he had continuously found himself.

The death of his father had shocked Ian, and the fact that he had caused it made him look for a reason or an excuse for his actions. Charles was never far from his thoughts and the reason for the duel.

Ian did not seem to comprehend that he had caused the trouble in the first place. His mind was in a turmoil. His father's death and the injury from the duel clouded his thinking. All he could think of was revenge. His hatred for Charles grew worse daily. Ian considered ambushing and shooting him, not realising Charles had left the district and had gone to the Australian colonies.

Several times he rode to a sheltered place near the manor and sat waiting to see Charles. After a dozen or so visits, he stopped going there.

Once he saw the earl and contemplated shooting him, but, for once, common sense prevailed. He realised that would galvanise the whole community into action against him. The earl was very popular.

Ian roamed the forests searching for food and snaring game. The fishing hut had a small dinghy which he often used. Fish were plentiful and a good size. He spent hours each day just walking in the forest. It was a picturesque place. Three streams joined The Loch within a mile of each other. The nearest village was over ten miles away to the north and few locals came to the streams' junction.

Several times Ian went to the lookout and just sat there. He spent hours trying to decide what he was going to do. He had to move on, but he had no idea what to do or where to go.

Sometimes he went near to his home in the early morning. He viewed it from a small hill overlooking it. He even took a small amount of food from the outside store. It was not noticed by the cooks or staff. Sometimes he felt an urge to visit his mother, but he still felt ashamed of what he had done to his family.

Generally, he lived on venison and fish. Both were plentiful and easy to obtain. He fished the lake and snared deer in the forest and would cut their throat as he did not want to use a gun. It would echo throughout The Loch. One evening he even went into the village disguised as a shepherd clad in deer hides. No one gave him a second look.

He sold several deer hides and used the money for food stocks. He enjoyed the thrill of the deer hunting. The animals were very alert, and the slightest noise would send them running into the dense forest.

Naturally, this helped Ian to be patient. He had time on his hands. Often, he would sit for hours near a snare, just waiting. He would follow the deer dung trails and then decide the best place to position a leg snare and then wait. The snare was a simple wire noose hidden under some topsoil and grass. Ian would wait until a deer placed a leg in the centre of the soil and grass and then he quickly pulled it tight. The other end was tied to a tree. Ian would sit there waiting until the deer had exhausted itself, trying to free itself from the snare wire. He then slit its throat and left it to bleed. He removed the pelt and then he cut the shoulders, ribs and rump. The sections he did not require, he put in the dinghy, rowed to the centre of The Loch and dumped the deer carcase remains in deep water.

Cooking was basic. He made a small open fireplace with stones from the forest. He selected the stones to match the previous stone's flat surface. He stacked the stones in layers until he made a semicircle of around three feet diameter and three feet high. He then placed a metal grill on top, allowing the meat juices to feed the fire. A large cast iron kettle was always on the grill ready for a cup of tea.

Wood was plentiful but Ian made sure it was dry. He wanted to avoid excessive smoke coming from the hut chimney. He kept a small fire going, for not only cooking but also for warmth. The hut was small and well made. There were no draughts, even with the strongest winds coming down The Loch. To an extent, Ian was happy with his lot. He craved isolation and where better to have it than here!

The earl's cook asked Shamus to slay a deer as meat stocks were low. The forests were full of herds of them up in the trees. At times they were difficult to track. The slightest sound would see them scatter and run to higher ground. Shamus used a bow and arrow to kill them. His arrows were made from lightweight metal and were pointed, they did not have fluted arrow heads. They were renowned for accuracy in the hands of a skilled hunter.

Ian watched as the dinghy headed towards him. As it came closer, he saw that it was Shamus McLeod, and he could feel his anger rising. This man was a Stuart man – an employee of the family who he blamed for his misfortunes.

Shamus rowed to the opposite side of the stream, disembarked and pulled the dinghy up onto the bank. He headed up into the hills, carrying his bow and arrows.

Ian collected his rifle and walked down the path to the stream bank, waded out from shore and climbed up onto a rock close to where the dinghy had been dragged – and waited.

After a few hours Shamus returned, carrying several large meat sections cut from a deer he had killed with his bow and arrow.

Ian raised his rifle and fired at him. The bullet hit a meat section on Shamus' shoulder. Ian yelled. 'I won't miss next time.'

Shamus grabbed his bow and arrow and ducked behind the dinghy. He waited for a minute or so and then ran to shelter behind a large tree. He saw Ian standing on the rock about fifty yards from him. He decided to fire an arrow and then run to higher ground, up into the forest.

Ian scanned the bank and saw Shamus behind a tree, arrow aimed at him. He laughed. 'You're not that good.'

Shamus fired and the arrow struck Ian in the shoulder.

Ian dropped his rifle, blood streaming from his wound. He then slowly fell back off the rock into the stream.

Shamus waited until the sun set, watching for Ian. Eventually he rowed to the rock and, seeing no evidence of Ian, rowed home. He told no one of the encounter between them and put the incident to the back of his mind.

The following year a fishing group entered Flint's hut and found evidence that Ian had been living there for a time. Amongst the rubbish, they found a note addressed to Ian by his mother. It had been an old shopping list. To all and sundry, it appeared Ian had disappeared from the face of the earth. The locals presumed he had died in the forest and animals had taken his remains.

CHAPTER TWO

The New Inspector

Charles thanked the crew as he disembarked from the barge. He had been to the port before and knew where the shipping agents' offices were. He had dealt with one of them before, when he had arranged a shipment of tartans to Sydney.

The agent recognised Charles immediately and invited him to enter. He advised that a ship was due to depart the next day and had berths available all the way to Melbourne in the Colony of Victoria, via the Cape of Good Hope. It was the only stop planned en route.

Charles met the ship's captain, who arranged for his baggage to be stowed in his cabin and for the horses to be loaded. He was advised that there were only six passengers, as the ship was mainly carrying cargo. The SS Arrow sailed the following morning, on the high tide flowing from the river.

His fellow passengers were a mixed group. Two were military officers, a farmer, a civil servant and a Colony of

Victoria police officer. Except for the farmer, the others had accepted postings to the Colonial Army and Civil Service. They were introduced during the first evening meal and enjoyed the banter as they got to know each other.

John Major, the civil servant was a magistrate who had been posted to Melbourne to join the Victorian legal department. Melbourne had sufficient trained legal officers, but the countryside was lacking sufficient trained legal personnel. When John heard of Charles 'qualifications, he asked him what his employment intentions were when he arrived in Melbourne. John encouraged Charles to consider a legal career.

Charles told him he might be interested but he felt he should first spend some time with his uncle at his sheep station on the Victorian side of the Murray River near the town of Kahuna.

Charles intended to stay and learn more about breeding livestock, but he was flexible in his future career direction.

Ironically, George Mason was a Victorian police officer who had been to England on a recruiting drive, to bolster the senior ranks and to increase the Victorian Police Force numbers. He wanted experienced men, who he considered could live in the Victorian far country, which he called the 'bush' or the 'outback', as the locals did.

George was interested in Charles. He came across as a personable and well-educated young man. Perhaps he could find a place for him in the Victorian Mounted Police Force. George had the rank of superintendent and had the authority to hire new personnel. He pondered whether this young man could handle working in the bush by himself.

Co-incidentally, Charles' uncle lived in a district where they needed more of a police presence. George assumed Charles could ride a horse, as he had seen him load three horses at their departure port. George had a map of Victoria, and it showed Kahuna as a port on the Murray River. He thought about hiring Charles as a mounted policeman and wondered if he could also use his legal expertise, perhaps as a prosecutor.

One evening, two days sailing out from Melbourne, George raised the potential employment subject at dinner. Charles was interested. George understood Charles wanted to spend some time with his uncle first and suggested if he was still interested, after visiting his uncle, to contact him at the police barracks in Melbourne within a month. Alternatively, he could visit the barracks when they disembarked in Melbourne and stay a few days to discuss the offer in depth, including the colony court procedures and general police training. The barracks had accommodation available for visiting V.I.P.s or policemen from the bush attending training courses.

John had been listening intently and commented to no one in particular. 'If Charles accepts your offer, he could keep his eye open for potential justice of the peace officers; men held in high esteem in the community.'

They laughed when George said, 'Possibly three jobs for the cost of one.'

Charles replied, 'It makes sense to stay in Melbourne for a few days. Let me think about it.'

The coast of Victoria appeared off the port bow. As the ship sailed closer, they could see a few small dwellings with smoke emanating from their chimneys and livestock grazing in the green countryside. The sea was calm, and the sunshine encouraged the passengers and off duty crew to be on deck and enjoy the view.

After the SS Arrow picked up the inward tide, as the seas poured through the Heads into Port Phillip Bay, the ship then headed north to Hobson's Bay. At the same time, Charles sat in a quiet corner on the main deck and began to seriously consider George's offer.

Charles had been on deck since daylight considering the offer and now he had made his decision. 'Yes,' he told George, 'I will accept the offer to join the Colony of Victoria Mounted Police Force.'

He then sat back, relaxed and began to enjoy seeing the coastal towns of Port Phillip Bay. Melbourne and Hobson's Bay were in the distance. The sun was shining; it looked to be a promising start for an immigrant.

The ship had furled its sails and was slowly being moved to a wharf. Two row boats were dragging mooring ropes attached to the bow and stern of the ship to some dock workers. The dockyard workers attached the ropes to the wharf bollards. The ship's crew then slowly moved the ship alongside the wharf. Once alongside the wharf, the ship became a hive of activity.

A walkway was lifted onto the ship's side, and the customs officers and ship's agent boarded the ship. The captain had all the shipment consignment documents ready. As soon as the customs formalities were completed, the unloading commenced.

When the ship berthed, Charles went to where his three horses were kept. They had endured the voyage without any drama and were none the worse for wear.

The horses had been supported by loose slings which helped keep them upright in rough seas. During calm seas, they had been walked around the deck several times.

A seaman approached Charles and advised that they were ready to offload the horses. The horses did not panic during the lift. They just calmly gazed around with their ears pricked, looking at their surroundings. Charles left them tied to a rail to let them get their shore legs again, while he collected his baggage.

The ship's agent approached him and handed him two letters. One was from the bank and the other from his uncle. The bank advised that he had a credit of three hundred pounds available in either Melbourne or Sydney. The other letter, from his Uncle Stephen, gave him the address of a solicitor, a friend of his uncle for many years. Charles also had the address of another college friend from years gone by, who he intended to meet.

After feeding and watering the horses, he saddled Rob Roy and strapped his travel bags onto the other two horses. He joined George and John and headed for Melbourne, crossing over by ferry. Charles mounted Rob Roy and followed George and John, in their hired cab.

His first sight of the City of Melbourne was an eye opener. It was much larger than he expected. The river was busy with ferry boats as there were few bridges.

The city buildings ranged from several multi-storied bluestone buildings, a generous number of shops, to a hundred or so various size homes or single room huts. A few streets were levelled but others had potholes from rainwater that could not drain away.

The cab stopped and John alighted and shook Charles' hand. 'You can contact me here at the Melbourne Court. I'd like to meet with you again. Goodbye for now.'

With a cheery wave, he turned and walked up the stairs to the court doors, where a constable opened them for him.

Charles continued on with George, and it wasn't long before George remarked, 'We're nearly at the barracks.'

Charles saw them and was impressed. The barracks consisted of a square of two-storied buildings enclosing a large open area.

They entered the barracks through two large iron gates which were opened to reveal a parade ground.

George stopped in front of the imposing entry of the largest building. He was in his uniform and a constable on porter duty ran down and saluted him. 'Welcome back, sir.'

George smiled. 'It's good to be back. I missed the sunshine.'

Charles dismounted and looked around, nodding. *This is impressive. I believe I made the right decision,* he thought.

George interrupted his thoughts. 'The constable will take your horses and stable them and take your luggage to a room. Come with me while I report back. It won't take long.' True to his word, he soon returned. 'I'll give you a quick tour and then leave you to settle in.

'The barracks has been divided into four separate buildings. The northern one is for accommodation and has lecture and training rooms. The southern building is for stables, fodder, tack room and carriages. The west building is the administration area, and the eastern building is for entertaining, dining and official functions.'

He pointed. 'The wind is mainly from the west. In summer, hot northerly winds occur. That's why the stables are in the south. The parade ground is used for training purposes – horse riding, drills, Passing out Parades, etc.'

After the quick tour, George took Charles to his room. 'Dinner is a six p.m. I'll collect you and take you to the dining room. If you have formal wear, feel free to wear it. You have three hours to relax. Bye for now.'

Charles' room was a reasonable size. It had a view of several houses, and, in the distance, there were forests and a few green paddocks with livestock. The room had a bed, a desk and chair, two lounge chairs and a large wardrobe. The wooden floor was polished Baltic pine.

After unpacking and stowing his clothes, he lay on the bed and dozed. It had been an interesting but tiring day.

A knock on the door signalled George's return. He was dressed in evening uniform, looking every inch an officer. Charles was dressed in his Highland Dress – kilt and sporran. George nodded approval.

The dining room had tables with two-chair, four-chair and six-chair settings. For a formal dinner the tables would be arranged in three long sets with a head table for six senior officers or V.I.P.s. George opted for a table of two.

A waiter appeared and offered the menu to each of them. After a quick glance at meals offered, Charles returned his to the waiter and asked George to order for him, commenting, 'I don't recognise any of these dishes.'

While waiting for their meals, George said, 'I wanted to have a quick chat tonight as I may be busy tomorrow. I'm never too sure what awaits me, and I need to make a formal report of my overseas visit to the commissioner and his team.'

He continued, 'However, I will get you your identification documents first thing. This will allow you access within the barracks to dine and tend to your horses. I will also arrange for you to be sworn in aa a temporary member of the Victorian Mounted Police Force. You can wander around at your leisure for the rest of the week.

'I have drafted you a training program, which starts next Monday.' He handed Charles a list. 'You will start at the bottom. Your initial training will be the same as for all recruits. This is for four weeks and includes street patrols with experienced officers.'

Charles nodded.

'Secondly, you will attend four weeks at Melbourne University for specific legal courses and finally you will attend the county court as an observer for two weeks; one week as a court clerk and one week as a prosecutor. After these three months, we will sit down and discuss your future role.'

Charles nodded in agreement. 'Thank you. I look forward to this training.'

They then enjoyed a few ales and, after a general chat, went their separate ways. George said he would meet with him at dinner each evening.

Charles was unsure whether to write to Mary or wait to hear from her. Her previous letter, via the Melbourne Bank, had taken three months to arrive.

The next morning, he met with George to finalise his swearing in and to collect his identification documents.

After feeding the horses, he went for a wander through the various buildings in the barracks. He was challenged several times by constables on guard duty. In the afternoon, he unpacked his trunk, removing his legal reference books, which he had studied at university.

He had correctly presumed that the legal structure in the colonies was based on English Law. The next two days he refreshed his memory by reading the English court procedures.

At the weekend he saddled a mare and rode into the centre of Melbourne to familiarise himself with the city.

Monday morning Charles walked to the classroom and found an empty seat. There were twenty students of various ages in the class. Some appeared to be teenagers and others up to forty years of age.

Their instructor had a commanding presence, a no nonsense person. His role was not only to teach, but also to identify any persons unsuitable for the police force. The lectures were easy to understand, mainly common sense. Charles made written notes of key points, both on policing and procedures.

The instructor noticed this and accordingly noted this in his class report to the chief inspector. Charles later found out three of the potential recruits had been dismissed as "unsuitable for the rating thereof".

Two of the recruits were in the same dormitory as he was and he introduced himself to them. They were of a similar age and, as sons of farmers, they had something in common.

William James was from Echuca, a major town on the Murray River, known for its paddle steamer port used to ship wool and grain down river. The other recruit was Fred Knowles from Ballarat in the centre of Victoria. The three would dine together in the general mess when George was away on business.

* * *

The new recruits were in uniform and assembled for allocation to a city night patrol team, consisting of an experienced constable and two recruits. They were briefed by the duty sergeant and then issued with a truncheon and handcuffs.

The briefing consisted of warning the patrols that a whaling fleet had arrived in Hobson Bay, and that they needed to be on their toes. It could be a long and demanding night.

Charles was happy to be doing something more exciting than sitting in a classroom. A coach dropped the team opposite the town hall in the centre of the city.

The team had a quiet time until sunset, when the dark streets began to fill with all sorts of riff-raff – both male and female. The local taverns filled with drinkers. Within an hour trouble loomed. First there was the noise of loud singing and breaking glass. Then the fights started. The police coach was soon taking drunks to the Russell Street lock-up for the night.

Charles' baptism of fire occurred on this first night patrol. A fight spilled out into the street from a tavern. Four drunks were arguing with each other and then started to fight each other. The police team watched and did nothing until one of the drunks was knocked unconscious. Then the senior constable stepped in and told them to stop.

The three then turned on him and struck him and he fell to the pavement. Charles and Fred Knowles then joined the affray. Charles' opponent was bigger than Charles and landed a few punches, knocking him down. Charles got to a kneeling position and raised his truncheon. He struck his assailant, hard on the outside of his knee. The assailant bellowed in pain and fell to the ground. Charles then struck him on the shoulder with the truncheon, rendering that arm useless.

In the meantime, the constable and Fred Knowles had overcome the other two drunks and handcuffed them. The fourth drunk had recovered and fled the scene.

A police cart was called to take the three offenders to gaol for the night when a man stepped forward and introduced himself as a ship's captain.

He asked politely, 'I could take these men back to my ship. We are due to sail on the early morning tide.' He pointed to one of the men. 'The one limping, is my navigator. I have a boat at the river now ready to go back to Hobson Bay.'

The senior constable quickly made up his mind and nodded, telling the police cart reinsman to take the drunks to the captain's boat.

The next day the senior constable asked Charles where he had learnt to strike the knee the way he did with his truncheon.

He replied, 'I saw a brawl in a village and saw one of the brawlers use this technique most successfully on a larger opponent.'

The constable replied, 'All recruits should be taught it as a defence technique.' He continued, 'Incidentally, if you're wondering why I let the drunks go, it saves us feeding them, paperwork, generally wasting our time, costing us money and they have now left Victoria. End of story.'

Charles agreed with the constable's logic. He stowed this lesson in his memory bank for future use.

The city patrols were often boring, doing the same daily routine. The majority of residents were normal law abiding citizens. Pickpockets and drunks were the most offenders.

The senior constable normally gave them a clip in the ear or a boot up the bum and told them to bugger off out of his sight.

There was one task Charles did not enjoy – going to private homes to sort out domestic arguments. At times it was difficult to decide who was the guilty party, with all the verbal abuse they would yell at each other. Then there could be physical abuse. Separating the parties was often challenging and sometimes dangerous.

The daily patrols did, however, allow him to become familiar with local landmarks, buildings of note and small lanes. This was to stand him in good stead when a daylight robbery occurred.

There were several banks in Melbourne. One morning the police team heard someone yelling with the cry of – 'Robbery!' When the team ran towards the noise, they saw three men running towards them. One was armed and waving a pistol at them, firing a shot in the air. Chasing them were two bank guards.

Charles' team watched as they turned and ran into a laneway.

Charles said to the senior constable, 'We can intercept them if we go this way.' The two constables followed him and then waited in a doorway. As the robbers ran past them, they tackled them. Charles' opponent had the pistol but dropped it in surprise, when he was confronted by him. The three robbers were soon overcome and handcuffed.

The senior constable wrote a report of the robbery and praised Charles for his local knowledge and initiative.

Another time, the team was confronted by an

agitated gold assayer. He said he had a man locked in his storeroom. The assayer said the man had tried to sell him bogus gold coins. When he refused to buy the coins, the man had attacked him. He and his assistant then tackled the man and locked him in the storeroom. When the team arrived, they could hear the man shouting from the storeroom, threatening to kill the assayer and his assistant.

When the storeroom door was opened and the man saw the police, he immediately stopped his tirade. 'Good morning, constable. I think there has been a misunderstanding.'

The senior constable, replied, 'I want all of you to come with us to the watch house to sort this matter out.' He told Charles to collect the alleged bogus coins and bring them with him.

At the watch house, the alleged offender said he did not know they were not genuine gold coins. They were given to him by a friend to cover a debt he owed him.

When the duty sergeant asked for his friend's name and address, the alleged offender said he would prefer not. His friend was the son of a parliamentarian.

This did not impress the sergeant, who told him he could stay in a cell until he gave him the name. The next morning after a sleep on a hard bed in a cold cell, the alleged offender gave the name, who surprisingly was the son of the state premier.

This information was advised to the commissioner, who was a personal friend of the Premier. Whilst the Premier was not impressed by his son's involvement, he said he would not interfere in the police process. Fortunately for the alleged offender, he came before a benevolent judge, who dismissed the case when the

Premier's son stated that he also had been frauded, when he purchased the coins from a money dealer.

Charles learnt from these cases. They would have been handled differently in England. The law was viewed more liberally in the colony. It seemed to work well and appeared adequate to govern the many new settlers in this land, far from their native homes.

Police were generally viewed favourably in Victoria and treated with respect. Attitudes had changed dramatically since the Eureka Stockade confrontation, when the police were too heavy handed in their carrying out of the unpopular government gold mining licence searches. This rebellion by the miners brought matters to a head, culminating in forcing the governor of the day to reduce the licence fee and introduce a new set of sensible and realistic licence regulations.

As part of their training the recruits were taken to the gun range for firearms tuition. Revolvers and rifles were the order of the day. Both guns fired the latest ammunition.

Charles was an experienced shotgun exponent and had been regarded as a skilled marksman. Several others had rifle and shotgun experience, but no one had fired a revolver.

The exercise started with each recruit being taught to dismantle, and assemble a revolver and rifle and being shown how to clean the parts, then to oil the metal parts to protect the metal from corrosion and the wooden parts from cracking.

The instructor was a former British Army sergeant and stressed the rule, "To treat every and any firearm as loaded and ready to fire". That is, never point a gun at anyone, unless you are going to fire it.

He advised he was going to give each recruit three

shots to fire at a three foot diameter target, with four different size coloured rings marked on it. The target distance was twenty feet for the revolver. The first three recruits only hit their target once. Charles realized this was going to be difficult. He hit his target twice but in the outer circle. Only one recruit hit his target three times.

The instructor then showed them how to hold the revolver correctly, brace their wrist and not to rush the shot. 'Take aim and slowly squeeze the trigger.'

In the next round of target shooting, each constable hit their target three times. He then had the recruits run two hundred yards around a circular track as fast as they could and when they returned, to immediately fire three shots at their target. Not one recruit hit his target three times.

The instructor advised, 'Let that be a lesson to you. If you're going to fire your revolver, relax and wait until your breathing has settled down.'

The rifle target was set at one hundred yards distance with a slightly larger target than the revolver one. The country recruits each hit their target three times from a prone position. The two city ones only hit theirs once. The instructor moved their legs to an offset position and altered their front hand grip.

These changes immediately improved their accuracy. When the instructor was satisfied with each recruit's performance, he signed their competence forms and allowed them to return to the barracks. All passed their gunnery test.

George had watched Charles' progress, and he was pleased. He had performed up to his expectations. His role in the bank robbery showed initiative and observation.

The first four weeks went quickly. Charles had enjoyed the patrols in the open air and outdoor activities. Now he would have four weeks indoors.

The university lectures identified the differences between the British Laws and the Victorian Laws. There were important differences. Of particular interest were the laws and regulations relating to land control and customs. Both had been abused in the early days of settlement in New South Wales and Victoria and the respective governments learned from these anomalies. These were entirely new to him, and he listened intently, as he knew he would be out in the country eventually and possibly near the borders of other colonies and would need this knowledge.

Some of the lectures were refresher courses from his days at university in London. The other students were mainly Englishmen, who had attended English universities similar to Charles and were employed either by the Victorian Government or intended to go into private practices. Some students were from other countries and found that they needed more time to study than the English students. This was due to the difficulties associated with learning the English language and its differing interpretations of some words.

Charles found the lectures interesting, but he still studied in his room, using the reference books he brought with him. Some topics were not covered in depth, so he wrote notes during classes.

In the evening, he rewrote the lecture notes he had written during the day. Most times he abbreviated the main points on the topic of discussion, writing only key words. By the time he had rewritten the notes, he found he had virtually a complete precis on each subject.

At the end of the course, he spent a few hours compiling the notes into a reference book. Charles' study consisted of rereading the reference books and his own notes. He felt confident he would pass the examinations. When the big day arrived, his optimism was correct. He achieved second place in the overall class results. He was presented with an appropriate certificate. He smiled, musing another wall hanging.

George had left a note for him to meet for a six o'clock dinner on the next day. That morning, Charles walked into Melbourne city to talk with the bank. When he left his father had given him a cheque and three hundred pounds.

The bank manager welcomed him into his office, he had received another letter from his father. After Charles opened his account he was advised the bank would be pleased to handle any of his future businesses or investments on his behalf.

Tea was then served. The bank manager was born in Sydney and had been promoted to the Melbourne branch of the bank. He enjoyed living in Melbourne and had travelled to some areas in the remote Victorian countryside. He believed that the colonies had a great future, with its potential mining wealth, agriculture and livestock.

Charles listened intently, particularly when the manager mentioned the Victorian countryside. After a pleasant hour Charles departed. The manager invited him back if he needed any information regarding his posting in the police force.

George arrived on time for dinner as always. After greeting each other, he asked Charles how his training was progressing. George already had prior knowledge of his examination results.

Charles had his certificate with him and showed George. He answered. 'A picture is worth a thousand words.'

George laughed, saying, 'Well done.' He continued, 'I have changed our previous arrangement for you to be an observer at court from Monday, only for one week. Following that period, you will have two weeks as the clerk of court and then the final week as a prosecutor.

'There will be a retired prosecutor with you to assist, if needed. Your training has been exemplary. Keep it up. You will enjoy this part, and I can assure you it will be an eye opener. The people you will see and meet, with their different persona, will amaze you. They are from all walks of life and countries, high born and low born, law abiding and born criminals.'

They ordered their meals. George started talking of the potential of the development of the Victorian bush. Livestock, sheep in particular, and general agriculture. The land was fertile with good rains and ample sunshine.

Charles listened intently. He could see George believed in Victoria and, indeed, he believed each of the colonies had bright futures.

George paused and said, 'The reason I'm speaking like this is because I want you to seriously consider taking a posting up on the Murray River, which, as you know, is the border of New South Wales. If things go as I've planned, you will be sworn in as an inspector and have a roving position as a prosecutor for the various courts near and along the Murray River. The choice will be yours. You have a month or so to consider this offer. If you agree, you could choose where you would wish to be domiciled.

'However, if you have other thoughts, we do have other choices.' Their meals arrived, and they both resorted to small talk – politics, the weather and family.

Charles told George of Mary and his hope that they would soon meet again.

George nodded. He understood. He had experienced a similar situation when he was a young man and had been posted to India and left his sweetheart in England for a year before they married.

They had been married for ten years and had been most content with his lot. Unfortunately, she died of typhoid. He hoped Charles would be as happy in the years to come as he had been.

As they departed the dining room, George told him to report to the doorman at Melbourne Court House next Monday at nine a.m. ready for his next assignment.

Charles walked up the steps to the impressive courthouse double doors. A smartly dressed police constable opened them and requested his name. After referring to a clipboard, he nodded, telling him to proceed to room number ten, where he was expected.

Nervously he rapped twice on the door. It was opened by an attractive young lady. 'You must be Mr Charles Stuart. Please come in, and I will introduce you.'

There were five persons siting at a round table. They each rose as he approached them. A tall impressive, man offered his hand saying, 'I'm Justice Sir John Wily. These two gentlemen are magistrates – William Barlow and Sydney Parks.' More hand shaking. 'Next our two senior court clerks – Michael Keough and Patrick Symons. Last, but not least, Shirley O'Dea, our secretary. We are the main members of the court.

'There are others, but you won't be involved with any of them. Now, please be seated and we will go over some protocols with you. Shirley, teas please.'

The meeting was brief but informative. The judge and the magistrates departed, leaving the two clerks with Charles.

Charles asked a few general questions. Then the clerks explained their weekly routine:

- Monday morning 0900 hrs. Meeting of the staff.
- Receive a briefing from the Deputy Commissioner of Police of any major crimes that had occurred over the weekend, requiring a hearing.
- Court cases outstanding from previous week, criminal or not. (There was always a backlog of cases).
- Prioritise cases on hand with the other clerks.
- Decide which judge or magistrate does what.
- Assign courtrooms.
- Ensure alleged offender(s) has been delivered to holding cells.
- Ensure prosecutor has arrived.
- Friday afternoon 1600 hrs. Assess and collate weekly court cases and file reports ready for Monday and identify carryover cases.

Charles arrived ten minutes early but did not sit at the table. He felt it would be presumptive. He waited until the others arrived and pointed him to a chair. The judge made a mental note of this. The briefing was interesting. The weekend had three murders. Each alleged murderer had been apprehended. One had been shot dead. The other two had pleaded guilty and had been remanded.

Sir John had a quiet chat to Charles before they commenced. He suggested that he should observe the murder cases first. 'Even though these two cases are straightforward with guilty pleas, their lawyers will probably bring up extenuating reasons for their actions, due to the possibility of them receiving a lesser sentence. You should concentrate on studying the people in court – the witnesses, the alleged offenders and the legal persons. Even hecklers in the gallery can be of interest in a major crime.'

He continued, 'You need to be aware of the differences in the presentation of alleged offenders – their attitude, their mood swings, the change in their speech and body language when they are under pressure, such as folded arms which means, "I'm not going to co-operate with your questions". If you hand them a folded piece of paper, they will normally be curious and open it up to read the contents. This is your chance to encourage them to talk. It works nine times out of ten.'

He paused. 'If their hands are clasped behind their head, it means "I'm smarter than you" and if they avoid eye to eye contact or speak with their hand over their mouth, this generally means "I'm lying". You will then know how to frame your questions.'

Charles nodded. 'Thank you for the advice.' It was good advice, and it would stand him in good stead in the future.

Charles sat opposite the main door where the alleged offender entered with his police guard. It was a heavy wooden door. Next to it was a second door with an iron grill inserted in it. The alleged offender had been held in the remand cell at the main city police station and then moved to a holding cell at the rear of the courthouse.

As soon as the doors were opened, people started to enter and select a seat. It was difficult identifying observers who were related to the alleged offender or if they were just curious to see a court hearing.

The judge and the alleged offender entered the court at the same time. The judge came via a door behind his chair from his chambers, as the alleged offender entered from the cells. The clerk stood and called 'All rise. The court is now in session.'

The judge bowed and after he sat down, all the persons in the court sat down. The charge was read out. "Jim Furity, you are charged with the murder of David Smith on the 8th of May. How do you plead?'

Jim Furity replied, 'Not guilty.' This answer surprised both the judge and the prosecutor.

The clerk then handed Mr Furity the bible for him to take the oath. The judge looked up as Jim Furity's lawyer stood up. He explained. 'Your Honour, my client admits to killing Mr Smith but claims it was an accident. We seek to have the charge downgraded to manslaughter.'

The judge asked, 'Why wasn't this done sooner?'

His lawyer responded. 'My client was not aware of the difference between murder and manslaughter. I was unaware of his claim until I first met with him this morning.'

After the alleged offender had taken the oath, The prosecutor asked him to tell the court what had happened to cause the death of the deceased.

Mr Furity answered, 'I was drinking in the Travellers Arms Inn at dinner time and the deceased bumped into me, spilling my drink. I asked him to buy me another drink and he declined. He was drunk and he then pushed me and hit me in the face. I reacted and knocked him down and he died.'

Charles could see that Mr Furity was educated but while he spoke, he kept fidgeting and did not look at the prosecutor. Nerves or guilt?

The prosecutor then called a witness, the landlord of the inn.

After he was sworn in, the prosecutor asked him, 'Did you see the altercation?'

The landlord asked, 'Do you mean, did I see the fight?'

The prosecutor smiled and answered, 'Yes.'

The landlord said, 'I saw the fight and the bloke in the dock knocked him down and then kicked the dead bloke in the head several times. I had to stop him. He was drunk too, but he's a mongrel. I held him until the police arrived.'

The alleged offender's lawyer then asked him, 'Did you see the whole fight?'

'Yes, sir, I did.' The defence lawyer sat down.

The prosecutor then stood up and said, 'I have a medical report which states the deceased had been subjected to severe trauma to the skull resulting in his death. The injuries are consistent with the deceased being kicked several times to the skull. I rest my case, Your Honour.'

The judge nodded. He then stated, 'Unless there is other evidence to be produced. I will give you my verdict tomorrow.' Both the prosecutor and the defence lawyer answered, 'No, nothing further.'

The next day, the verdict from the judge was, 'Guilty' and the defendant was sentenced to life imprisonment.

Charles attended three other trials on his first day. They were simple and straightforward without any complications. He soon learned to understand the reasoning for the judges' decisions.

He decided to concentrate on watching the senior prosecutors' technics. Some were slow and deliberate, searching for one or two tangible answers.

Others were quick, with more general questions. He began to see how the prosecutors eventually came to focus on the actual reason for the charge. There was nearly always a prior reason; only a few were an accident. The police officers' evidence was vital in nearly all cases, as were their answers when in the dock. He could see he needed to establish a rapport with a witness in the dock to obtain calm and confident answers.

He noted the deliberate avoidance of eye contact by the alleged offender during questioning by the prosecutor.

The court hearings had taken three days and had been a formality. The other cases were minor civil cases, such as domestic violence, petty theft and pick pocketing.

Charles was surprised at the short hearings, but he soon got used to them. It was indicative of the performance of the courts in the colonies. They always had a backlog of cases.

Family violence was difficult to resolve to the satisfaction of all affected parties. Why family violence occurred was often a dilemma. It was often difficult to determine who in the family caused the violence to occur.

The reasons were many. It could be due to one party being drunk, committing adultery, spending money excessively, denying conjugal rights, uncontrollable children or a person who had mental problems and was inherently violent. Regardless of the reason, the courts took a dim view of women suffering violence.

A violent incident occurred during a wedding party. The wife of a well-to-do farmer was caught kissing a neighbour. The farmer pulled them apart with such ferocity, she fell and broke her arm. The farmer thrashed the neighbour, who then went home. The farmer took his wife to the hospital to have her arm examined. He then stayed the night with her.

In the meantime, the police had been called to the wedding and been told of the farmer's wife's injury. When the farmer arrived home, they arrested him and charged him with assault. When the wife found out her husband had been arrested for assaulting her, she was filled with remorse.

The kiss had not meant anything to her. She had had a few drinks and had not given thought to what the kiss would look like to her husband.

The man she kissed had been a boyfriend several years before she met her husband. She was now in a quandary in how to explain the situation to their three children. On her discharge from the hospital, she went to the police and asked to have the charge dropped.

She said it was her fault that she was injured. The police said the case must go to court. The court was full on the day of the trial.

The farmer was well-liked in the district. He was an officer in the local militia and a prominent sportsman.

The judge had read all the editorials in the press plus the police and hospital reports. Before the hearing, the prosecutor said to the judge. 'There will be no winners in this case, only losers. There always is when families are involved and he's the breadwinner.'

The judge opened the court with a speech. 'Before we start this hearing, I want the prosecutor and the defence lawyer to appreciate that I have read every word I could obtain relevant to this charge. Will either party be going to introduce more evidence?'

The defence lawyer stood up. 'Last night I received a doctor's report on the lady's health.'

The judge nodded to him and replied, 'Please hand it to the clerk.' He did and the clerk passed it to the judge. The judge read it and handed it to the clerk for the prosecutor to read.

After reading the report, the prosecutor asked the judge if he and the defence could approach the bench. The three of them spoke quietly for five minutes. Then they returned to their seats.

The judge spoke, 'This case is one that can destroy a family or help it become stronger. I have been presented with a doctor's report that has shed some light on the lady's arm injury. The report details several injuries to her. She has had six broken arm bones from falls over the last eight years and a broken bone in the lower right leg.'

He paused, 'The doctor advises that she suffers from brittle bones due to lack of calcium. Even though she is on a calcium rich diet she has not improved. This is a lifetime affliction for her. In the light of this doctor's report, I agree with the prosecutor, who wishes the charge be withdrawn.'

He looked up and said, 'I do not believe that her husband would intentionally wish her to fall knowing the medical condition of his wife. He took her to hospital. It shows he cares for her. I believe this was a spur of the moment event. Which he now regrets.' He looked at the defendant in the dock and said, 'You are free to go.' The gallery of onlookers cheered and clapped at his decision.

As the judge began to collect his paperwork, the wife stood up and, in tears, she sobbed, 'Sir, you are right. He would never hurt me intentionally. Thank you.'

The judge nodded and left the bench. It was a lesson for Charles. If the prosecutor had investigated her medical history earlier, there would not have been a court hearing.

The last case he attended as an observer, was that of three bushrangers. They had held up a stagecoach, robbing the passengers and killing the driver. One passenger recognised one of the bushrangers. They had been captured two days later at a nearby farm. One bushranger was shot dead during the subsequent gun battle. The other two were then arrested and brought before the court.

Again, Charles was surprised at the speed of the hearing. It was completed in five days. Judges were ruthless with bushrangers in general, but when a killing was involved, they moved the hearing along quickly. The passengers, as witnesses, were reliable and identified the two offenders, even with their masks on. They were hardened criminals. The defence had no evidence to request leniency from the court.

The verdict was predictable – death by hanging. The hanging would be carried out at Pentridge, the main prison in Victoria.

Charles began to feel comfortable in a court hearing. Even as an observer he could see how he could fit into the position as a police prosecutor.

On his first day as a court clerk, he was shown his duties by the senior clerk. He had been told them previously but politely listened. Primarily, he was responsible to open the court hearing and close the hearing. Other duties required him to ensure the courtroom was prepared and the bible available, the alleged offender was delivered to the holding cell and the prosecutor had arrived.

Also, he had to make sure that the charge sheet had been seen by the presiding judge and pertinent paperwork, writing material and pens etc. were available on the judge's bench.

His time as a clerk passed quickly and without any drama.

At dinner with George, they chatted about the training. Charles was happy with his exposure to the system and said that he believed he was ready for his prosecutor role. George nodded and said that he had spoken to some of the court staff, and they commented that he appeared comfortable in court.

George continued, 'If you're happy after your role as prosecutor, we'll need to select a suitable posting for you. If you have a preference for a particular area, let me know.'

Charles nodded and answered, 'I have an uncle who manages a property near Kahuna, up near the Murray River. Perhaps, a position near there?'

George nodded. 'Yes, I'll look into it.'

The following week, Charles reported to the clerk and the judge, who knew of his training role. The judge welcomed him and wished him a successful performance.

The trial concerned a Mr Jack Smith, who had been

driving a single horse cart and had hit a woman near the local school and killed her. He was charged with culpable driving. The case hinged on a "Slow down" sign which it was alleged was ignored by Mr Smith. Witnesses testified he had been travelling too fast.

Charles asked the alleged offender to tell the court what happened to cause the death of the lady.

Mr Smith said, 'She stepped out in front of me and I couldn't stop. I'm sorry, but it was her fault.' Charles then sat down.

The defence lawyer asked Mr Smith, 'Could you see the sign?'

Mr Smith replied, 'Yes.'

'Could you read the sign from the cart?' asked the lawyer.

'No,' answered Mr Smith. The lawyer sat down.

Charles had visited the site of the accident and knew the sign was in good condition and was readable. Further he was advised by the town clerk, that it had been there for twenty-odd years.

He stood up. 'Mr Smith, how long have you lived in the town?'

He answered, 'I was born here and went to school here.'

'Obviously, you know the position of the sign in question.'

'Yes, I have already answered the questions relating to the sign.'

'Yes, I know, but you weren't asked if you know the words on the sign.'

Mr Smith did not answer and looked away.

'Mr Smith, was that sign there when you went to school?'

Mr Smith replied, 'I'm not sure. It's been ten years since I went to school.'

'Mr Smith, you are under oath. What are the words on the sign?'

Mr Smith looked at his lawyer for help. The judge said, 'Please answer the question.' Mr Smith mumbled some words with his hand over his mouth.

The judge said firmly, 'Answer the question now!'

Mr Smith said, 'I think it's something to do with speed.'

Charles asked, 'Would you agree the words are – "School - Slow down"? I have witnesses who will testify you were travelling at a very fast trot.'

Mr Smith sat down in the witness box with his head in his hands. 'I'm sorry. It was my fault.'

Charles sat down, feeling pleased with himself.

After a few questions from the defence lawyer, eventually the judge spoke. 'On your admission of guilt, I find the charge proven. I will defer sentencing until tomorrow at noon. I have a minor case in the morning.'

The clerk called, 'All rise', as the judge left the bench.

The next morning, the participants were all in court, as the judge gave his ruling. 'It is unfortunate when any life is lost, but when it occurs due to the lack of observance of a road safety sign, it is unacceptable.

'You have not presented any reason or excuse for your action and no extenuating circumstances have been produced. Therefore, I sentence you, Mr Smith to ten years gaol.'

Charles had several other cases and was successful in each prosecution. Only one case was a challenge. It involved a paternity situation.

A single mother, Susan Lang, had a daughter named

Sharon. Susan's sister, Jane, had a jealous streak. The father of baby Sharon had previously been her boyfriend. Out of spite, she wanted the baby to go to an orphanage. Jane alleged the baby had been neglected and Susan was incapable of looking after the child.

Charles had met with Susan before the trial and found her to be a pleasant and level-headed young lady. But Jane had produced written reports, quoting examples of mistreatment and neglect, one by a Mr James.

When the hearing commenced, Charles could feel the tension in the courtroom. After the preliminaries were over, it was obvious that the case hinged on two reports of abuse and neglect of the child. Initially, Charles only asked a few rudimentary questions of Mr James and then sat down.

He wanted to see what would evolve. He felt uncomfortable and was not satisfied with the allegations associated with the charge. The defence lawyer decided to obtain some more information. He looked at the author of the first report for several long seconds. Bill James was a farmer who had three children of his own. He alleged he had seen Susan strike the baby several times.

When the defence lawyer asked him to tell the court where and when these instances had occurred, as this detail was not in the written report, Bill James was vague and had a mental lapse and would not, or could not, answer the question.

The second witness was Jane, the sister of the mother of the child and the one making the allegations. She was married but had not had any children of her own. When she entered the witness box, she was already angry. Charles intended to use this anger to find out if she was telling the truth.

He asked her, 'How long have you been married?'

She answered, 'Six years.'

'And you have no children?'

Angrily, she answered, 'No, my bitch sister has one and doesn't know how to look after her. It's wrong!'

Charles asked, 'What's wrong?'

'Why should she have a baby and not me.'

'You say in your letter that the baby is neglected. Could you give us some examples?'

'I've seen the baby in dirty clothes, she smells and is thin.'

'When was this?'

'Whenever I see the baby.'

Charles continued, 'When was the last time you saw the baby?'

She replied, 'I forget.'

'Come now, have a guess,' coaxed Charles.

Silence from Jane.

'How many times have you been to Susan's home since the baby was born?' More silence. Charles sat down.

The defence lawyer stood up. 'You must answer this question. Are you telling the truth?'

Jane started crying and could not stop. The judge told her to leave the witness box.

The defence lawyer called Mr James back to the witness box. 'Mr James, what's going on?' Mr James began to look uncomfortable. 'Did you see Susan Lang harm the child or not.'

Mr James looked up at the courtroom ceiling. He answered, 'Well not really. Jane told me of this and asked me to support her complaint against her sister.'

The lawyer replied, 'Do you realise where you are? This is a court hearing.'

Mr James asked, 'Can I have the report back? I want to withdraw it.'

The judge looked at Mr James and shook his head. 'You're either a fool or a liar or maybe both. Now please leave the box.'

'Mr Stuart, as prosecutor do you place any credence on these reports?'

'No, Your Honour, but I would like to get to the bottom of this fiasco.'

The judge agreed. 'Yes, I think we all would. Tomorrow, I want Susan Williams to bring her child to court. Also, arrange to have the police doctor in attendance here. Clerk, we are finished for the day.'

The clerk stood up and called, 'All rise.'

The following day, the courtroom soon filled. The hearing had been a feature in the local newspaper and was of interest to the public. When Susan and her baby arrived, the judge had them ushered to his chambers. The police doctor was already there.

The judge asked the mother if she objected to having her baby checked by the doctor.

She answered, 'No, please do.' Susan undressed the baby and laid her on a couch. The doctor took his time examining the child.

When he had finished, he told Susan to dress the child as he was finished with his examination. They waited with bated breath for his comments. The doctor said, 'This child is as healthy as you could want. It has been well-fed, has unmarked skin, not even a nappy rash. The mother has done an excellent job of rearing this child. I will send you a report in writing by tomorrow.' The judge thanked the doctor and the hearing recommenced.

The judge was angry that his court had been used for such a puerile and vindictive allegation. He called Mr James to the witness box and reminded him that he was still under oath. 'Mr James, we have had the police doctor examine the child and he is of the opinion the child is unmarked and well-nourished. Do you wish to tell us more? It would be in your best interest to help the court understand your letter. What was the reason?'

'Your Honour, I was trapped into writing this letter by Jane. One night I was drunk, and I fondled her.' He continued, 'She threatened me, saying she would report me to the police for sexual assault. A month later she asked me to write the letter saying I had seen Susan hitting the child. I had no choice.' He took a deep breath. 'She said the police would believe us and she would then, as a relative, apply to have custody of the baby. She did not believe we would end up in court.'

The judge answered dryly. 'Yes, there is no doubt of that. Before I give a ruling on this case, I would like Susan Lang to enter the witness box.'

When Susan was seated, the judge asked her, 'Do you live at home with your parents?'

'Yes, I do,' she responded.

'Do you work?'

'Yes, I do.'

The judge continued. 'Who looks after the child when you are at work?'

'I do. I work at home doing tapestry work for the Melbourne Emporium.' When she said these words, the judge leant back in his chair.

Everyone in the court watched as he decided his ruling. He sat there quietly, looking at his notes. He looked up and said, 'I don't need the wisdom of Solomon to make my determination. The doctor has stated the child is in good health. The mother lives with her parents, and she is gainfully employed working at home and looking after her child. Most importantly, the evidence presented is tainted and will be referred to the public prosecutor to decide what action he recommends be taken against Mrs Jane Williams and Mr Bill James. My ruling is that Miss Susan Lang's child remains with her as the natural mother and the case is dismissed.'

Charles had anticipated the ruling. Jane started to cry, while Mr James just stared into space, wondering what was going to happen next. Susan Lang stood up, her child in her arms and left the courtroom without looking at her sister.

A month later, Charles found out Jane Williams had been gaoled for six months for perjury. Mr James was fined two pounds for obstruction. The blackmail issue saved him from a charge of perjury. Miss Susan Lang married the child's father two months later.

A messy family feud had ended reasonably well. Although there were always going to be winners and losers.

Charles' time as a prosecutor had been completed. The judges he had worked with gave good reports on his performance to the police commissioner. Charles had now completed George's training schedule to the satisfaction of the senior police staff. George was away on business, giving Charles a few days to himself.

He had written to his Uncle Stephen in Kahuna and was eagerly waiting for a reply. Charles used these days and leisurely visited the city and the various buildings of interest.

In its short history, Melbourne had grown dramatically after the discovery of gold at Ballarat and the surrounding districts, although for several years afterwards many city businesses and country farms struggled to remain financially viable, due to the lack of staff and workers. The gold rush had caused sailors to desert their ships. Shop attendants and tradesmen had headed west to seek their fortune. Very few miners became wealthy, but many city businesses and farms did recover eventually. Stability again returned to the colony.

Charles received an invitation to attend the Passing Out Ceremony. After a few inquiries, he discovered the ceremony would be in two parts, namely a parade followed by an evening dinner.

George arrived the next day and invited him to lunch. He started the conversation, advising Charles he had received a letter from the Inspector General with a list of the latest promotions.

The list included new constables, sergeants, sub inspectors and inspectors. He then handed Charles an envelope with the Victorian Police crest, addressed to him.

It was his Certificate of Appointment to the position of inspector and included two unique collar number badges.

Charles looked at George, who offered his hand. 'Congratulations. You are now a confirmed member of the Victorian Mounted Police Force.

'Tomorrow, I'll take you to be issued with your uniform. Also, I have found a position for you in Kahuna.

It has a sergeant, two constables and access to an aborigine tracker. They have proven to be invaluable in the bush with their local knowledge and extraordinary eyesight. Your primary role is that of District Prosecutor with the police rank of inspector. You are due to leave here in seven days.

'It will take you at least week to reach there. You will need to select two sturdy horses for the trip. Now, I've spoken enough. Your turn for comment.'

Charles had been listening intently and nodding at times. 'Thank you for all you have done for me. I am indebted to you. Yes, I'm delighted you have found a position for me in Kahuna. It will be good to see my uncle again. I haven't seen him for over ten years. What time do you want me to meet with you for the uniform fit and issue?'

'I will come via your room at ten a.m. Now, let's eat and drink your health to celebrate your appointment.'

The day dawned with the sun rising over the barracks. Exactly at ten a.m. George arrived. They walked to the uniform issue room. There the orderly checked Charles' body measurements including shoe size. He was issued with two sets of riding uniforms including high boots and spurs. A hat, under clothes and shirts etc. He was taken to another room where he was further issued with a belt, a holster with a revolver, a bridle, saddle and cloth, a Carbine rifle with a saddle holster and, finally a sword.

George said, 'You are also entitled to a mess uniform, but we can get that later. In the meantime, you can use your Highland dress in the officers' mess.' The orderly advised he would arrange to have the issued items taken to Charles' room.

George asked, 'Have you given any thought to the selection of horses?'

'Yes, the stable sergeant recommends the Waler breed from New South Wales, and he speaks from experience. He was posted to Northwest Victoria for five years and he found they had good stamina, strength and were easy to manage. The country out there is very dry with large areas that are virtually deserts.'

George nodded, 'Yes, I agree with him. He's a good judge.'

'Also, he said my own horses could remain here, until I make other arrangements. He will see they are ridden and well looked after.'

The next day Charles selected his two horses. They were five-year-old mares. Oddly enough they were similarly marked. They were both brown and each had four white hocks and a brown tail.

The Passing out Parade had been rehearsed to ensure the March Past was understood by all participants. The day arrived, with part of the barracks courtyard arranged with seating for the VIPs, senior police officers, guests and relatives. The marchers and riders were assembled outside the barrack's gates, behind the police band.

The beat of the drums heralded the commencement of proceedings. Exactly on time, the band marched into the courtyard. The new constables led the parade, followed by the promoted sergeants. The new sub-inspectors were next, riding horses and finally the new inspectors also on horseback.

'Eyes right,' was called by the leader of each group when they paraded past the Governor and the official party.

The parade was perfectly executed. Charles felt a little overwhelmed but enjoyed the occasion. The crowd showed their appreciation and clapped energetically. Some waved to their policeman of interest.

After Charles unsaddled his horse and handed him over to a stable hand, he rested and then dressed, ready for the evening.

He felt comfortable wearing the Highland dress as he was not going to be the only person wearing a kilt. Another inspector and a new sergeant were also Highlanders.

When Charles arrived, he was shown to a table for six persons. Two fellow inspectors had their wives with them. George, who was still unattached, and Charles made up the table.

The evening went smoothly. The meal was excellent, and the background music was pleasing to the ear. English melodies with some Irish and Scottish airs were the order of the night.

After the speeches, the inspector-general, Sir Giles Gideon, visited the tables to converse with the occupants. When he reached Charles' table, they all stood. George introduced them. When he introduced Charles Stuart, the inspector-general mused, 'I knew a Scottish Stuart at university, the Honourable Keith Stuart. He was from Belcannon. I think that was the name. He was the son of an earl. Do you know the family?'

'Yes, my father is Sir Keith Stuart, the current Earl of Belcannon.'

'Well now, we have the son of a Scottish earl in the Victorian Police Force. Things are looking up. I trust your father is well.'

'Yes, thank you, sir.' The inspector-general smiled and wandered to the next table.

When they sat down, George said, 'You never cease to amaze me. Why didn't tell me?'

'Why, that's easy; I wanted to succeed on my own merits, not because I'm the eldest son of an earl.'

George nodded. 'Yes, I can see your point of view. It's a good thing that you were already an inspector, before anyone knew of your father. How should I address you now?'

'Nothing has changed between you and I; I'm still Charles.'

Arrangements commenced for Charles' departure to Kahuna. He was sorry he had to leave his three horses behind, but he was confident they would be looked after very well. Indeed, they would often be used in official parades.

On his final night in the barracks, Charles dined with George and the deputy inspector general. He thanked them both for his training and their encouragement to achieve his role in the Victorian Mounted Police Force. After several toasts, they wished him well in his future career.

The following morning, Charles arose early and packed his possessions onto one of his police Waler horses and saddled the other. George was there to farewell him. They agreed to keep in contact. Charles waved back as he rode from the barracks, heading to his new venture. He felt proud riding through the streets in his new uniform with his two Waler horses. Some people even waved to him.

The departure day was overcast but not cold. It was typical Victorian November weather. He decided to ride for around two hours at a time, which seemed to coincide with the distance between way stops with small villages or just an inn and a few shops.

At night he would water the horses and find a snack or meal for himself. His accommodation was varied from a room to a stable with a straw mattress. He didn't mind, just so long as he had a good night sleep. Although he did find in the country the early morning roosters crowing was a little annoying.

After ten days travelling, he was sitting at a table in a wayside inn, when a farmer rushed in, with a severe head injury. He was yelling. 'The blacksmith has gone berserk. He's chasing me and wants to kill me.'

Charles stood up as the blacksmith rushed into the inn with an iron bar in his hand. Charles drew his revolver and called, 'Stop. Put the bar down on the table.'

The blacksmith put the bar on the table, saying, 'This man has just cheated me. Look! He paid me this and said it was gold. It's not real gold; it's fool's gold. I've been a goldminer, and I know.'

Charles asked the injured man, 'Is that true?'

The injured man nodded.

Charles continued, 'Have you enough money to pay the blacksmith?'

'Yes,' was the answer.

'Well, pay the blacksmith and be on your way.' After he was paid, Charles said to the blacksmith, 'Be on your way. You're lucky I don't arrest you.'

He mused, arresting either of them would have been a waste of time for the court. He had remembered what the Melbourne sergeant had said during his street training.

The trip had become boring; the countryside had a sameness about it. At times, he could see large flocks of sheep, or scattered cattle or some paddocks that had been tilled and sown. The grass was still green and lush. Livestock appeared to thrive on it. Most rivers he crossed had wooden bridges, and a few had a ferry. Only once, had he needed to ford a river.

The final part of Charles' journey had seen the country landscape change. The northern country was dryer and hotter. The grass was less dense and not as green.

Finally, he saw a signpost that read "Kahuna – 10 miles". Charles was pleased to see the sign.

He had begun to feel at home in this new land. It was very different from his native Scotland but pleasantly so with the warmer weather. He had no regrets – so far.

He sat on his horse, on a hill looking down over Kahuna. A river flowed not far away from the town. The town had been planned and not just happened. Many small country towns had been allowed to expand without any long-term plans.

Kahuna was a planned square, with a very wide main street, designed to allow drovers to bring their stock through the town, using the main road when travelling to the next town.

A stockman would ride into a town and warn the locals of their herds or flocks coming. This allowed the locals to move their horses and gigs from the main street. The cattle were kept tight by the drovers and their dogs stopped them from escaping from the herd into side streets.

Sheep were different, they tended to go where they could see any opening. The flocks were large, sometimes in the thousands.

Often a few sheep simply vanished if they wandered from the flock down a side street. A day or so later some families would celebrate the visit of the sheep flocks, by inviting friends to share a lamb dinner or two. The sheep skins made good sleeveless jackets.

There was a variety of shops on either side of the main street with two larger buildings in the middle. Charles could also see a large paddock with buildings around a circular area. He presumed this would be the local Agriculture Showground. Most councils of growing towns reserved an area for a showground and sometimes even a racehorse track.

It was noon when he rode into Kahuna. Few people were on the street. He was wearing his police uniform and some waved to him. Charles immediately thought it would be a happy community. He was right.

The police station and the courthouse were combined. It was a two storied building. The top floor was for council offices and the lower floor was for the police operation, with stables and a small holding paddock in the rear.

He dismounted and walked into the foyer where a constable was seated. The constable immediately stood up. 'Welcome, Inspector Stuart. We have been expecting you. Please come through.' He knocked on the door with the word "Sergeant" painted on it. They entered the office.

The sergeant had his back to them, closing a filing cabinet. He turned and then smiled. 'Welcome, sir. I received a letter advising of your imminent arrival. I hope you had a good journey. It's a long way by horse. I know; I did it once.' They shook hands. 'Please be seated, sir.'

The sergeant was a tall, solidly built man. He appeared to be a person who would take no nonsense from a mischief maker or alleged offender. Charles considered him and decided he would be a good man to have on his team. The sergeant introduced himself. 'I'm Tim Cosbie and this is Fred Smith.'

He then asked the constable to "boil the billy", as the locals called it. He meant serve tea.

The three sat down. Charles spoke of his role in the district, to ensure they were aware his primary role was as a prosecutor when a magistrate visited the local towns. They then chatted about the local scene. It was a quiet area.

The only time they had problems was when the local shearing season was over, and the shearing teams cashed their cheques at the local hotel, staying until their money was spent.

Mainly, the problems were drunkenness and brawling, but very little major crime. The other constable and the blacktracker, who was called Murray, were out bush arresting a cattle duffer, who had been caught branding young cattle. They were expected back tomorrow. It might be Charles' first case as the district prosecutor, if the sergeant decided to charge the man.

Charles asked about his Uncle Stephen's property. The sergeant pulled out a local map and pointed it out. It was only an hour's ride, and he knew Stephen Stuart personally. They often had a drink when he came to town for supplies. He advised the property was called "Belcannon". Charles laughed and told the sergeant that was the name of the Stuart family home.

After Charles settled into his temporary accommodation at the hotel, he decided to visit his uncle the next day. He left his spare horse at the police stable. The ride was easy. He alternated between cantering and walking the horse.

He suddenly realised he had not given either of the horses a name. The one he was riding now always carried her head high, so he called her Princess and the horse in the stable, he named her Beauty.

The only difference between the horses was Princess had a small white section in her brown tail, where Beauty had a pure brown tail.

The signpost read, "Belcannon", with an arrow directing the way. There were only a few fences and yet sheep were everywhere. Buildings soon appeared in the distance. The largest and grandest was obviously the homestead. The other buildings were all similar in design and were made of wood with metal roofs. He presumed they were shearing and carriage sheds. Another building he presumed would be the shearers' quarters. Several holding yards were attached to the shearing sheds.

As he approached the homestead, some dogs ran out, barking. A man appeared on the verandah and stepped forward calling the dogs to heel.

Charles was in uniform and dismounted as his uncle walked closer smiling and said, 'I presume you are Charles, my nephew.' Charles smiled and nodded. 'Well about time. I've been expecting you for weeks.' They hugged each other.

Charles replied, 'It's a long story. It will take time telling.'

'Come in and meet the family. They will love to meet their cousin.'

Several people had gathered on the verandah. Stephen said, 'This is my family. Allow me to introduce you. This is the Honourable Charles Cornelius Bartholomew Stuart, your cousin, Uncle Keith's son. This lady is my wife, Clara. Our daughter, Isobel, and last, but not least, is our son Finlay.' More hugs and some kisses.

Charles could see a very happy family. The family group adjourned to a large sitting room. Stephen had decorated it as a Scottish memorabilia room. Swords, painting, kilts, sporrans even a set of bagpipes adorned the walls. Naturally, whisky was the drink of the day to celebrate the reunion.

Charles stayed for dinner and agreed to remain at the homestead overnight. At dinner he found himself answering question after question, mainly about Belcannon. He could sense his uncle was homesick. But as his uncle said 'I've been here so long; I'm now a colonial with a family of colonials. Maybe one day I will take a trip to the land of my birth. It is just a maybe.'

After a pleasant breakfast, Charles departed. He said, 'I will stay longer next time, as I would like to have a good look around your station.'

His uncle replied, 'You're welcome anytime.' A few kisses and hugs again. He rode away, both parties promising to visit each other.

CHAPTER THREE

The New Arrivals

Summer had been long and hot. The paddock grasses were brown with most dams and lagoons now dry. Livestock sheltered under whatever shade was available. They looked forlorn and listless with their heads down.

Charles watched the dark clouds forming in the north, hoping that the clouds would bring in the expected rain. He watched for a while and then returned to his desk to attend to some paperwork.

The thunder made him look out of his office window. Then the rain started, and it pelted down. It was running down the window distorting his view. He walked to the building's entry and saw the daily stagecoach appear out of the heavy rain and stop in front of the building. The coach driver jumped down from his seat carrying a mail bag and opened the coach door. He then ran to the building, quickly followed by his passengers. He waved to Charles and handed the mail bag to the local Cobb and Co. representative. Charles waited for an hour, then went and asked if he had any mail. Charles had ten letters. Six in official envelopes, two from his father and two from Mary. Two of the official letters were office tasks and the other four, updates on police procedures.

He decided to read Mary's letters at home.

After arriving home and pouring himself a drink, he sat down and first read his father's letters. His father was an excellent writer and gave an update on the local events and occurrences. Both letters had the same format. Charles was delighted his ageing parents were both well and Nicola had a boyfriend, Gavin McIntosh, who was the son of a farmer.

When Charles had left, Mary turned her attention to keeping busy. She became more involved in looking after their property and livestock. The horses were her main interest. She checked their health daily for condition. Most times it was unnecessary. Occasionally she found a minor injury such as a cut or a stone in a hoof.

Once a fortnight she visited town for shopping, whenever the weather permitted. The town often had dance nights, and she would attend with her parents. She was asked out a few times by men her age, however, she declined. She would never forget Charles.

Charles opened Mary's letter after checking the dates. She had received Charles' letter telling her of his escapade with the bank robbery. Her first letter advised, she had been successful at some horse shows and her father had won prizes for his bred horses. The weather had been unpleasant. Snow and freezing winds. She had not been to the village for four weeks, but food stocks were getting low. She and her father would have no choice but to brave the elements and go shopping soon.

Mary said Stella, her mother, was not very well. She had chest problems and had difficulty breathing with the cold weather. Her second letter was a surprise. It had been written three months ago. Her mother's health had worsened, and the doctor said she needed to move to a warmer climate to improve her quality of life.

Mary's father, Thomas Webster, had sold his business and property, and she said she was trying to talk her father into emigrating to Australia. He had first thought of Spain but decided against going there, due to the unstable political situation. He then considered going to South Africa and breeding horses, but again he was undecided, due to Boers and British settlers clashing. Mary said she was still hopeful of coming to Australia, after telling him of Charles' comments about the warmer climate. She advised future letters to her should be addressed to his Belcannon home, for his family to onforward them to her. Then she gave him her love. There the letter finished. Charles wondered what her father had decided.

Mary's father had eventually decided to emigrate to Australia. A friend who had lived three months in Australia helped him make up his mind. Her mother brightened up when he told her where they were going. He planned to open a farrier-blacksmith business and breed horses. He intended to take several horses with him. His friend told him of the reasonably priced land sales in the colonies. Her father had profited quite well from his business and property sales and intended to buy land or a business. Maybe both!

The travel planning for them to emigrate from Scotland had been tasked to Mary, while her mother packed their clothing, and her father selected and arranged the packaging of their favourite items, valuable furniture and prized possessions. Her father had four large horse stalls manufactured.

They were collapsible and easily erected. Slings were made to support the horses in heavy seas.

The Webster's farewell dinner was held at the earl's manor. Charles' family knew of his friendship with Mary and had met her previously. The meal was served with a background of Celtic tunes and airs. After some speeches, handshakes and kisses, the Websters departed for home.

Within a month of Mary's father making his decision, the family boarded the steamship SS Goliath. Mary wrote to Charles via his uncle's address, immediately after the decision had been made. She advised that she would write to him on arrival in Sydney, via the Melbourne Bank.

The ship would stop for twenty-four hours at St Vincent, Cape Town and Perth to take on coal for her steam engines and was expected to allow up to nine to ten weeks steaming. Her father had assembled the horses' stalls and loaded water barrels and fodder on the main deck. It was not unusual for livestock to be carried. They also carried cargo and some twenty passengers.

The voyage was interesting and when they berthed at a harbour, they hired a coach to show them the sights of local note.

Soon though, the endless ocean became boring. She had brought novels to read and when she finished them, she swapped them with other passengers. She befriended another lass the same age and from the same district. Fortunately, they had similar interests, namely in show horses.

Joan Jessop had heard of Mary's successes and asked her how she had achieved her wins.

Mary answered, 'There's no secret; just riding practice and more practice doing circuits.'

Mary's mother was very skilled with a crochet needle. During the voyage she produced countless doilies, table settings, milk jug covers, dress collars etc. She intended to donate them to a hospital fundraising committee.

The weeks rolled on. Mary was standing on the bow when the coast of Western Australia appeared on the horizon. She thought, *Not long now!* But she had no idea how large the continent was. They still had a few more weeks before they arrived in Sydney.

The great day eventually arrived. They sailed into Sydney Harbour following two other vessels. The day was cloudless with a slight breeze. It was a perfect day. The sun was warm, not hot. It encouraged women to carry their sun umbrellas. Thomas helped his wife to come on deck to enjoy the view and the sun. She had endured the voyage quite well and was happy. Her breathing seemed to have improved.

After the ship moored, it took five hours before the horses were unloaded. They had travelled well and were in good condition. Joan and Mary promised to keep in contact with each other after they were settled.

Thomas Webster soon found some stables for the horses. They then went to a nearby inn for accommodation.

The next day Thomas visited several land dealers, looking for a suitable block to commence his new venture in Sydney Town. If he had no luck there, he would try Melbourne.

Mary wrote to Charles advising him of their arrival but, as yet, she had no permanent mailing address. She promised to provide immediate details as soon as her father had made up his mind.

Thomas found a blacksmith business for sale. It was on a three acre block of land on a hill, close to Sydney Town. It had a small hut alongside the business, which could be added to a future residence.

Mary now had an address and true to her word, immediately wrote to Charles. The family stayed at the inn until a new building was erected alongside the hut and made into a four roomed residence. The hut became the kitchen.

Thomas had been approached by the military to maintain some of their parade horses. The commandant had seen his horses and had been impressed by their appearance. Obviously due to his professional care and attention.

Mary had been busy trying to locate information on persons owning show horses or hunters.

One day an army officer's wife rode into the blacksmith shop and enquired about the horses Thomas had bought from Scotland. Mary introduced herself and the lady replied, 'I'm Alice Howard and I believe you are a gymkhana competitor. Your father mentioned it to my husband when he visited here yesterday.

Mary nodded. 'I competed for three years in Scotland, and we brought four horses with us, as you probably already know. Are there competitions in Sydney Town yet?'

Alice said, 'No, we do have fox hunts, and we have been considering having gymkhanas in the future. I have five friends interested and, with you and I, we would be seven, if you wish to join us. I wonder if you would like to meet everyone.'

Mary answered, 'Yes, I would be delighted.'

Alice replied, 'If you are free Sunday at three p.m. I will send a gig for you.'

Mary said, 'Thank you. I look forward to it.' Alice then departed, leaving a very pleased Mary.

The gig duly arrived and took Mary to the army barracks. It was situated on a hill overlooking Sydney Harbour. The view was spectacular.

Sunday afternoons the harbour always had a variety of sailing vessels. They varied from small skiffs and yachts with coloured sails, to multi sailed vessels arriving from overseas. The sun was shining on the blue waters creating a scene of perfection and making her feel blessed with life in the colonies.

Alice was waiting in front of a large building. After a friendly greeting, Alice escorted Mary into a small dining room and introduced her to her friends. They were all wives of military officers. They made her feel comfortable and told of their time in Sydney.

Mary listened carefully to their conversation and their comments regarding the day-to-day activity in Sydney. Alice soon led the conversation to the potential of organising a gymkhana. A quick election saw Alice elected President and Mary as Secretary, as she had the most experience at competing in these events.

Alice had spoken to the commandant, and he gave his full support and even allocated some land to be developed into a horse rink. He commented that the military would have some use for it. Primarily, to train new officers from England. Secondly, the hunt club riders could ensure they kept their skills by practising over the obstacles. After a pleasant afternoon tea, the group set an inaugural meeting date. Mary was then driven home in a gig.

The Webster family attended the monthly dances at the military base. They were popular and always well attended. Mary, an attractive young lady and seemingly unattached, never missed a dance. She was often invited to dine by unattached officers. Unfortunately, Charles had not officially proposed to her. Consequently, he had not given her a ring to wear. But Mary had been true to Charles and always went home with her parents. She was pleased, having been accepted by the officers wives and made to feel welcome.

Mary wrote to Charles care of the Melbourne Bank address and eagerly looked forward to his reply.

When Charles received her letter, he wrote to her immediately and she was absolutely delighted they had been able to maintain such a strong communication. He wrote of his love for her and how he had missed her over these long months. He advised he would come to Sydney Town as soon as he had decided how he would travel.

Charles spoke with the sergeant and asked for his advice on what was the quickest means to travel to Sydney. He replied, 'The best way would be to link up with the Sydney-bound stagecoach.' He suggested, 'Ride to Albury and catch a coach there. Leave your horse with the local police and collect it when you return. Riding overland is risky. It would be a long ride. An injury to yourself or your horse could be a disaster in the vast lonely outback country.' Charles then wrote another letter advising Mary of a possible arrival date within three weeks.

The deputy inspector general agreed with Charles' request for four weeks leave of absence. He packed a few clothes and headed off with best wishes from the team. Fortunately, a strong wind blew from the west his entire travel time and helped him make good time to Albury. At Albury, the local NSW police inspector was pleased to be of help in looking after his horse in their paddock with their own horses. The stagecoach arrived on time with a driver and a shotgun guard.

He was one of three passengers who were heading to Sydney. Their first stop was Holbrook, and a problem occurred. The following morning, the driver arrived for work, but the guard did not. The local manager saw that Charles was a police officer and asked if he would ride as guard. He offered to pay him. Charles agreed to act as guard but declined the money offer. He still had the money his father gave him.

The journey was uneventful. Although at the next town, he noticed three men lurking in the shadows of a small building at the end of the town. He was later to learn that these three men had kidnapped the wife of the guard and forced him to miss his job as the guard on this trip.

When the offenders saw an armed police officer on board, they panicked and abandoned their plans to rob the coach. The guard's wife had not been harmed by the kidnappers, who had blindfolded her and returned her to her home.

Charles reverted to being a passenger at Jugiong, another small town en route to Sydney and remained so for the rest of the journey. The miles rolled on. Sydney was getting closer, and he was eagerly looking forward to meeting Mary again.

The stagecoach continued on through the days and through the nights. Rocking and rolling. This coach was an American design with leather suspension in lieu of the British metal type. They gave the coach a more improved ride. One could even sleep when travelling on some graded roads.

When they reached the outskirts of Sydney, more dwellings began appearing. Charles could see paddocks with grain growing and/or livestock grazing. Within the next three hours, the passengers could see the sea and Sydney. They had arrived safe and sound. When they alighted, he first needed to stretch his legs and he then approached the stagecoach terminal manager and asked, 'Where can I hire a horse. I need to find Webster's Blacksmiths. Have you heard of it?'

The manager laughed, 'You don't need a horse. Shanks pony will do. There it is, next to the church.' He pointed. Charles could read the sign. *Webster's Blacksmith's – Farrier (late of Scotland)*.

He walked to the building and stood there a while. It was on a large fenced-in block of land where several horses grazed. The building was in two joined parts; one an old dwelling, attached to a new three-roomed residence. Smoke was wafting from its single chimney. He entered the foundry and looked around and called, 'Hello, anyone here?'

A voice answered behind him. It was Mary's father. 'No, it can't be. Charles is that you? I don't believe it.

Well now, what a surprise. Does Mary know? She has been a little secretive lately. You look smart dressed in your uniform. Mary is in the kitchen. Go through. I'll talk with you later.'

Mary was baking bread and was kneading dough when Charles opened the kitchen door. She looked up. Seeing him, she squealed in delight and rushed to him. She put her arms around him and hugged him, her hands covered in flour. They kissed and then she spoke, 'You're finally here. It's been such a long time.'

Charles replied, 'Yes, you look great. You're prettier than ever.' They sat down still holding hands. 'Well, you go first. I want to hear what you've been doing over these long months.'

Mary laughed and answered, 'Well, mainly I've been thinking of you. When father decided to come to the colonies, we sold everything we didn't want, packed what we needed and brought it with us, including some horses and, after a long boring journey, arrived several months later. Father was lucky and purchased this property, which as you can see, has a few large paddocks, a workshop and a one room residence. We have added three rooms, and the business has been successful. That's my story. Now what's yours?'

Charles nodded. 'Yes, my life here has been interesting, challenging at times, but I enjoy it. Most of it you already know through my letters.' He continued, 'Currently, I am a prosecutor as well as a Victorian Mounted Police Inspector.'

Mary stood up. 'Let's go for a walk, after I dust you down. I have put flour all over your impressive uniform.' They strolled down to the river, hand in hand, not talking. They were just enjoying each other's company again.

That night Charles stayed at a nearby inn and joined Mary and her parents for breakfast, the next morning. They were a happy family and believed they had made the correct choice in selecting the colonies for their new life. Her mother's health had stabilised and improved.

Their business had soon become established and profitable. The military contract was a bonus and had attracted more businesses to use their services.

Charles and Mary sat in the garden and began to plan their future together. Laughingly he said, 'I don't think I have asked you to marry me. Let's make it formal. Will you marry me?'

Mary smiled and nodded. 'Yes, I will marry you. There, we are now official engaged. Do I get a ring?'

He kissed her and answered, 'Yes, but not today. I forgot.' They decided to marry in Sydney when he could have some more leave.

However, Charles had a dilemma. Should he stay in Victoria or move to New South Wales and seek a new career?

When he said this, Mary answered, 'Why do that? You have a good position. I would be disappointed if you did that. No, I'll join you in Victoria. My parents don't need me around anymore.'

Charles shook his head. 'Think about it. I do love the country life and my job, but I'm thinking of you. I'll be going back in a few days and hopefully I'll be able to return in about a month and then we can decide.'

Mary replied, 'Yes, but I'm sure I will want you to stay in the Victorian Police Force and in the country.'

The remaining days soon passed and helped them confirm their feelings for each other. After a few kisses and handshakes, Charles boarded the Melbourne-bound coach and with a final wave to Mary, it headed south.

The trip was long and boring, but it surprised him; the coach was nearly always within ten minutes of its planned arrival time at its next destination. He dozed on and off most of the trip to Albury. After collecting his horse from the border police, he began the long ride west to Kahuna. He was once joined by a mob of kangaroos who hopped alongside him for a mile or two, then vanished into the trees.

The sergeant greeted him with a smile. 'Welcome back. I hope it was a good trip. It's a long way, isn't it?'

Charles nodded. 'Yes, I'm a bit saddle sore.'

Mary and Alice had been busy arranging a gymkhana. The arena had been laid out and the obstacles placed into position. Mary rode one of her horses to the arena and slowly cantered around the course allowing the horse to see the obstacles. After a few circuits, they cleared the first three jumps successfully but at the fourth jump her horse shied.

She tried three times before the mare cleared the jump. Mary was happy with their first day's efforts. She would try again in a few days.

Alice had been watching and was impressed. She clapped her hands as Mary dismounted. 'We have five riders to date and if the weather is sunny, we'll have a picnic atmosphere, and it will definitely attract many spectators.'

Gymkhana day arrived, with the sun shining brightly. Alice had been right; a crowd had arrived. Several food stalls had been erected and a bar. Spectators were resplendent in their weekend refinery, carrying colourful parasols. The riders were introduced to the crowd amid claps and cheers. There were two events with slightly different courses. Most riders scored high marks and only one horse caused her owner some discomfort.

Mary took a tumble once, but only her pride was injured. She won one event and was second in the other competition. Alice deemed it a successful day and gave a small speech.

During the day, Mary had noticed an officer looking at her several times which made her feel uncomfortable. He was the husband of one of the other riders.

Later that afternoon, he approached her and introduced himself as Lt Gary Low. He said he wanted to compliment her on her riding skills. Grudgingly, she spoke with him and thanked him for his comments. He offered to buy her a drink, but she declined, saying she had to meet with Alice and the committee for a summary of the day as she was their secretary. He politely bid her good afternoon and left. Mary noticed Alice looking her way but thought nothing more about the encounter.

Two weeks later, at a hunt meeting, Mary saw him looking at her again. She nodded to him and turned away. After the hunt, Mary made sure she was not alone. She had a bad feeling about Lt Low. His wife was at the hunt, but he appeared to ignore her.

She was going to say something to Alice but decided not to make an issue of her feeling. At the next hunt, as she was dismounting, Lt Low was standing alongside her. As she turned to lower herself to the ground, she felt a hand touch her breast and a voice say, 'Allow me to help you down.' When she had completely dismounted and saw it was Lt Low, she hit him hard on his arm with her crop. She was furious. He quickly realised this and mumbled an apology before walking away.

Unknown to Mary at the time, Alice saw the incident. She walked across to Mary and said, 'I saw that. That's the third time he's done something like this. I'll see the commandant and have him moved to the outstation.' Mary felt sorry for his wife. She was a quiet lady with two children.

Two days later, Alice invited Mary to visit the military headquarters. On arrival she was met by an officer and escorted to the commandant's office. The officer opened the door, and Mary saw Alice standing alongside a tall and distinguished officer.

Alice said, 'Mary met my husband, Major General Thomas Howard.'

Mary had no idea Alice was the commandant's wife. She was invited to be seated. An orderly served tea.

The major general said, 'Hello, Mary. My wife speaks highly of you. Call me Thomas. Alice told me of your incident with Lt Low. This is the third incident I am aware of; no doubt there have been others. Tell me exactly what happened. I have Alice's comments as a witness, but I need yours as well. Wait until I get a scribe here.' He called out loudly and the waiting scribe entered the room and sat alongside Thomas. As Mary spoke, the scribe wrote every word into a large journal.

The commandant made a quick decision. He asked the scribe to send in the duty officer. The commandant ordered him to have Lt Low and his family posted to an outstation. 'They are to leave the barracks by noon tomorrow.'

Mary felt sorry for Mrs Low, but she had told the truth about what had happened. Lt Low was a disgrace to the military. She was surprised he had not been sent back to England. She was unaware that a posting to an outpost was regarded as a worse punishment.

Learning that Alice, her friend and mentor, was the wife of the second most powerful military person in the colony, after the Governor, had been a pleasant surprise.

Charles wrote to the deputy inspector general requesting time off to go to Sydney to be married. The answer was, '*Go now and return as soon as possible. You will be needed as a prosecutor soon. We have several cases due within the next month.*' Charles left the next day for Sydney.

When he arrived, Mary's family was sitting down for dinner. They had made some arrangements for the two to marry but only a tentative date had been planned. Her parents understood the rush due to his police commitments and did not complain.

Charles arrived in time for the tentative wedding date to be confirmed. Mary's dress had already been made and now Mary could send out her written invitations to her riding friends and to her parents' new acquaintances.

The wedding was idly watched by many of the settlers, who had been out and about having a weekend stroll. Joan Jessop and Mary had managed to find each other and had kept in contact. Joan had been delighted when she was asked to be her bridesmaid. Most of their guests were military wives and their husbands and her father's business acquaintances. The military band provided pipers and drummers who added to the spectacle when they left the church. That evening was a culmination of many months of waiting for each other. They retired that evening as one, after waiting for so long.

After breakfast the next day, Charles farewelled a tearful Mary and his in-laws and headed back to Kahuna as required by the deputy inspector of police. Mary planned to follow on within the week.

Mary packed her clothing and her knick knacks on her dressing table. Her mother gave her some family heirlooms. Several years ago, her mother purchased a glory box for her. Over that time, she had collected sheets, towels and other manchester items for her marriage home. Her riding gear and saddle would follow later, together with her horses. After she had booked her seat on the stagecoach, she wrote to Charles advising him of her date of arrival.

The military wives planned a farewell dinner for her and presented her with a gold necklace with a small enamel medallion with a military crest on it. She would miss their chatter and their goodwill.

The departure day soon arrived and amid hugs and kisses, Mary promised her mother she would not forget to write home. She then boarded the southbound stagecoach for Albury.

With a crack of his whip, the driver sent the four horses galloping down the road. At first the journey was interesting. She had not been outside Sydney before. During the first four hours, she saw animals that she had only read about – kangaroos, emus and countless different birds, including the noisy kookaburra. At one stop she watched as a large wedge-tailed eagle floated in the wind currents, gliding effortlessly in the sky.

She was intrigued to see the speed the kangaroos could achieve, bounding alongside the coach. Another animal new to her was the emu. She watched a female and a younger bird running into the trees, after being startled by the noise of the coach and horses.

The coach stopped frequently to change the four horses for fresh animals and drop off or collect new passengers. Conversations between them revealed a mixed group of nationalities.

They were from all walks of life. Wealthy or just battlers, they were each seeking to find their niche in the colonies. Generally, it was only small talk. Some passengers were interesting to listen to.

One was a member of the Russian Royal family. He had been sent to the colonies to investigate the possibility of purchasing a goldmine. He had visited several sites, but he believed all the gold had been found and was now heading home. Another passenger was listening and said, 'I think you will be proved wrong in years to come. The colonies are still being explored.'

The Russian answered, 'Yes, you could be correct. But I can't wait.'

The journey had now become boring. The countryside had a sameness about it, and the coach rocking and rolling had become annoying. She disembarked halfway through the trip and stayed at a guest house just to have a good night's sleep and to freshen up.

The next morning, she rejoined another coach and headed further south. At the next horse change-over station, the passengers were advised that a bridge over a river on their route had collapsed. A large log from upstream had hit the centre support pole and caused the section to fall into the deep river water.

The coach driver said, 'I know another way across the river at a ford further upstream. I'll try to cross the river there.' The passengers looked at each other, wondering what this meant.

When they reached the river ford, the driver stopped the horses and he and the guard climbed down and walked to the ford. Water was slowly flowing over it, but it was hard to see how deep it was.

The guard started to walk across the ford and stopped halfway, the water up to his waist. He shouted to the driver, 'It will be risky. The coach might float.'

The coach driver asked, 'What's on the riverbed?'

He called back, 'Gravel stones.'

The driver replied, 'Good. We'll need to make sure the coach doesn't float.'

When the guard returned to the riverbank, he nodded. 'There are plenty of logs on the riverbank. We could put some of them on the roof of the coach and open the coach doors to allow the water to flow through.'

The guard had an axe under his seat and headed to the logs on the riverbank. After half an hour the logs were ready to be placed on the coach roof. They recruited the four male passengers to help lift the logs into place. The driver had spare reins, and he used them to tie the logs into position.

One of the passengers interrupted and said, 'With the logs on the roof, if the coach becomes buoyant, the logs will make the coach top heavy. I suggest you put the biggest log through the coach doors and lay it on to the coach floor.'

The driver nodded. 'Yes, good idea. I agree.' They carried the log and slid it through the two coach doors. The passengers helped the two ladies to climb back on board and sat them sideways on the seats, to keep them dry. The men sat on the log.

The driver called, 'Here we go.' The horses trotted into the water. The driver kept yelling, 'Come on, come on, keep going,' continuously cracking his whip. The horses continued to walk on the gravel and kept their footing. Halfway across, the coach started going sideways but the horses kept going, making progress. Soon they had the coach on solid ground on the other riverbank.

After unloading the logs, the guard suggested a break and he boiled the billy for a well-earned cup of tea for all. They all praised each other for a successful team effort. Even the women, who did not get wet due to sitting sideways on the seats.

Mary thought that now she would have something exciting to tell Charles.

The driver said, 'That's the pioneer spirit in action.'

The driver said to Mary, 'This is Albury, the end of your coach journey. The riverboat leaves from over there.' He pointed to a large, impressive building. It was a warehouse for storing wool bales. At the front of the building, she saw the booking office for the paddle steamers. Her timing was fortunate, a steamer was due to leave in three hours, heading down river to Kahuna.

Mary was delighted to have a cabin on the top deck. Her view of the gumtrees captured her attention. They were on the edge of riverbanks. Some had their roots exposed due to flood waters scouring the soil from them over the years.

There was a variety of trees, with different types of bark on their trunks and with lush green foliage. The river gums were impressive, towering high into the sky. Birds of all colours, making differing sounds, filled the air. Sometimes they settled on the steamer's safety rails. The outstanding sound was that of the kookaburra. Its laughing call would echo through the trees and soon other kookaburras would join in. Their sounds filled the air.

The chug chug of the engine and the noise of the splashing paddle wheels pushing through the water, made her think she was in another world. Peaceful and serene.

There were several other passengers, mainly farmers returning from either land or livestock sales. One was James Freeman, the town mayor. The steamer had a small bar on board. She joined some of them for a sundowner drink.

It was an Australian term and appropriate to the colony's pioneers enjoying the end of a working day. As they chattered with each other, with the sunlight filtering through the trees, she began to understand Charles' happiness in this environment. She had no intention of allowing him to leave it.

The captain was laying down the law to a drunken passenger, who had been sitting by himself most of the afternoon and drinking from a whisky bottle. He had now become boisterous and annoying to the other passengers.

Suddenly the captain picked him up and threw him overboard into the river. Mary looked at the captain horrified and said, 'Maybe he can't swim.'

'Don't worry, madam, he won't drown.' The drunk was floundering and waving his arms in distress. The captain looked at Mary and said, 'He's on a sandbank. The water there is only four feet deep.' He turned and went to the steering bridge. Mary looked back and had to laugh. The drunk was standing up chest deep in the water, angrily waving his fist in the air.

The days rolled on. Not all passengers disembarked at a wharf. Several minutes before approaching a small beach, a known drop off or pickup spot, the captain would sound his siren and slow the boat. Soon a person would be seen running to the riverbank to meet the boat. A dinghy would be rowed out to be alongside the boat to collect a returning passenger or mail and maybe uplift a new passenger or mail. With a farewell wave the dingy would be rowed back to shore.

Mary was surprised at the number of small beaches along the meandering Murray River. Towns were few and far between but there were farmhouses every few miles.

The captain called Mary to the bridge and advised her they would be berthing at Kahuna in the next hour or so. She went to pack her belongings and became excited at the prospect of seeing Charles again. The captain surprised her when he presented her with a small model of the paddle boat as a souvenir. She was delighted and thanked him.

The paddle steamer slowly approached the wharf. The crewman at the bow cast a rope to a wharf hand, who lopped it over a wharf bollard as the boat stopped moving. After the stern rope was secured, the crew pushed out a ramp for passengers to disembark onto the wharf.

Mary looked for Charles on the wharf, which had a large crowd, welcoming James Freeman, the mayor, home. Mary began to panic wondering where Charles was.

A voice soon allayed her fear. It was Charles.

As he approached her, the mayor turned and asked, 'Do you know Charles? He and I are good friends.'

'Yes. He's my husband,' she proudly replied.

Then he waved to her, saying, 'We'll meet again,' as he was moved on, surrounded by his happy welcoming crowd.

Charles said, 'You look great.' Then he kissed her. Together again, the happy couple walked arm in arm to collect her baggage and then stroll to the hotel. Charles had changed his hotel room for a double room. After unpacking, he took Mary to the police station to meet his team. Even shy Murray welcomed her, saying, 'H'llo, missus.'

That evening, they had been invited to dinner at Belcannon Station. Mary was soon made to feel at home with Charles' relatives.

Isobel was the same age as Mary and soon began chatting. She asked about Scotland and Mary asked about Kahuna.

Charles and his uncle, Stephen, with Finlay, sat on the porch and enjoyed a few whiskies, while Clara sorted out dinner with their chef. During their conversation, Stephen asked, 'Have you decided where you two will live?'

Charles shook his head. 'I haven't given it any thought yet. I'll look around next week. I'm in no hurry.'

Stephen said, 'If you like, you can stay in the head stockman's house down by the river. It's vacant, as Finlay is doing that job now. I'd like someone to stay there and use it. I don't want it to go to rack and ruin as deserted houses often do. It's yours if you want it. Stay the night and have a look at it tomorrow.' When he told Mary of the offer, she became excited – to live by the river - wow!

After breakfast, Charles, Mary and Stephen rode to the river house. It could be seen from the homestead and was only a leisurely five-minute ride. Immediately Mary saw the house she made up her mind and thought, *This is for me.* The house had two bedrooms, a parlour, a kitchen, a separate dining room and a large storeroom. The furniture was minimal, but they could purchase items and include them in the home as they felt necessary.

Outside, there was a stable for four horses, a tack room for saddles and harnesses and an annex for a gig. While Charles and Stephen were talking, Mary strolled to the riverbank, clapping her hands in delight when she saw the view.

The river water was twinkling, with the sunlight shining through the tree branches and reflecting on its surface. Birds were chirping and skimming over the water. Even a few fish were jumping out of the water, completing the scene.

Charles and Stephen had followed Mary and were enjoying Mary's happiness. Charles turned to Stephen and laughingly said, 'Well it looks like you have new tenants.'

Stephen nodded, 'We'll enjoy having you as neighbours.'

The couple headed back to town to arrange for their belongings to be transported to their new home. The next day they moved in. Mary had been shopping for food, cutlery and manchester. Within two days they were settled.

Mary rode to Stephen's homestead, to invite the family to lunch. As she dismounted, she saw a bitch suckling six pups. She had always wanted a pet dog and asked Stephen if she could buy a pup. Stephen said, 'Take your pick. They are seven weeks old and are due to be weaned now. We don't need any more cattle dogs.'

Mary selected a male who was a black blue in colour with a white chest. She named him "Toby". She kept him in the storeroom at first and took him for a walk on a leash in the morning and the afternoon. After a month Toby was let run free. He had been easily trained to obey the commands of 'sit', 'stop', 'drop', 'heel', 'come here', and most importantly, to 'bark' when ordered.

When he was six months old, Toby had been laying under the seat with Mary in the gig, when he showed his protective side. She was in town and had stopped the gig and was about to alight. A man who knew her to nod hello, stepped forward and put his arm out to help her alight. Toby stood up and began barking fiercely. The man withdrew his arm as Mary shouted at the dog, 'Stop,' which he did and lay down under the seat again.

The man said to her, 'You're safe with your cattle dog as a bodyguard. I wouldn't like to be bitten by him.' Mary apologised.

The house had been built on a small hill and was safe from flooding. When the snow in the alps melted it sent down a deluge of water into the river. Just to the right of the path to the river was a billabong or lagoon.

It had been formed when the river had previously flooded and filled a low lying land area with water, leaving it full of water when the flood waters receded. The billabong was about fifty yards in diameter and five feet deep in the middle.

The night was balmy; it had been a very hot day. They walked hand in hand down to the river and sat on the bank just enjoying the peace and stillness of the night. As they walked back to the house, Mary said, 'Let's go for a swim in the billabong?'

Charles answered, 'What, are you serious?'

Mary was already undressing and just said, 'Hurry up!' She was now naked and in the water. Charles just shrugged his shoulders and undressed. The water temperature was just right. They swam a little and splashed each other as would children. Charles had his arms around her and felt the warmth of her breasts against him. They dried themselves with their clothes and then laid together. It was inevitable that their feelings would become amorous and eventually they made love under the stars twinkling through the branches.

Charles looked at her naked body and said, 'You are my Venus De Milo and Mona Lisa rolled into one. No wonder I love you.' He kissed her and helped her up. They walked back to the house naked, carrying their clothes, but wearing their shoes.

A couple of days later, Mary went into town with Charles to do some shopping and to have lunch with Isobel. When she returned to the police station to go home, she asked the sergeant, 'What is the best way for me to bring my horses to Kahuna?'

He suggested, 'Put them on a ship from Sydney to Melbourne, then train to Echuca and paddle steamer to Kahuna. It's a long trip but it's the safest way.'

Mary raised the subject on the way home and asked Charles, 'What do you think?'

'Well, it needs to be done, sooner or later. Yes, do it.'

Mary then said, 'I think I should travel with them.'

Charles nodded. 'They are valuable. When do you want to go?'

She replied, 'Next week.' The next day she booked a seat on the paddle steamer to Albury.

After travelling the same coach route as before, it was now just a long boring trip. She eventually arrived in Sydney. Her parents were delighted to see her. Her mother could not stop asking questions about her new home and location. Her father sat there listening. That night she slept soundly, ready for a long and busy day tomorrow.

She booked herself and three of the horses to sail to Melbourne within one week. Her father kept a mare for breeding with some quality stallions he knew were in Sydney Town. That night she wrote a letter to Charles advising of her expected time and date of arrival on the SS Orian.

The next few days Mary spent visiting the military wives and was invited to dinner twice. The women were all keen to learn of Mary's experiences in the Australian bush.

Departure day arrived and, with her father's help, she took the three horses to the dock and supervised their loading. She also checked there was sufficient fodder and fresh water available for her to feed the horses en route. After a few kisses and a few tears, Mary boarded the ship and waved goodbye.

The voyage started with sunshine and moderate breezes as they sailed out of Sydney Harbour. It was a magnificent harbour. Houses were built on prime positions on the waterfront with magnificent views across the water. She was surprised to see so many boats in the harbour. Sydney had rapidly expanded to the northside of the waterway and now needed water taxies to serve the northside of the harbour to bring their residents to work in Sydney.

When her ship steered south after leaving the harbour, she went to check that the horses were settled. She then went to her cabin and lay down looking out at the sea through her round porthole glass window. She eventually went to sleep due to the calm rocking movement of the ship.

She was awakened by the ship lurching. Looking out the porthole, she could see white capped waves and heavy rain. She immediately put on a heavy shawl and went to check the horses. A sailor saw her and said, 'It's dangerous out here. What are you doing?'

She answered, 'I want to check my horses are safe.'

The sailor said, 'Come with me,' and led her to the horse stalls. It took a few minutes to check they were secure and out of the rain, then the sailor took her back to her cabin. 'Don't worry about them. I was born on a farm and know how to look after animals. I'll keep an eye on them for you.'

The shawl Mary had on was wringing wet and so was she. She stripped off her clothes and put on dry ones. Her hair was wet, she tried to dry it but with little success. She then retired to her bunk and soon fell asleep.

The next morning, Mary awoke with a heavy cold. Coughing and sneezing and feeling unwell. By afternoon she began shivering and perspiring.

At dinner that evening, the captain's wife wondered why she had not come to dine. She went to her cabin and found her distraught with a fever. The captain's wife went back to her cabin and returned with dry clothes.

She then helped Mary change out of her saturated clothes.

She then fetched a bowl of broth and some medicine called Laudanum. She stayed with her until she went to sleep again. Before going to bed, the captain's wife looked in on her again. She was not perspiring, but she still had a fever.

The next few days were of concern for Mary. When the SS Orion entered Port Phillip Bay, Mary's fever had abated. She had been ill for five days and had lost weight, not having eaten a main meal, only broth. The captain's wife had tended her constantly with cold towels on her brow. This helped reduce the fever. She helped Mary get dressed and to leave her cabin to check her horses. She was very weak and needed the help of the sailor who had watched over her horses while she was incapacitated. They were in good condition and quite lively.

Charles was waiting on the wharf. The first person ashore was the captain's wife. She knew Charles by his uniform as Mary had described it. Charles sensed something was wrong, when he saw her heading towards him.

She introduced herself and quickly said, 'Mary's alright, but she's had a very bad cold, with a fever. She is quite weak and will need you to help her ashore. I'll take you to her.'

Charles quickly followed her on board the ship and to Mary's cabin. He was shocked when he saw her drawn face and sunken eyes.

Mary started to cry. 'Take me home. My bags are packed ready to go.' Charles picked her up and carried her ashore, placing her in the small police gig he had borrowed. After thanking the captain's wife, he approached two mounted police constables and asked them to collect the three horses and take them to the police barracks. Charles waited until the horses were ashore safely.

He drove Mary to the hospital first for a doctor to inspect her.

The doctor advised, 'The worst is over, but until she gains some weight, she must take things easy and rest up. Plenty of broth and fresh fruit and she will be back to normal in no time.'

Charles and Mary went to the police barracks and stayed for two days before catching a stagecoach to go home. After he saw the horse master, it was decided her horses could remain in the police holding paddock and could be used, as he decided, for police duty. Charles was more interested in Mary's wellbeing.

The stagecoach journey home was uncomfortable for Mary. But it was much quicker than by train and then a ferry to Kahuna.

The sergeant was there as usual and immediately had Constable Smith arrange a gig for them to travel home. As they drove up to their home, Mary asked Charles to stop on the rise. She pointed to the river and said, 'Once when I was sick, I wondered if I would see the river again.'

Charles lent over and kissed her. 'I'm pleased you were wrong.'

After two weeks Mary was back to her old self again and began to think of her horses at the Melbourne Police Barracks. They decided to transport them by train to Echuca and then by steamer to Kahuna.

Mary invited Isobel to travel to Melbourne with her. Isobel readily accepted the invitation. She had not been to Melbourne for six years. The women would make the trip a shopping visit, as well as bring the three horses to Kahuna.

They booked into the Empire Hotel in the centre of Melbourne. The city had grown considerably since Isobel's last visit. The first day they visited the shops until they were exhausted from walking. After a good night's sleep, they decided on one more day's shopping.

They then arranged for the horses to be taken to the train station and loaded.

The horse master greeted them with a smile. 'They were easy to look after and have been no trouble. We used them once for a Passing Out Parade and they behaved themselves. I'll be sorry to see them leave.'

Mary presented him with a silver ring with a horse head on it. 'Thank you for looking after them and I hope the ring fits one of your fingers,' she said laughing. They waved goodbye and led her three horses to the nearby station where they supervised their loading.

An hour later they were headed home with their purchases. Luckily, they had a compartment to themselves. The rocking of the train soon had them dozing. The train stopped several times. At one long station stop, they had time to have a cup of tea. At long last they arrived in Echuca. The ferry was a day late, due to a boiler problem.

Loading the horses was easy. The deck hands were used to handling prize livestock. The horses were easier to move around than the large bulls they sometimes carried. Charles was there to meet them. He guessed they would arrive on this day or the next. Charles and Mary drove Isobel to the homestead with the horses tied to the gig.

They continued to the new paddock which she and
Charles had fenced. When she released the horses, they
began prancing and buckjumping, happy to be free in a
paddock with water and plenty of grass.

Mary advertised "Interests in a local Gymkhana"
in the local paper. She was delighted to receive ten
answers. Some had competed previously, and others
just wanted to be involved. Mary asked James Freeman,
the mayor, if she could use a room at the local shire hall
for an initial meeting. He had no hesitation in agreeing.
He offered his full support to attend to whatever would
be needed to stage such an event.

The first meeting attracted twenty local citizens.
Mary opened the meeting, suggesting a committee be
formed. She was nominated to be the president, which
she gratefully accepted. She had prepared an agenda
and handed out copies to the gathering. The priority
was to find a block of land to establish a course and
erect the gymkhana obstacles. The mayor suggested
the centre area of the local showground. It was large
enough to have the gymkhana course in the middle and
leave sufficient area around it for the parade of livestock
on show days. Mary had anticipated his answer and
thanked hm accordingly. This had been her main worry.

Mary began to plan the layout of the course. She sat
on the porch, wondering if it should be a simple course
or a complex one. She was worried if the course was
too difficult she could lose some potential permanent
members. She decided to have a simple five-obstacle
course. First a simple brush fence, then a single pole
jump followed by a water jump, next a high jump
and finally a three pole jump with the poles set at
progressively different heights. The course would have

to be completed within two minutes. The competitors were allowed two attempts over the jumps. The obstacles were made and erected by volunteers, some were council employees, in two weeks. All was ready for Kahuna's inaugural gymkhana.

The mayor issued a bulletin advertising Gymkhana Day, inviting all to attend. Local businesses were encouraged to open stalls on the day, selling drinks, food or souvenirs of the event.

Gymkhana Day arrived with the hot sun shining, and Mary feeling a little apprehensive. Most of the riders had trialled during the week and most were successful. A few horses had baulked and refused to jump, embarrassing their riders. Mary had been watching and was happy to see the high standard of riding. The event would be competitive.

The local band started the day's proceedings with a few appropriate tunes such as *Garryowen*. This was followed by the mayor giving a short welcoming speech. The first two riders were experienced and guided their horses successfully over the jumps within two minutes.

Mary was next to compete and jumped the first two. At the water jump, her horse slowed down and turned away. Mary tried again to make him jump, but at the jump he baulked very late, and Mary went flying over the jump and ended up in the water. The audience gasped; afraid she might be injured. Mary stood up and after a few seconds, she left the water and turned to the audience. She then curtsied with outstretched arms. The crowd clapped and cheered at her response to being thrown. Mary took off her coat and stood in the hot sun. By the time for her next attempt, she was reasonably dry.

The day progressed with the crowd enjoying the jumping. The competition was exciting. There were ten riders and three were outstanding. Mary saddled a different horse for her second attempt. This time she was successful and cleared the water jump.

Her time placed her in third place. The day ended with the mayor presenting the winner with a cup and a blue rosette. The second placed rider receive a red rosette, and Mary collected a green rosette. He advised the crowd the next gymkhana would be held in three months. The local paper wrote a glowing article of the Gymkhana and complimented Mary on her initiative in establishing such a high profile community event in a small country town.

CHAPTER FOUR

Another Emigrant

When the arrow struck Ian, momentarily he did not realize what had happened. He stepped back and lost his footing and fell backwards from the rock into the river. The cold water shocked him back to reality. The arrow had penetrated the flesh under his armpit. No bones had been hit. He looked at the arrow and saw it was a lightweight metal type with no fluted arrowhead. He gritted his teeth and pulled the arrow out from under his arm. It was a small injury and there was little bleeding due to the cold water. Ian sat in the water collecting his thoughts, deciding what to do next. Immediately behind him and in line with the rock, was a large clump of undergrowth. He crawled low in the water to the undergrowth and when he reached it, he was able to climb out, still hidden from Shamus. Ian stayed there until he saw Shamus row away, heading back to the manor with his venison cuts.

While Ian waited for his wound to heal, he considered his future move. He knew he had to leave The Loch area forever and start a new life far from Scotland. But where? America, Canada, South Africa or the most distant country of all – the Australia colonies. He decided to ride to the port and join the first ship requiring a crewman and go where it was heading.

Leaving early evening, Ian saddled his two horses and rode into the trees along the riverbank. He had a final look at his home from the opposite bank. He mused about whether he would ever see it again.

He rode nonstop until he reached the port road. It was still dark, which suited him. He wanted to avoid contact with anyone who might possibly know him. In the daylight he left the road and rode into the forest. At noon he stopped by a creek and watered the horses and had meal of precooked cold venison and some fruit. He rested until dark and then joined the port road again and rode on.

It took him four days to reach the port. He sat on a hill overlooking the moored ships. There were three in port. Only one was active, with men loading timber into its holds. He decided to venture into the port and sell his horses to a farrier near the loading wharf.

The farrier purchased them cheaply; Ian didn't try to negotiate. He just wanted some cash. If he was unsuccessful in obtaining a berth on a ship, he would need to have money for food and accommodation.

Ian approached the ship being loaded and looked for a person who appeared to have some authority. He saw a tall man shouting orders to the loaders and walked over to him. The tall man looked at him enquiringly. Ian asked him if he needed any extra crewmen.

The tall man gave him a quick look and answered 'Yes, can you start now?'

Ian nodded. 'Yes'. The tall man was the ship's bosun. He pointed to the timber. 'Go and help them. We're running late for the tide.'

Ian couldn't believe his luck. The work was demanding, but he was capable of assisting to move the timber, even with his damaged arm. By late afternoon the ship was ready to sail. The bosun told Ian to follow the other crewmen and come aboard. He would talk with him in the morning. The ship sailed on the evening tide.

Some of the crewmen introduced themselves to Ian. Others were quiet and kept to themselves. After finding a spot in the sail locker, he bedded down on some sails and went to sleep. He finally felt a sense of mental relief and freedom.

He heard the ship's bell ringing and as it was still dark, he rolled over and went back to sleep. Half awake, he heard men shouting and running on the deck above him.

A loud voice, accompanied by a kick to his ribs, made him sit up angrily. He saw it was the bosun. 'This is not a pleasure cruise. Get up and report to the little bloke with the red headband. He's the crew chief. I'll talk with you later. Now move it!'

Ian nodded angrily to the bosun. He soon simmered down and went up to the main deck. Normally he would have become engaged in a fight, being treated like this. But he was sensible enough to realise that this was a new environment for him.

The man with the red headband saw Ian coming out of the hatch and waved to him to come over. He was a Welshman and appropriately called Taffy.

Ian found his accent difficult to understand and had to listen intently to his instructions. Taffy was the deck chief, and he knew it. Do it or else! He asked Ian a few questions. When he realised Ian had not been to sea before, he told him to report to the sailmaker in the sail locker, where he had slept last night. He had been assigned to assist the sail master, who was responsible for the condition of the sails.

An elderly man was leaning over a large table sewing the corner of a sail. He looked up and asked, 'Hello. Who are you, young fellow?'

Ian replied, 'I'm Ian. The bosun sent me to assist you.'

The sailmaker nodded. 'Call me Eric. Do you know what I do here?'

Ian answered, 'No, but I can learn.'

'Simply, we need to have sails ready to replace, depending on what the weather dictates, and those that have been torn or have worn corner sections. We cut out the damaged corner and sew a new corner section in its place. Sail repairs are difficult. Both time consuming and difficult. You can start by watching me today. Tomorrow you will earn your living by being of use to me, by helping me to reposition some spare sails.'

Ian watched as Eric sewed a corner replacement section onto a large sail. He had large powerful hands, developed from years of sewing canvas sails. It was not easy pushing the needle through several layers of canvas and leather.

At noon he followed him to the mess deck. The food was basic and generally wholesome. He noticed all sailors had a drink of lime juice. He learnt later that this was to prevent scurvy, a very serious illness which could cause death. It was caused by a lack of vitamin C in their normal at-sea diet of limited fresh fruit and vegetables.

On their way back to the sail locker, he stopped and looked at the sea. There was a light swell, causing the ship to sway gently. The sun was shining with very little wind. It was a pleasant day. Suddenly he realised he didn't know the ship's destination. At the sail locker, he embarrassedly asked Eric, 'To where are we heading?'

Eric laughed and answered, 'Well, you are on the SS Lark, and we are sailing to Sydney in Australia, in the Colony of New South Wales. We will only stop once at Cape Town for water and food, then sail nonstop to Sydney. You will have enough time to make up your mind if you want to stay on for the return voyage. We will be at sea for over a month before we reach Cape Town. I've been at sea over forty years, and I believe the Australian colonies will grow and be prosperous in years to come. If I were twenty years younger, that's the country where I would settle. Cape Town is fine, but Sydney is better, in my opinion. I've travelled the world in the Royal Navy as Bosun, but I don't want to be ordering crews around anymore and settling arguments. I prefer the easy life of mending sails. I have no family, so I do as I please. The captain knew me from my ten years in the Royal Navy, and he was happy for me to join this ship. I've been on the Lark for eight years next month, and I'm content with my lot.'

Ian soon settled into a daily routine of inspecting the installed sails with Eric. He pointed out what to look for in the corner areas, where possible and or potential damage could occur, and repair it before it failed.

After a week, he had learned to climb the rigging and carry out an inspection of the sails' corners for wear deterioration. He was nervous at first but soon became used to the height and felt comfortable with the swaying of the ship and the riggings' movements.

He soon proved his worth when he reported to Eric that he had noticed a sail was showing signs of wear in a corner eyelet. It had torn away from the sail in two corners. Eric kept a record of when each sail was installed. This sail was the oldest one installed. He spoke to the captain with the bosun listening. The captain called his second in command and told him the sail was to be replaced and to oversee the task. Eric and Ian went to the sail locker and selected the replacement sail.

The bosun was already arranging his deck crew to be ready to lower the sail and sent several crewmen to help carry the replacement sail up on deck. The second in command ordered the sail to be lowered and reefed. The bosun ordered his crew to release the halyards and lower the sail for the reefing to be completed. When the sail was collapsed, the reef lines were tied to hold the sail wrapped. The sail corner ropes were then untied, and the sail was removed.

The new sail was attached to two wooden beams or yardarms, with ropes tying the corner sections of the sail. The reef ties were undone and the crew pulled on the halyards to raise the yardarms and sail into position. As the sail was rising the wind began to fill it. When fully raised, the halyards were secured. The last task was to lift and carry the old sail to the locker. Carrying the sail was heavy and difficult. Six men were required, and they were exhausted by the time they reached the sail locker.

The next day Eric and Ian examined the sail's corners. Eric decided to cut out the damaged corner and replace it with a larger corner section.

Eric sat on a small stool and pulled on a leather glove. It was a necessity when forcing the needle through the multi layers of canvas. He was slow but methodical.

His skill at sewing canvas was impressive. Ian watched carefully how each stich was pulled tight and equally spaced. After he had sewn one side, he looked at Ian. 'Now it's your turn. Don't try to hurry, just take your time. Tell me when you want to change over.'

Ian moved his stool to the bench and sat down. Initially, he found it difficult to push the needle through the canvas layers. After the first six stiches, he gathered confidence. When he had sewn half a side, his hands were starting to ache.

He said to Eric, 'I need to swap. I didn't realise it was so difficult to push the needle through!'

Eric laughed. 'After forty years, you'll be good at it.' He nodded. 'I'll take over now.' By late that evening, the new corner had been stitched into place. It took Ian two days for his hands to stop hurting.

The SS Lark sailed on, heading south along the coast of Africa. Cape Town was two weeks distant. The seas were mainly moderate. Ian enjoyed his leisure time, sitting on deck watching the occasional albatross gliding and turning into the wind; some even settled on the sea. He often saw dolphins diving across the bows, then vanishing as quickly as they had appeared.

Seamen often fished when off watch and sometimes caught a shark. The cook was always happy to provide a fresh new meal for the crew, and shark was excellent eating.

The crew were generally happy. Only a few arguments occurred, and these were mainly due to gambling losses. Gambling was banned by the captain, but it was still quietly carried out by some sailors during their free time.

Neither Eric or Ian gambled, and they kept clear of the gamblers. A gambler lost heavily one night and accused another player of cheating. The violence that then occurred cost the sailor his life. A knife was produced and the resulting wound from the fight, killed him. He was buried at sea wrapped in a section of an old sail. The captain had the culprit taken to the brig in the bows, ready to be handed over to the British authorities in Cape Town. It was thought he would be hanged, based on the written report from the captain and witnesses.

When the ship reached Cape Town, they had a full day to unload and load new cargo. Eric and Ian had some free time and saw a few of the sights. The next leg of their voyage was the longest nonstop section. Destination Sydney.

Ian had now started to consider what to do when they arrived. He had no intention of staying on board the ship. The novelty of travelling on long sea voyages had worn off. Even working, he still found sea life boring.

The coast of Western Australian appeared on the horizon. It looked bleak and uninteresting. Ian viewed the new land from high up on a mast and was unimpressed with the brown cliffs and stunted desert growth.

It wasn't until the coast of Tasmania appeared and he saw the lush green countryside of that island, that he began to look forward to landing in the colonies.

The leg to Sydney was rough. Seas were breaking over the bow stinging the sailors' eyes. A strong westerly wind had the ship healed over constantly and it was difficult moving around the deck.

The wind abated when the ship arrived at the entry to Sydney Harbour. They turned to port and sailed between the two cliffs at the entrance to the harbour. Farmhouses and livestock were dotted along the shoreline. The further they sailed into the harbour, the denser became the houses. The ship continued to enjoy calm water as it tacked up to the mooring area off the city of Sydney

As soon as the ship anchored, officials boarded the ship. The captain presented the custom officers his Bills of Laden and the ship was cleared to unload. The ship was not due to depart for seven days.

After the unloading was completed, the crew were paid. This was Ian's decision time. He said goodbye to Eric who wished him good luck, saying he was unsure if he would return. He wanted to look around Sydney to see what employment opportunities were available.

He booked in at a small inn for three days. Strolling around the town, he saw an advertisement for stockmen, needed for two months droving two thousand sheep inland. When he approached the head drover, George Jones, he immediately signed him on. He was having trouble recruiting men, as most young men were rushing to the goldfields to seek their fortune.

When Ian reported to the head stockman at the stockyards, it was in shambles. It took George several hours to organise drovers with their horses, the cook's wagon with food and rounding up the sheep for a head count. As soon as these tasks were completed, the drive commenced. Drovers shouted, cracking whips and dogs barked running to and fro, as they headed due west.

It was a new thrill for Ian. The sheep flocks in Scotland were never this big. He rode along one side to help keep the sheep bunched together. Once all the sheep were moving, there was less whip cracking, and the dogs soon settled down. The next morning Ian awoke to the clanging of the cook's saucepan. He could hardly walk due to saddle soreness.

It would take a few days for him to feel comfortable in the saddle. The days rolled on, with the country becoming dryer the further they travelled west. Ian was surprised at the number of small towns they passed and the isolated homesteads with large cattle herds or flocks of sheep. More importantly, he became aware of the toughness of the outback people.

Most nights, after a good meal, Ian would sit listening to a drover and his harmonica, playing Irish and Scottish airs. He enjoyed sleeping under the stars and the stillness of the outback.

The drove was uneventful, and only a few sheep were lost. The sheep dogs kept the dingoes away. The drovers shot them if they appeared during the day. When the drive was completed and the drovers had been paid off, Ian checked into a small inn for a few days.

One evening, Ian and two other drovers were drinking outside the inn, when they were approached by two armed men.

'Bail up and pay up,' they were ordered. Ian stood up and threw a glass at one of them, hitting him in the face, incurring a large cut to his nose and left cheek. The other fired his revolver and hit one of Ian's fellow drinkers. Ian put up his hands, as did the other drinker. The robbers searched their pockets and saddle bags. They had no choice but to allow themselves to be robbed of their earnings.

The armed robber helped his offsider onto his horse, and they rode away. They noted the horses were both bay mares and had light brown tails. Ian went berserk and yelled at the departing thieves. 'I'll get you one day, you bastards!'

Ian and his two friends sat there wondering what to do next. They still had their horses, and each had a revolver left in their saddle bag, but no money.

Ian was furious and irrational. He said to no one in particular, 'I think we should become highwaymen like them. They robbed us because we were not alert. We were easy targets.'

Sam, who was the drinker who had been shot in the forearm, was unconcerned with his wound; it was not serious. He had wrapped a cloth around his arm and promptly forgot about it. He nodded in agreement with Ian's comments.

The third of the trio, Bill, was also very angry and was inclined to agree with the comments. He sat quietly thinking. Finally he spoke. 'I have a wife and child to support. I want my money back.' Although Ian had been robbed, he still had a money belt under his shirt, which, the robbers in their hurry, had not noticed. He still had some money left.

The next day the trio headed in the direction their robbers had taken, fortunately the innkeeper had been generous and had given them some food. At the first town, they rode around the streets looking for the horses. They even visited the local stables, without any luck. They decided to keep riding to one more town and if they were unsuccessful, they would seek some employment. If not, they would find a soft target and rob them.

The next town decided their future when they located the thieves' horses outside the local pub. They could be seen laughing and drinking at the bar. The trio lay waiting in the dark for the two to appear. As soon as they walked out they saw Ian, Sam and Bill. The one with the cut on his face pulled out his revolver, but Ian had his revolver out and fired first and the robber collapsed to the ground, dead. Bill searched his pockets and found some money. The other robber ran back into the bar shouting, 'Bushrangers.'

The bar only had one other drinker, and he wasn't interested in leaving the bar room to chase bushrangers, nor was the bar attendant. The three new robbers left the town and headed back the way they came for an hour or so, then headed south for the Victorian border, several days ride.

CHAPTER FIVE

The Highwaymen

That night the Highwaymen were born and became infamous with the murder of the robber. It wasn't long before reward posters were on the colonies' community notice boards with vague descriptions of them. Possibly two Scotchmen and an Englishman, medium build, two with brown beards and one with a red beard. The notice promised five hundred pounds reward, leading to their arrest and conviction.

The money they recovered from their robber was enough to satisfy their needs for several weeks. They camped on a riverbank for a few days, resting and fishing near an old gold mine, while they decided what to do next.

The three had talked about becoming highwaymen. Now they were. The colonies were large open spaces and sparsely settled. They would be hard to locate and apprehend. They decided to visit some towns and select a vulnerable business such as a bank.

After a visit to four small towns, they selected a bank on a corner at the end of its main street. The escape route would be via a small track leading to a large forest. They marked several trees high up in the branches. Easy to see, if you knew where to look for the marks, but not if you didn't know what to look for!

It was agreed Ian would enter the bank just prior to closing time and only take the teller's cash drawer holdings and quickly leave. Other robberies had failed when the robbers had been greedy and waited to empty the bank's vaults, and they had been apprehended. Sam would guard the main door, and Bill would have the horses ready.

Bill said to Ian, 'Make sure the customers do not raise their arms, in case passersby look in the bank window and see them.' They performed a few trial runs and were satisfied the plan was workable.

Ian walked into the bank, pulled up his scarf and drew his revolver, pointing it at the young male teller, who sensibly realised immediately what was happening and, in accordance with the bank's procedure, handed over his cash drawer contents. Not a word was spoken. Ian immediately ran back to the horses and the trio were gone in a matter of minutes. The exit plan worked. The trio were miles away and it was dark before the town officials could organise a search.

The Highwaymen simply vanished, when really, they were posing nearby, as goldminers, in full view of the everyone.

The proceeds from the robbery totalled two thousand pounds. They now had the feeling of success and would continue their dangerous career. They had made the authorities sit up and take notice.

Their next venture was similar to their initial crime. They selected another small town, near a forest and with a similar escape route. The execution of the plan was nearly perfect, except two men who were on the other side of the street saw them ride away. Sam had not covered his red beard with his tartan scarf, as it was a hot day. The trio netted over fifteen hundred pounds and again vanished.

Their next venture, to the south, nearly brought them undone. When Ian entered the bank and pulled out his revolver, the male teller fainted. Ian left immediately and the gang left empty-handed.

The manager hearing the teller fall, entered the counter area. When he saw Ian leaving, he ran back to his office for his revolver and chased them around the corner. He fired a few shots but with no success.

The gang had only selected banks with male tellers for that very reason. They were not expected to faint. While the teller was embarrassed that he had fainted, the manager was unconcerned. He was happy his bank had not been robbed.

This set the trio back, making the Highwaymen rethink their bank robbery plan. A month later, they decided to move north and agreed to rob a gold assayer's office for cash only, not gold or other items.

Gold would have to be sold to a third party, and this could reveal their identity. They expected the proceeds to be small, but it was safer to only collect cash.

The assayer's office was a mile or so from a major gold mining area and was next to a small general store. After watching the assayer's office for a few days, they saw he had a set daily routine. He left at four p.m. exactly. Ian decided to enter at three forty-five p.m.

When Ian entered the office, the assayer had his head down. When he looked up, he was smiling until he saw the masked man with a revolver in his hand. Angrily he said, 'What do you want?'

'I only want your cash, not your gold. Give it to me and you won't be hurt.'

The assayer opened the drawer and handed over all his cash. Ian immediately put it into a canvas bag, turned, left the office and the three of them galloped away. The assayer was fuming because he had felt so helpless during the robbery. He had kept his gold, but he had been robbed of thousands of pounds.

That night the trio had a chat about their future. Surprisingly the haul from the assayer's office was large – twenty-two hundred pounds.

Bill decided to return home to his family, sell his small farm and go north. He said, 'I've had enough. The money I have now will give me a new start. You won't see me again.' They shook hands and waved to him as he disappeared into the distance. Bill was right, they would never meet again. He simply vanished into the vast country of the Australian colonies.

Ian and Sam went back to the goldmine and idled around for a month carrying a pick and a shovel but did very little digging. The police activity had increased in the area.

One day they were visited by two constables who questioned them. Ian and Sam were dressed in dirty work clothes and looked to be just another pair of struggling miners. When questioned, they laughed,

'I wish we were thieves and had robbed someone; we wouldn't be here.'

The constables smiled and departed. One looked back and said, 'I hope you have a change of luck.'

Detective Stephenson of the New South Wales Police Force was co-ordinating the search for the Highwaymen. A newspaper reporter started calling them that name and now it was being used by all and sundry.

Stephenson visited each of the robbery sites and interviewed witnesses to the crimes. Most reports were of very little value. One manager commented, 'The one who carried the cash out of the bank, seemed to have trouble mounting his horse.' This comment didn't seem relevant and was ignored.

Their next robbery was in Victoria. The two travelled together and were ignored in towns in which they stayed. Police were looking for three men. They selected a small bank in a town on the Murray River. It was between two shops in a wide main street. They selected Wednesday as the day for their robbery. They had seen the police escorting a gold shipment out, after they stopped at the bank, on the previous Thursday.

Wednesday was very cold and raining. Few people were in town. Ian looked inside the bank and saw only one customer.

When Ian walked into the bank with his face covered with his scarf, the teller just glanced at him and said, 'It's a miserable day.' He then looked more closely at him and saw Ian's revolver pointed at him.

Ian said, 'Give me the money from your cash drawer quickly and there will be no trouble.' The teller did not speak and handed over two handfuls of bank notes. Ian immediately turned and ran outside to his horse, mounted it and they both galloped out of town.

The teller called out to the manager. 'We've been robbed.'

The customer, an elderly lady was in shock and had collapsed onto the bank floor. The manager ran to her first, as the teller ran to the bank door to see the robbers ride away.

Inspector Stephenson arrived four days later. He was surprised to hear there were only two robbers, not three, and wondered if they were the same men or copycats. The teller commented, that the one with the revolver seemed to favour one arm and he spoke correct English with an accent, possibly a Scot. He couldn't explain what it was about the arm, but it was unusual. The horses had no distinguishing colours, not that he had much of chance of getting a good look at them. But he did recall seeing a blue scarf on the robber. The whole incident was over in a matter of minutes.

The two robbers headed east, following the river upstream into the high country. They rode almost non-stop for six hours until they found an old wagon track. The country was rugged and steep. They stopped occasionally to give the horses a rest. They had purchased a pack horse, some bedding and some new clothes. When they found a vacant hut, they decided to stay there for a few weeks. Later they rode separately into a nearby town and bought food stocks for a month.

They had been lucky so far. They decided to rest and stop robbing for a while. They had spent very little of the stolen money and now began to think of what to do with the cash. They had more than they thought. They had around three thousand pounds each.

Sam wanted to buy a small property but was worried that it might look suspicious to purchase one with cash.

They decided to head back to New South Wales and buy gold ingots from individual assayers and deposit them in different towns' banks.

Charles was most surprised to see a New South Wales police inspector enter his office. He said, 'I'm Inspector Peter Stephenson.' After greeting each other they went to the local pub for lunch and to talk.

Charles asked, 'To what do I owe the pleasure for this visit?'

'I suppose you have heard of the Highwaymen robberies.'

Charles nodded. 'Yes, I believe they are now in Victoria. But I know very little about them. We have received no description of them or their horses.'

'Yes, neither have we. We believe there are three of them. One a Scot and one with a red beard and two with brown beards, the horses are bay coloured, and one man has an arm injury, or that's what some witnesses think! Also, they have distinctive scarves. One blue and one tartan. The latest robbery involved only two men, so they may not be the same gang I'm trying to locate.'

They walked back to Charles' office, wondering what they should do next. They had no idea where the robbers were. Inspector Stephenson and his two constables decided to stay for week or so. Perhaps something would occur.

The trip back to New South Wales was uneventful. Ian and Sam agreed that the deserted hut in the high country would be their hideout. It had some basic furniture, was dry and had two small rooms. The surrounding country was heavily treed. Numerous birds nested high above ground, and in the morning gave forth a symphony of sounds – galahs, kookaburras and cockatoos. They lay in their bunks enjoying the birds. They had a small creek adjacent the hut.

If they sat quietly for an hour or so on the bank, occasionally a platypus would break the water surface and shake its head before vanishing again in the dark water. The thumps of kangaroos were heard at dusk, when they came bounding down to the creek to drink. The nights were cold outside, but a log fire inside made for a comfortable habitat for them both.

They went to a small town to put their plans into action. Ian purchased some gold bars from the government assayer. and they then went to the next town, where he deposited them in the local bank, as Sam went to buy some gold.

As Sam was entering the assayer's office, one of the two New South Wales townsmen, who had previously seen the Highwaymen robbing and leaving his local bank, noticed him.

He recognised him because of his red beard and tartan scarf. He hailed a passing constable, and Sam was arrested on suspicion of robbery. Ian was walking to the bank and saw the commotion and slowly turned around, watching from behind a wagon. Sam was led away in handcuffs and taken to the local jail.

Ian began to panic, wondering if Sam would talk about their exploits. He immediately left the town and headed back to the hut. The hut was on a small hill in a clearing where the trees had been removed by the timber cutters who had stayed there previously. It gave him a clear view in all directions for a hundred yards or so. He would stay there for a few weeks, but he knew he would be required to be alert. He regarded Sam as a friend and felt he could trust him to say nothing, but he was not completely sure. Ian nervously remained alert, unsure whether to stay or go.

If Sam said nothing, Ian would be safe in the high country. Even if he told them where he was, the hut would not be easy to find.

When Charles and Inspector Stephenson were advised of the arrest, they immediately departed and headed to the town. Sam had not answered any questions and was being defiant. He had not been charged yet. When the two inspectors arrived, Inspector Stephenson immediately charged Sam with armed robbery in New South Wales. The witness was adamant with his identification of Sam as one of the robbers. Sam knew if he was found guilty of armed robbery, he could be hanged. Sam began to answer some minor questions but would not fully co-operate with them.

When asked about his partner, Sam replied, 'I don't know much about him. We met on the road, and he wasn't a good talker. He came from the highlands of Scotland. That's all I know. He did not speak of any family.'

Charles asked, 'What did he look like?'

Sam replied, 'Same as me, but with a dark beard.'

'Anything else?'

Sam replied, 'He had an injured right arm. He couldn't straighten it. I'm not saying anymore.'

Charles persisted, 'You wear a Stuart Clan scarf. Where are you from?' Charles asked again. 'Where did you get the scarf?'

Sam said, 'He gave it to me.'

Charles looked at Sam. What he had said made him think! It couldn't be Ian! This must be an extraordinary coincidence.

Nevertheless, Charles continued, 'Who is he? Does he have a name?'

'I called him Scotty, but I think his name was Ian something.'

The answer astonished Charles. Ian in Australia and now a notorious fugitive from justice!

Inspector Stephenson interrupted. 'Where would he be now? If you help us find him, it will be to your benefit at your trial. You are only charged with robbery under arms. No one was injured during the bank and gold dealer robberies.'

Sam said nothing and was returned to his cell. Sam lay on his bunk thinking about the whereabouts of Ian. He guessed he had seen him get arrested and then quickly left town.

Charles, Inspector Stephenson and the local constable sat down to discuss the evidence they had.

Charles said, 'Sam was arrested at ten thirty a.m. We can assume he would have left his hideout just after sunrise. He would have cantered his horse, so how far would he have travelled in that time?' He asked the constable for a local map and drew a circle with a radius of some twenty miles.

He asked him, 'What is the most likely area he would have come from?'

The constable pointed to the map and said, 'Three quarters of the area is farmland. Three large farms with station hands.'

'The other quarter is thick forest. Years ago, timber cutters were in there, but not now. I suggest we try there, but we could use a good blacktracker.' They nodded. Charles immediately sent for Murray.

The constable suggested that they ride to the forest and have an initial look while they waited for Murray to arrive.

The following morning, they rode along the main road bordering the dense trees. They followed a few overgrown tracks that soon petered out. It soon became obvious a rider could pass a person hiding only a few yards from them and not be seen. Only one track looked as if it could still be used. As the sun set, the trio returned to the town.

Murray arrived two days later, and the team headed to the forest. With Murray leading the way, they started up the only track they had located. After two days riding, they found it had become overgrown and showed no sign of recent horses' movements. When they returned to their starting point, they circled the forest, searching for any other old tracks.

Murray signalled to them. He had found some recent signs of horseshoe imprints in the soil.

The team became excited and quietly followed Murray. Sometimes he dismounted for a closer look. Nodding and pointing forward, he would remount and continue his slow progress. Eventually he signalled – Stop! He pointed to a small hut in the distance. It was in a large clearing. The sun was setting. They decided to wait until daylight and then approach the hut at dawn, from several directions. Unfortunately, they disturbed some forest birds. Murray signalled – Quiet! They all hoped if someone was in the hut, they had not heard them.

* * *

Ian was sitting watching the sun go down when he saw the flock of birds fly up from the treeline. He knew they would normally have been settled for the night. Something had disturbed them. He immediately began his evacuation plan. His horse was nearby in the trees with a saddle, bags and reins on an adjacent branch. He waited until it was dark and keeping low, he slowly crept to the horse. Animal night sounds echoing in the forest helped cover his escape. He knew the pathway leading away from the original path. Within two hours Ian was out of the forest and had vanished into the night.

The following morning, according to their plan, at daybreak, they separated and crept forward with pistols drawn.

On reaching the shelter of the outside of the hut, Inspector Stephenson shouted, 'Surrender in the Queen's name.' He called once more. They then each entered the hut. It was vacant. When they searched the hut, their suspicions were confirmed. It had been occupied very recently. They found food, water and an empty bank bag.

Murray found where the horse had been kept. The horse manure was less than a day old. They believed they had just missed the second robber. Murray then followed Ian's exit track. The team had not given up on catching him.

Ian rode as quickly as he could after leaving the forest. Both he and the horse suffered scratches from the many branches they encountered from the dense foliage. He kept riding north. He criss-crossed several streams to avoid leaving any tracks, until he reached a small town on the Cobb and Co. stagecoach route to Sydney. He stayed at the local hotel for two days, as he tried to figure out what to do next.

He finally decided the best thing for him to do was to go to Sydney and sign on as a crew member on a merchant ship, leaving the colonies for good. He had enough money for a new start in another country or even return home to Scotland.

While wandering around town, he saw an advertisement for Cobb and Co. coach guards. When he asked about a job as a guard, the manager asked, 'When can you start?'

Ian answered, 'I can start now. I'm out of a job.'

'The next coach leaves in one hour. You will save me having to do it. You'll be paid after each trip, and you'll get free meals.'

Ian left his horse at the local animal pound paddock and his saddle at the hotel tack room. He had no intention of returning for them.

Ian slung his saddle bags up onto the coach and collected a double barrel shotgun from the manager. With a crack of his whip, the coach driver soon had the horses doing a slow gallop out of town heading east.

Murray soon found the track Ian had taken. But they lost time when they reached the creeks. After a few days they found his single tracks heading north until Ian had started following a cattle drive. The next town they visited was the one Ian had joined as a stagecoach guard, several days ago. They asked around the town if anyone had met a Scotsman with an injured right arm. The Cobb & Co. manager remembered him and complained a Scotsman only did one trip outbound and did not return. That was a week ago. Ian was long gone.

The inspectors stopped the pursuit and they each returned to their home base. Ian had eluded them, and they had no further leads.

Ian, together with his saddle bags, left the stagecoach at the Cobb & Co. office at the Sydney-Melbourne road junction and purchased a ticket to Sydney. On arrival in Sydney, he went to the harbourmaster's office to ask about shipping movements. He was advised none were expected to arrive and only one was scheduled to leave in the next twenty-four hours, bound for Liverpool – the SS Lightning.

When Ian approached the ship, he could see the crew were loading wool bales. He asked a sailor, 'Where can I find the ship's captain?'

The sailor pointed to a nearby inn and said, 'He's having his midday tot of rum.'

Ian looked across and saw a large bearded man, who looked to be a sailor, sitting outside the inn.

He saw Ian approach and anticipated his request. 'I have a full crew, bad luck. I have a spare cabin if you want to become a passenger.'

Ian thought quickly. He wanted to leave the colony as soon as possible. He had plenty of ill-gotten gains with him and could afford to travel as a passenger. He replied, 'Yes, I'll be happy to travel as a passenger. When do you sail?'

'Sunup tomorrow. You can go aboard when you like, but don't be late. You can pay me now, just in case you don't show.'

Ian laughed. 'I'll go aboard now. Here's your money.'

The captain asked, 'What should I call you?'

Ian replied, 'Ian, just Ian.'

As they left the inn a drunk approached them, asking for money.

The captain pushed him away. 'Bugger off!'

The drunk swung a fist at Ian and hit him in the face. Ian's temper flared. He hit the drunk several times and when he collapsed, he kicked him.

The captain grabbed Ian's arm. 'That's enough. Do you want to kill him?'

Ian stopped his assault on the drunk. 'Sorry I did that to him. I lost my temper.' There was a woman screaming and in the distance a police whistle was sounding. She had seen the one-sided fight.

The captain said, 'Let's get out of here before the police arrive.' They ran up a small lane and back to the ship.

The captain showed Ian to his cabin. It was small but comfortable.

Ian had been invited to join the captain for dinner at six p.m. He was introduced to three other passengers. Each of them was returning to England after spending some time in the Australian colonies.

Joe Sole had been selling home merchandise to the larger stores. William Morris was an ex-Army officer, who had finished a tour of service with his battalion. The third passenger, Hamish McDonald, was a Scottish stagecoach business owner, who had been evaluating the value of establishing a stagecoach business in Australia and had decided against it. Cobb and Co. were too well entrenched. It would be a difficult task competing with them. The risk was not worth the effort.

The SS Lighting departed as planned. The wind was from the west and gusting. The waves had white caps as the ship sailed down Sydney Harbour towards the two cliffs at the exit into the Tasman Sea. When the ship turned to a south-easterly course, the ship began to pitch and roll uncomfortably. Ian retired to his cabin and lay on his bunk, wondering where his wanderings would take him this time. He still had money from his highwayman days. Perhaps he could start a business, but where?

The ship was bound for Liverpool via Cape Horn. Its first port of call would be Rio De Janeiro on the east coast of South America. He had heard of the city but knew little about it.

After they turned east around the bottom of New Zealand, the captain advised they were making good time. Ian passed his time reading books the captain had purchased over his years at sea. He was an avid reader. At times Ian played cards with the other passengers but neither of the four gambled.

The days became weeks with boredom setting in. One evening Ian was chatting generally with Hamish McDonald when Hamish mentioned he was considering extending his stagecoach route further north into the Scottish Highlands. Ian listened as he said, 'I just hope the banks will support my business plans and extend my current loan.' He said his company was financially sound, but he needed more cash to expand to three more towns.

Ian casually asked, 'How much money are you talking about?'

Hamish replied, 'I would need four more coaches and horses plus I would need to lease some office space and stables. Probably around one thousand pounds as a minimum.'

Ian had fifteen hundred pounds in his money belt and saddle bags. Unfortunately, he had not been confident enough to try to retrieve his gold bars from the bank after Sam was arrested. That night he lay in his bunk, thinking if this could be the answer to his future. He kept mulling over the idea, thinking about it for a few days.

The two of them were having a drink watching the whales ploughing through the sea, when Ian said abruptly, 'If I loaned you the money to extend your coach service, what could you offer me?'

Hamish was taken completely by surprise at Ian's words and sat looking at him. He responded, 'Well now let me think about it. I'm sure we can come to mutually agreed terms. I'll let you know tomorrow night.'

After dinner the following day, Hamish visited Ian's cabin. 'I'm interested in your offer, but you really need to give me an idea of what you would want or expect. Is it interest on the money, a share in my company or a job with me?'

Ian replied, 'I'm happy to be a silent partner. I've nothing planned, so perhaps a job and a share of the profits generated by the extended service.'

Hamish nodded, 'That sounds reasonable. I'll give it some thought, and we can talk again.'

In the meantime, the captain had advised at dinner, they would be rounding Cape Horn in two days and to expect the weather to change dramatically. The passengers were told to secure any loose items in their cabins likely to cause damage to themselves when the ship was in rough seas. The Cape Horn seas near

Terra Del Fuego were notorious for their savage and unpredictable waves.

Hamish came back to Ian the next day. 'I would be happy to consider your idea. I will talk with my lawyer on arrival at Liverpool to formalise the arrangement, viz. a job as a manager and fifty per cent of the profits on the new route.' Ian agreed.

The wind increased in strength and began gusting. The captain reefed the topsails and the jib to reduce the ship's speed. In the distance they could see the seas churned into large white caps with foam flying from the tops of the waves. Th seamen had difficulty walking on the main deck, even with their rope soled shoes. They all held onto the rope safety guards.

The captain was on the quarter deck standing alongside the helmsman, watching the sails and the wind direction. The closer the ship got to Cape Horn the rougher the seas became. The ship pitched and rolled uncomfortably.

Ian lay on his bunk with his arms and legs outstretched to counter the ship's rolling.

He closed his eyes and tried to sleep, unsuccessfully. Dinner was not served that evening at the captain's table. A rain soaked cook delivered some bread and slices of ham and cheese to his cabin. Ian wasn't seasick and managed to keep the food down.

The wind whistled through the rigging. One felt sorry for the sailors who had deck duty, altering the rigging of the sails as directed by the bosun. The other passengers were in similar cabins to Ian's. They each had retired to their bunk and lay there. Joe Sole and William Morris read, while Hamish tried to write a draft agreement between Ian and himself. He gave up after a while, due to the excessive pitching and rolling of the ship.

The weather raged for another day and showed no sign of abating. A rogue wave occurred which was much stronger than the usual rough waves and rolled the ship violently, causing Joe to fall from his bunk. He landed on his cabin deck with one arm outstretched. He fell with the other arm under him and landing heavily, he broke a bone in his forearm. He suffered the pain for over twelve hours, before the steward found him lying on the deck of his cabin. William had acquired some medical knowledge during his military service. After obtaining a small wooden slat from the shipwright, he strapped the forearm flat to the slat, as Hamish pulled his wrist lengthways and hopefully aligned the broken bone. Joe had been in pain as the bone was aligned, but it soon subsided to a throbbing ache. A few whiskies helped to dull the pain.

The wind changed and the ship began to steady. It was still a strong westerly, but it was no longer gusting. To the east, the clouds were vanishing, and sunlight appeared. That afternoon the ship turned to port and headed north bound for Rio De Janeiro in much calmer seas.

When the ship arrived in Rio's magnificent Copacabana Bay, it anchored offshore. The beach was wide and long, complimented by the blue sea. It had beautiful golden sands where the locals were swimming and enjoying the sun.

The longboat was lowered and the captain and two sailors, together with the four passengers, went ashore. Ashore, the captain was met by the ship owner's local agent to collect mail and some valuable parcels.

The ship was only laying over for twenty-four hours, to load water, fresh vegetables and fruit. The food loaded on board at Sydney had deteriorated and had been thrown overboard before they arrived in the bay.

The four passengers hired a coach and visited the tourist sights and sampled the local cuisine. Late afternoon they returned to the ship via the waiting longboat.

Joe had gone looking for a doctor. He had kept his arm strapped until the ship docked at Rio De Janeiro. Eventually he located a doctor who reset the splint and commented, 'Your arm was well looked after. It will be as good as gold after a month or two.'

Hamish had drafted a proposal for Ian to view and give his opinion. The draft proposed: "On acceptance of the loan of one thousand pounds from Ian Flint, Ian Flint shall be entitled to fifty per cent of the profits on the new route and he shall be hired as a manager. The agreement shall be for twelve months only and renewed subject to both parties' mutual agreement."

Ian nodded his agreeance. 'Yes, have your lawyer view the document and we will take it from there.' Ian went to his cabin pleased with the agreement. If the new route failed to make a profit, he would still get his money back. Also, he would be paid as a manager. It was win–win for him.

CHAPTER SIX

Quick Justice

The sergeant looked up as Charles entered the office. 'Good morning. It's been a quiet weekend for a change. No paperwork needed.'

Just then, a horseman ran into the office, breathless. 'Bushrangers have taken over Waroo Station. I was in a barn and managed to escape. There are four of them. Shots were fired, but I don't know if anyone was injured. I had a good look at them. They're not from around here.'

The sergeant said calmly, 'Sit down, relax and have a cup of tea. Constable Smith, have the horses saddled and get some rations. We will leave in half an hour and bring Constable Lang and Murray here.'

Charles asked, 'How far is Waroo Station?

The sergeant answered, 'A two-hour ride. We can be there by late afternoon. Sir, I suggest the five of us go, together with the station hand as well.'

Charles nodded in agreement. 'Yes, we'll need his knowledge of the layout of the homestead.'

When they walked to the stables, Charles met Constable John Lane and Murray the black tracker. They shook hands. Murray was a tall lithe man with an air of confidence around him. Charles was impressed.

Charles noticed John Lane carried an unusual rifle holster. He asked John about it and John replied, 'I was a marksman in the British Army, and I have an extra-long barrel, which I use for target shooting. Perhaps, we'll need it for this situation.'

The team mounted and headed out of town at a canter. They were wondering what to expect. This would be the first time any of them had tackled an incident such as this.

They arrived at Waroo late afternoon with the sun just above the horizon. They could see four horses at a hitching rail in front of the homestead but no riders. All was quiet. The station hand said the building had three outside doors. One was the kitchen door, another door led to a hall and then there was the main door.

Charles said to John Lane, 'Get your rifle long barrel ready.' John nodded and fitted the barrel. Charles continued, 'We'll wait until dark and try to set the horses free.' He looked at Murray and asked, 'Do you think you could get to the verandah?' Murray nodded.

'Unwrap the horses bridles and leave them loosely draped over the hitching rail. The horses will think they are still restrained and will not move. This will give you time to get back here without bring noticed.'

Murray headed towards a large barn. He waited for darkness to descend then quietly approached the homestead and waited for a few minutes. Slowly he approached the horses and unwrapped their bridles. The horses did not move.

Murray returned and said, 'H'm done, boss.'

Charles nodded. 'Well done.' They waited. Then a horse shook his mane, and the bridle fell to the ground. The horse realised it was free and walked away to a nearby paddock. Soon the other horses followed.

The team waited for someone to appear. An hour later a man appeared on the verandah, lighting a cigarette. When he saw the horses were no longer tied up but were in the paddock, he ran to catch them, but he spooked them, and they scattered. He ran back to the homestead, shouting.

Charles said calmly, 'John, shoot him.'

John aimed and fired. The man dropped to the ground and did not move.

There was movement inside the homestead. Through the open windows people could be seen moving. Another man appeared at the main door with a rifle in his hand. He called loudly, 'The horses are gone!'

The sergeant shot him. Charles said to Fred Smith, 'Cover the hall back door.'

The homestead was quiet. They waited. Two shots were heard. Soon after they heard the sounds of a horse galloping away into the distance.

A woman appeared on the porch screaming, 'Please help me!'

Constable Smith appeared behind her shouting, 'I shot one; he's in the hall. The last one got away. I fired at him; I think I hit him. There was a saddled horse outside the kitchen.'

The team ran into the homestead and escorted the lady into her parlour. A man was lying on a couch bleeding from a shoulder bullet wound. He was the woman's husband. Constable Lake found some sheets which he cut into strips. He then made a pad and bound the wound, tightly. It soon stopped the bleeding.

Charles sat down with the team and summarised the happenings. John shot the first bushranger, the sergeant the second and Fred shot the third. Charles looked at the station hand and asked, 'Where did the fourth bushranger get the horse?'

The lady interrupted, 'My husband was going out to check the fences when those *animals* arrived. His horse was already saddled and close to the back door.'

Charles decided to get the station hand to harness a single horse coach to take the lady and her husband into town and find the doctor for him. Their maid had hidden in a clothes closet and now reappeared. The lady of the house had her serve well-deserved meals to the police team.

During the meal the sergeant commented, 'I was surprised at your decision making. Being a prosecutor, I thought you were going to try and apprehend them.'

Charles responded, 'Sergeant, their crime would have incurred the death sentence.' He paused and looked at him. 'If you follow my logic.' The team nodded in agreement. They stayed overnight in the empty shearers' quarters.

As they departed after breakfast, the sergeant asked the station hand, 'What is the brand on the stolen horse?'

He replied, 'It is a distinctive double triangle over a number eight, and it's a light brown gelding.' He waved and the team headed towards the next nearest town.

The small town of Tallo had a population of around

four hundred. There was no police presence. The main buildings were an hotel and a Mechanics Institute. The sergeant told Charles, 'Nearly every town in Victoria has a Mechanics Institute. They serve as a local meeting hall for community meetings, weddings, weekend dances and even as a library.'

Murray had ridden in front of the team and came riding back excitedly. He pointed to the front of the hotel. 'Deem horse, look!' It was the stolen horse. It was tied up outside the hotel with three other horses.

The team dismounted, guns ready. The sergeant went to cover the back of the building. Charles and the others entered the bar quickly and went to opposite ends. The drawn guns startled four slightly drunk customers and the barman. They looked at Charles.

The barman asked, 'What's going on?'

Charles asked, 'Who owns the brown gelding outside?'

They each said, 'It's not mine.'

Charles asked, 'Come outside and show me your horses.'

Three of the horses were owned by three of the customers. The fourth one said, 'My horse is gone. That's not my horse.' Charles was disappointed. The four customers were from the same sheep station and agreed with the fourth customer. He was telling the truth. After obtaining the brand on his horse, the team headed to the next closest town of Willmot, another small town.

The brand on the second stolen horse was a large OAAs all in a row and it was a black gelding.

The owner said, 'He has a funny gait. Your tracker will soon find him.'

Charles decided to send the sergeant and Constable Smith back to Kahuna. He would press on for a few more days with Constable Lane and Murray. A quick wave and they split up and headed in different directions.

The owner of the horse was right, Murray soon identified the horse's unusual gait. It was slow going. At times the trail vanished, and it took Murray some time to find it again.

The rider was heading in an easterly direction but at times he wandered. Charles began to think the rider might have been hit by a bullet from Constable Smith's revolver.

On the second day, Murray said, 'He fall off horse dere.' He pointed to some marks on the ground. Some grass appeared to have dry blood stains.

Suddenly the crack of a rifle shot rang out, followed by a puff of soil in front of the horses. The trio quickly dismounted and took cover behind some tree trunks. A second shot hit a tree.

Murray pointed. 'Big rock.'

Constable Lane nodded and aimed his rifle.

Charles said, 'Wait until you get a clear shot. We've chased him long enough.' They waited for half an hour for him to appear. He stood up and looked towards the area where the police were hidden. Constable Lane fired his rifle, and the fugitive slowly fell forward and did not move.

When they reached the fugitive, he was dead. It was apparent he had previously sustained a serious bullet wound to his thigh from Constable Smith's shot on that fateful night. They returned to Tallo and buried him as an unknown in a grave in the local cemetery. They returned to Kahuna tired and saddle sore.

When Charles returned to the police station, the sergeant and Constable Smith were delighted that the fourth bushranger had had been accounted for and the case now closed, except for the paperwork.

The sergeant said, 'We've had some reports of cattle theft, but strangely only a few each time. Normally we would expect forty or fifty rustled.'

Charles asked, 'What do you suggest we do?'

He answered, 'Just wait and see. There's no value in trying to find them in this large district. It would be a waste of time.' Charles nodded at the sergeant's logic.

Charles and Mary received an invitation to his uncle's homestead for a Scottish evening, and to stay overnight. He rode to the sheep station in police uniform and carried his Highland uniform. When they arrived, several carriages and gigs were already there.

Finlay saw them driving up to the homestead and waved. He stepped down from the verandah and took their reins. 'I'll stable your horse and see you inside.' They shook hands and Charles and Mary walked to the hallway.

Highland reels were being played. His uncle saw them and came over, greeting them. 'Hello, you will look smart,' and a kiss for Mary. 'You have the same room as last time. We'll talk when you return.'

Charles would not be the only one in Highland dress. Several men and ladies were also wearing their tartan attire and looked resplendent. There were even a few Irish tartans.

When Charles and Mary entered, his uncle introduced him to his other guests.

Charles was surprised at the number of emigrants from Scotland and Ireland.

When he was introduced to Milton Miles, a local tailor who knew he was a policeman, made a comment which surprised him. He said, 'You have a reputation for clearing the country of bushrangers. I believe you take no prisoners. I'll make sure I don't upset you.' He laughed. No one else did.

The dinner gong summoned the guests to the dining room where their name tags had been placed on the table. Stephen made a short speech of welcome to the guests and introduced Charles as his nephew and the son of the Earl of Belcannon.

Charles counted a total of thirty guests. He and Mary were seated between a wealthy cattle station owner and the wife of a local hotel owner. The conversation was on local topics and was of interest to Charles, as he was still relatively new to the district.

During the evening, he became aware that there was friction between some large cattle stations. The cattle man mentioned about having a few cattle stolen and said, 'The three I had stolen were prize winners at the agriculture shows. Another owner had four of his best cattle stolen – a bull and some cows.'

Charles began to take an interest in the thefts. He asked, 'Would they be taken for breeding or showing.'

He answered, 'Could be both. Their brands would need to be altered. But, yes, it could be done.'

'Do you have any ideas who the thieves might be?' Charles asked.

'Well, I'm sure the stolen cattle have been stolen by a local who knew of the specific cattle and could move them out of the district quickly.'

Charles nodded. He decided to look further into these thefts.

The evening passed quickly. After the meal, dancing began. They varied from reels to waltzes with music mainly from violins, bagpipes and a solitary piano. Around midnight, the guests began to leave. Charles was invited to stand alongside Stephen and bid them goodnight as they left. Some guests had a two-hour journey to their home.

Milton Miles commented rather snidely, 'Well, an earl-apparent and a police officer who takes no prisoners, as well.' Charles did not reply.

Charles and Mary said goodnight to Stephen's family, then retired for the night.

A rooster awoke him at dawn. When they came to breakfast, they were first at the table. It was half an hour before the others came in. They all agreed the evening had been a success.

Charles asked about Milton Miles.

Stephen replied, 'He's our neighbour and sometimes helps with mustering our sheep. He's a strange person; he has a son and keeps to himself. I wouldn't be surprised if he has a history.'

Charles and Mary departed at noon and headed to Kahuna. The day was pleasant, full sunlight. They enjoyed the ride, and they were liking the colony more and more each and every day.

Charles and the team had a meeting the next day to discuss the cattle thefts. He was unsure where to start.

The sergeant suggested, 'Contact the Royal Agricultural Society of Victoria and advise them of the issue to obtain the cattle brands.'

Constable Smith suggested, 'We could ask the cattlemen if they were prepared to offer a reward?'

They were both good ideas. They soon received an answer from the society with an assurance they would be alert during show days for possible altered brands. Regarding the reward, each owner agreed to contribute one hundred pounds each leading to the capture and conviction of the thieves. A poster was soon distributed in the district.

Two weeks later a drover walked into the police station. He said he had driven a small flock of Merino sheep to the local wharf and remembered seeing three prime cattle being loaded on board a steamer late at night. He thought it was strange as the drover with them seemed to be in a great hurry to leave after they were boarded. Being prime cattle, he expected the drover would have waited to see if the cattle had quietly settled in their pens. He said, 'I may be wrong, but I suggest you talk with the manager of the wharf.'

Charles and Constable Smith visited the wharf and put the question to the manager regarding the events at that night.

The manager remembered the Merinos and the cattle. He said the cattle were booked to be off loaded at the first port over the border of South Australia. When he was asked, 'Did you know the cattle drover?' he answered, 'Well yes and no. Sometimes he works for the blacksmith, but I wouldn't say I know him. I don't know where he lives.'

They went to the blacksmith and received a similar answer. He was called Jed, but there was no address forthcoming. It seemed Jed would appear in town to work and receive some cash, get drunk and then vanish.

Constable Smith visited the pub, and a patron said he thought Jed lived in a shack along the river, but he did not know where.

The two of them returned to Kahuna. The sergeant sent Constable Smith and Murray back to the wharf to search along the river for a few days to find the elusive Jed and take him in for questioning. Charles decided to wait until they located Jed and had questioned him about where he obtained the three cattle.

Two days later Constable Smith and Murray returned with Jed in tow. He was a quiet man and did not appear to be a bushman. When questioned, he sat silently and refused to answer. He was left in his cell.

After a day and night, he agreed to talk. It was a strange tale. He was approached by two men who asked if he wanted to earn some easy money. All he had to do was to load three cattle on board a riverboat. The cattle would be handed over to him near the wharf in the evening. He just needed to act as if he was the owner and pay for their passage. He was paid five pounds for an hour's work. He did not see them again and could not give a good description of them. They were average height, weight and spoke English.

Charles released him. They had no evidence, other than what he had told them. They may not have even been the stolen cattle, although it did look very suspicious.

Charles wrote to George in Melbourne for him to pass the information onto the South Australian Police Force. It was two months before the South Australia police advised they had found the stolen cattle, with their brands still intact. They also provided a name with whom they were dealing and admitted they had received three consignments of stolen cattle. Only the last two could be returned to Kahuna.

The previous cattle had been sold on to other cattlemen who had properties in the outback country. Trying to locate these cattle would be almost impossible.

The person named as being responsible for planning the theft of the prize cattle was a well-known racehorse owner and gambler. He had been in trouble with the law previously on suspicion of several frauds. He had always managed to walk free. Henry Breakspear appeared to be a wealthy man, but with his gambling losses and the costs associated with managing several racehorses, he had been rendered almost bankrupt.

Charles was compiling a report on the stolen cattle when he received a letter advising of the visit of a magistrate. He was pleased to see it would be John Major, who he met on the voyage to Victoria.

Charles went to the Cobb and Co. Stagecoach office to greet him. He saw John alight the coach and waved to him. John smiled in recognition of his friend.

'I was wondering if I would see you. I met George at a function in Melbourne, and he told me of your promotion, and that this was your district. You look fit. Country life agrees with you,' greeted John. They shook hands, and Charles led him to the police station. The friends spent the next half hour telling of their work in Victoria

The main reason for John's visit was to oversee a preliminary trial of an alleged murderer in a nearby town. Charles was aware of the murder but had no details. The alleged offender had surrendered himself to the town's constable over a week ago.

Charles' copy of the murder report was with the

sergeant, and he had not considered it urgent. John asked Charles to accompany him to act as prosecutor as, and if, required. As he had already pleaded guilty, John might only have to check the accuracy of his guilty plea and see if the Brief of Evidence and associated paperwork were acceptable.

The two of them left next morning with John riding Charles' spare horse. The ride took two days. Fortunately, the weather was sunny with a light northerly wind blowing.

As they rode, John remarked, 'I can see why some people love the country life here. Listening to the birds and watching them circle and dive. The colours of their feathers make the scene even more attractive and, together with the green trees and grasslands as a background, make it an absolute delight.'

Charles nodded. 'I'm content here. I have Mary and family. The people are very open and friendly. It's a good life.'

CHAPTER SEVEN

The Assassin

Sydney Harbour was awash with colour. The harbour had ships sailing hither and thither. Some were even flying bunting in their rigging. The largest ship was sailing under full sail in the middle of the harbour. It was the HMS Archer, a Royal Navy ship, and it had the Duke of Cumberland on board for an official visit to the Colony of New South Wales.

Her sailors were in uniform lining the deck. Others were standing in the rigging. Sydney had been decorated with flags. Harbour side, people from all walks of life were enjoying the spectacle. Free settlers, public servants, soldiers, convicts and even some aborigines were watching as the ship slowed and finally stopped and then dropped anchor. A cutter was lowered for the duke and his entourage. The crew rowed the boat to a landing in a small cove where the official welcoming party were assembled.

The official party consisted of the governor, military officers and senior public servants. Behind them were a few hundred excited onlookers. As the boat reached the landing, and the duke stepped ashore, the military band played *God Save the Queen*. The duke was impressive in his uniform and his erect stance, as he saluted.

The governor walked forward, and they shook hands. As they turned for the governor to introduce the duke to the other officials, a shot rang out and an official collapsed to the ground. Military officers immediately moved forward and surrounded the duke, hurriedly escorting him to a waiting carriage and immediately taking him to the safety of Government House.

In the meantime, the attempted assassination gunman was quickly subdued by members of the crowd who also manhandled him. When the police came and arrested him, he had a broken arm, several teeth missing, a bloody nose and two broken ribs plus much bruising. When the gun was wrenched from his right hand. The trigger finger was virtually severed and needed to be removed. The gun was never found and obviously had been souvenired.

The duke appeared to be unfazed by the incident and enquired about the injured man's condition. Fortunately, the bullet had only grazed his scalp, and he was expected to be out of hospital within a few days.

The incident was the talk of Sydney town for days and the newspapers had a field day. The culprit was Gavin Maquire, an Irishman. He was charged with attempted murder. However, he was medically assessed as being mentally unstable and sent to an asylum. He escaped two weeks later and vanished into the wide Australian outback. Some believed he had been helped to escape by Irish loyalists.

The New South Wales Police sent out reward posters throughout the colony. As the fugitive had been born in Victoria, posters were also sent to the Victorian Police.

His distinguishing marks were – three missing front teeth, blue eyes, a slight limp and one missing trigger finger from his right hand. He was six feet tall and weighed twelve stone. Charles first saw the poster when the sergeant placed it on the notice board.

Charles was still learning from his sergeant's wisdom. The town had a remittance man, John Fisher, who, when he collected his monthly cheque, would hand it over to the hotel owner where John resided. The cheque would cover his lodging and meals. Unfortunately, the remainder of the cheque was spent on alcohol. John was the town drunk and eventually became a pest. He had already been barred from one town after he had been jailed for a month for assaulting another drinker.

The sergeant was getting fed up with the number of times he had been jailed overnight for being drunk and disorderly. One night the sergeant decided to act. He called Constable Smith into his office and said, 'In the middle of the night, I want you to waken Fisher and tell him I'm going to charge him and have him jailed. Then tell him the back door of the police station is unlocked, and his horse and saddle are in the stable and to leave now. He won't have another chance. Then leave him.' The next morning the cell was empty. John Fisher had departed Kahuna for good.

They heard later he went to Echuca and had gained

employment as a deck hand on a paddle steamer ferrying freight on the Murray River. He managed to change his ways and save some of his cheque and eventually married the daughter of the captain of the steamer. This was all due to the Kahuna's sergeant's creative thinking.

When Charles approached the police station, he saw four men waiting at the door. He sensed they were an official party.

He was correct. It was Inspector Peter Stephenson and three other members of the New South Wale Police Force.

Inspector Stephenson said, 'We met again,' and shook hands. 'We're hunting the attempted assassination gunman of the Duke, in Sydney.

'We have tracked him to this district and as we are over the border, we have no authority. We need your help.' Charles suggested a group conference and sent Constable Smith to book the hotel dining room. It wasn't used on Mondays.

Whey they had assembled, Charles invited Inspector Stephenson to start the discussions to explain the current situation.

The inspector started, 'We've been chasing him from Sydney. He initially headed west. At Bathurst, he headed south, and we lost track of him until last week when we were advised he had a relative living in Kahuna and Melbourne. The name given to us was, Milton Miles. Do you know of him?'

Charles laughed. 'Yes, we know him. He has a tailor's shop two doors from here. He's a bit of a smarty and has an attitude, but I think he's harmless. How do you want to approach the matter? You will have our support. But I will need to notify my seniors in Melbourne.'

The inspector nodded and thought for a moment. 'Well, we can't conduct a surveillance, as we are all strangers in town. We would soon be spotted in a town this size.'

Charles asked his sergeant, 'What do you think? Any ideas?'

'Constable Smith plays pool with his son in a pub competition. That could help us. He may know something. Do many people know the name of the assassination gunman?'

The inspector answered, 'We haven't mentioned his name to the public. It's Gavin Maquire and the newspapers have been warned against publishing it by the NSW Attorney General under the threat of being jailed.' The meeting closed with only the one positive idea. Fred was to see if Miles Milton's son knew of his notorious family member's whereabouts.

The New South Wales team stayed at the hotel and registered as mining surveyors. Early each day they would ride out of town and go fishing and then return late in the afternoon. After a week, Milton's son mentioned to Fred, an uncle from Sydney, had visited them yesterday.

Casually Fred asked, 'How long's he staying in Kahuna?'

The son replied, 'He's gone to Melbourne to visit my father's brother, somewhere in an outer suburb.' After being given this information, the four New South Wales police members plus Charles, Constable Lane and Murray headed south. They split into two teams. Charles, Murray and two New South Wales constables in one team. The other team with Inspector Stephenson, his constable and Constable Smith.

Passing through one town they were advised the gunman had been positively spotted by the local police but managed to escape. Charles' team immediately went directly to Melbourne to try to find the uncle.

It took a few days, but he was eventually found to have a small shop with a residence in a suburb. A surveillance commenced around the clock. Two days later, two riders were spotted at sundown, slowly riding up to the shop. The shop was closed but a light was on in the upstairs residence. They stopped and looked around.

All of a sudden one rider galloped his horse towards town. Most of the two teams galloped after them. Murray signalled to Charles, 'Him no one! Odder man we chasem.' Charles stayed with Murray and watched the second rider, who calmly rode away in the other direction. Charles and Murray followed him at a discrete distance.

Eventually, Inspector Stephenson and the team caught up to the rider, who surrendered. He was surprised that they were police officers. He told them he had been paid to divert their attention while the other rider escaped from debt collectors. At first, he was not believed.

When questioned at length, he admitted he was afraid of the other man and felt threatened. He agreed to his demand. He was unable to comment on the man's hand as he was wearing gloves, but he did notice he had some front teeth missing. Constable Smith arrested him, pending further enquires.

Charles and Murray followed the man for over an hour and eventually lost him in the darkness alongside a creek. However, they were satisfied they had not been spotted and decided to have a quick sleep and commence looking for his tracks next day.

They started as soon as the sun started to rise. Murray soon picked up his horse's tracks as they moved quickly in a northerly direction. Shortly after noon the suspect was seen. He was sitting alongside a fallen tree, eating a slice of bread. He stopped and looked up and saw the two of them close to him. He jumped up, drawing a pistol and commenced firing at them.

The first bullet skimmed Charles' shoulder without causing an injury. Charles returned fire. His first two revolver shots missed but the third bullet hit the suspect's left kneecap causing him to collapse. Murray ran forward and quickly took the revolver from the suspect's hand, while Charles handcuffed him. When he took off the suspect's righthand glove, he could see the trigger finger was missing.

They had captured the attempted assassination gunman. Murray had been correct. They went to a local farm and borrowed a small cart in which to carry the injured assassin.

Charles decided to take him to a jail in a small town and not take him to Melbourne. He knew there would be an argument over where he should be charged. He was right. When he confidentially reported to the Victorian Police Inspector General, he agreed there would be an argument concerning where the assassin would be tried – Sydney or Melbourne. As the injured party was on an official visit to New South Wales but had been captured in Victoria, it was a moot point.

When the Victorian Government issued an official bulletin, the letters between state government officials began fast and furious. The bulletin only stated: "The gunman associated with the attempted assassination of the duke has been apprehended after being shot."

Charles' name was leaked to the press and this caused a problem. Many assumed that Charles had shot the gunman dead. This was not denied by the police, even though few knew he was alive.

On his return to Kahuna, Charles was asked direct questions by all and sundry. He didn't even tell the sergeant; only Murray knew the whereabouts of the gunman, and he wouldn't talk.

When Milton Miles read of the capture and the non-disclosure of the details of the incident, he assumed that the gunman had been shot and killed by Charles. He then started writing letters to the major and local newspapers, calling for Charles to be sacked for the killing of another fugitive without a trial.

The New South Wales Attorney General wrote to his counterpart in Victoria requesting: "An inquiry be held into the circumstances surrounding Gavin Maguire's apprehension." After weeks of negotiations, the Victorian Government established a board of inquiry to examine the circumstances of the gunman's capture and what had really occurred.

Charles was summoned to appear in the Melbourne Court. He was to be the star witness. The court was filled with observers and newspaper reporters. After he was called to the dock and sworn in, he was immediately questioned by the Board of Inquiry Chairman as to where Gavin Maquire was or might be. He was also asked if he could produce him to the court.

Charles turned to the court entry door and nodded to the constable on duty. He opened the door and escorted the gunman into the court. The audience gasped in amazement. The majority thought Charles had shot him dead.

Even the chairman smiled and commented, 'You kept that secret very well.'

Charles nodded. 'Yes, I was under instruction.'

'So I gather. I have just received a letter explaining the situation. It also states that the Victorian Government has agreed to extradite Mr Maquire to New South Wales with immediate effect. I presume you will be involved as the main witness and will accompany him to Sydney.' Following normal formalities, the chairman closed the enquiry.

After the dramatic revelation, several newspapers had to rewrite their prepared headline stories. Milton Miles became the local joke because of his presumptive biased letters to the papers. He left Kahuna for a short time, hoping people would eventually forget his vicious, personal and stupid comments directed at Charles. He became even more depressed when a newspaper reporter found out he was a relative of the gunman and published that story.

Charles remained in Melbourne waiting for Inspector Stephenson to return, to escort the gunman to Sydney. The powers that be decided they would travel by sea. They felt he couldn't escape at sea. It was impossible as he was handcuffed and in ankle chains.

The trial in Sydney was swift. He didn't deny the charge. There were many reliable witnesses, and the gunman admitted he had tried to kill the duke. He was found guilty. At the end of the trial he read from a prepared script, giving his reason for the attempted assassination.

"Oppression of the Irish people and the duke is a

symbol of the oppressor." The attempted assassination gunman was named as Gavin Maquire, an Australian born from Irish immigrant parents in Victoria. He was hanged the next day.

When Charles returned to Kahuna, he spent more time at home. At the weekends, he and Mary worked on developing the vegetable garden and the orchid bed she had started, with the sunny weather, some rain and horse manure, and nature doing the rest. They had excellent results, bumper crops! They shared their vegetables and fruit with Stephen and Clare. Life was good.

CHAPTER EIGHT

Testing Times

Several weeks later, Charles was requested to return to Melbourne by George who wanted a meeting with him. It was only a ploy to have Charles in Melbourne for a specific reason. Unknown to him, he had been recommended for a New South Wales Government Award for his involvement in the capture of the gunman. George had been advised the medal would be presented at the next Passing Out Parade, in a month.

Charles and Mary travelled to Melbourne by coach and went to the barracks to a VIP room reserved for them by George. They had decided to take some time off.

The next morning, they walked into the city and were surprised at its rapid growth. The shops had almost doubled in numbers. Most shopping area footpaths and roads had been levelled and some even sealed. The river was busy with small boats ferrying people from shore to shore.

The day was a normal Friday shopping day. At ten a.m. there were a few shoppers around. Midday would see the streets crowded with pedestrians either buying or window shopping. Just another Friday in Melbourne.

The banks had queues of customers as expected, so the sight of three men entering together was of no concern until they each drew a revolver and began shouting. 'This is a robbery. Get on the floor and you will not be harmed.' Some women started screaming and men were either surprised or just stood there stunned. All the customers did as they were ordered and lay on the floor, the tellers doing likewise. Two robbers kept guard on the customers while the other jumped the counter and began filling a mail bag with notes from the cash drawers.

The manager saw the scene from his office and was seen by a robber. He then joined the others as another hostage. A passerby saw the robbery unfold and immediately advised the police. The bank was a two storied building which was on a corner. The police soon arrived and covered the main door and the two street windows. The robbers soon realised they had taken too long and now had a major problem. They were trapped.

Charles and Mary had returned from shopping and went to the barracks administration offices to check for mail, just as the police were advised of an attempted bank robbery.

Charles saw George run by shouting, 'Follow me. There's a hostage situation at a bank.' When they arrived, an inspector reported to George. He believed there were three robbers and an unknown number of hostages being held. As yet, no contact had been made with them.

George nodded and had a window smashed. Standing out of sight alongside the broken window, he asked to talk to the leader of the robbers.

A loud voice answered, 'We have not hurt anyone, but we want to make a deal. Five horses for us and two hostages.'

'No. we don't do deals. Just come on out and you will not be harmed,' George shouted.

The robbers did not answer, but they opened the front door and ushered all the women out before quickly closing it. George decided to wait for them to speak again. After two hours a voice called loudly, 'Come and get us, if you dare.'

Something had to be done. At that moment, it was a standoff. Charles suggested they enter through an upstairs window and proceed down the internal stairs. The idea was feasible, but George was still concerned about the hostages if there was a gun fight.

He agreed with the plan, but he wanted it to be co-ordinated with an attempted entry through the front door or street windows at the same time. Charles and two constables would make their way downstairs and wait until George began hammering on the front door to distract the three robbers.

He again asked the robbers to free all the hostages. Eventually they agreed, much to the amazement of the police. All the hostages had now been released unharmed. The standoff continued; they refused to surrender. When the police identified the robbers from the description they were given by the hostages, they found they were the notorious three escaped convicts who had carried out a gold bullion theft of a police escort. They had been wanted for several months. The three of them had little to lose now.

They placed a ladder below an upstairs window and Charles borrowed a revolver from another inspector. He and two constables climbed up into a storeroom. Ready with their revolvers, they slowly crept downstairs. Charles listened at the door, which opened into the bank's teller counter area. It was unlocked.

When he heard the team at the front door noisily attempting to enter, he and the two constables burst into the room. One robber was looking their way and fired his revolver. Charles was struck above the hip. He fell to the floor. The other two constables each fired their revolvers several times.

They killed two of the robbers and injured the third, who promptly dropped his pistol and surrendered. George and his team had now entered the bank.

It was all over in a few minutes. Charles was sitting up holding his right side. Blood was coming out between his fingers. The bullet had entered the fleshy part just above the hip where he had been injured in his dual with Ian. Fortunately, the bullet hadn't caused any major damage. A medic arrived at the scene and pronounced the two robbers deceased, tended to Charles' injury, and then the wounded robber. He had suffered a wound to his shoulder and his collarbone had been shattered.

The newspaper reporters had a field day with photographs and headlines praising the quick action of George and Charles. When it was revealed two of the robbers had been killed and Charles had been involved, a reporter from the Star raised the issue of Charles previously being called, "The policeman who takes no prisoners" with a headline 'How many did he kill this time?' Unfortunately, the article generated some adverse publicity for the Victorian Police Force. Other newspapers wrote articles on Charles' arrests, based on fact not fiction.

During a meeting, prior to the coroner's enquiry, a debrief was held at police headquarters. An independent inspector chaired the debrief. Initially he asked for details of the first notification of the bank robbery, who attended and who took charge. These questions were answered without any queries.

The next question was, 'What plan was instigated at this time to end the hostage siege, and did it get the hostages out of the bank safely?'

George read from a report he had drafted when he returned to the barracks. The chair asked a few questions such as, 'What did you consider the level of risk associated with the plan?'

George replied, 'After the hostages were freed, the risks were no different than those a policeman could face any day.' The chair nodded in agreement.

'We now come to the entry into the bank. Your report is quite clear. It states your plan. I support your idea. Now I have read the report from each of the policemen involved in the shooting and apprehension of the robbers. I presume the three policemen are here, even Inspector Stuart who was shot.'

The three stood up, although Charles was slower.

'Please be seated,' said the chair. 'Inspector Stuart what role did you take when the door was first opened?'

'I had only just stepped through the doorway when I was hit by a bullet and fell to the floor.'

'Now think carefully – did you fire your revolver?'

'Not that I recall. There were plenty of gunshots, but I think I dropped my revolver.'

'Thank you, Inspector. Next witness please come

forward.' The chair continued, 'Tell me what you recall happened and what you did.'

The first constable said, 'I followed the inspector through the door. An armed robber was standing near the counter. He turned towards me, as I fired my revolver at him several times. He collapsed to the floor and did not move. I then fired at the robber near the window. I think he was the one who had shot the inspector. My bullet hit him in the right shoulder and he dropped his revolver. He lifted up his left arm and surrendered.'

'Did Inspector Stuart fire his revolver?' asked the chair.'

'I don't think so. He was on the bank floor.'

'Thank you, Constable. Next witness please come forward. I want you to relate exactly what you recall during your involvement.'

He answered, 'I went through the door with the other constable and saw an armed robber listening at the front door of the bank. As he turned and saw me, he levelled his revolver at me, and I fired several shots. After a few seconds he slipped to the floor. I believe he was dead.'

'Did Inspector Stuart fire his revolver?'

'He could have. I don't know.'

'Thank you, Constable. I think with the written reports and the witnesses' statements, we have heard all we need to hear today. As it is Friday, we will adjourn now and will reconvene Monday morning to finalise the report for the Inspector General's office. Thank you. The meeting is now closed.'

George and Charles went to a locate tavern to have a drink and a chat. Charles had a nagging concern. The chair had not asked any questions regarding the revolvers.

George said, 'The revolvers concerned are under lock and key in the evidence room if he wants them checked. But why would he?' Charles just shrugged his shoulders.

The next morning Charles was awakened by a loud banging on his door. It was George with a Star newspaper in his hand.

'Read the headlines.'

Charles was soon wide awake. *"Inspector Stuart unsure if he shot one of the bank robbers. He has reputation of not taking prisoner live. Is this a police cover up?"* The newspaper article continued, *"We have this information from a reliable police source."*

When the meeting reconvened on Monday morning, the chair was fuming. He angrily asked, 'Who spoke to Bill Gunn, the Star newspaper reporter?' He asked each person in the room. When he received a negative answer from all he asked, 'Well someone has discussed this hearing with somebody.'

A female voice from the back of the room said, 'Excuse me, sir. It might have been me. I spoke to my brother at dinner, but I don't think he would say anything to anyone else.' Jane Lake then started to cry.

The chair had not considered their scribe could be the person who caused the report to be leaked to the press. He sat there thinking on how to handle this problem. This would not be good for the police force – a scribe revealing confidential information to a newspaper reporter.

George asked, 'Where does your brother work?'

She answered, 'At the weather bureau.'

'Is his office in the Star Newspaper building.'

She replied, 'I think so.'

The chair stood up. 'The meeting is convened until tomorrow morning. George, you and I are off to visit the Star. Charles, you and Jane go and find her brother and see what he has to say about this article.'

The Star building was very impressive. Thomas Batty was the owner. He had been one of the few who had struck it rich on the goldfields and had invested wisely by buying property. When he saw two uniformed senior police officers enter the building he immediately knew why. He had only seen Bill Gunn's article a few minutes ago. He knew that they would want to know the source of information regarding the attempted robbery at the bank.

The Star reporters held accredited police passes to access crime scenes and gather information on a preferred basis. The newspaper owner valued this priority access press. Thomas was not happy with Bill Gunn.

Thomas invited the two inspectors into his office and, after introductions, called for the tea lady to serve tea and biscuits. Thomas started the conversation. 'I can guess why you're here. I have just read the article myself and have yet to speak with Bill Gunn about his source of this police leak.'

The chair said, 'Yes, we are very concerned and want to find out who he spoke with over the weekend.'

Thomas stood up and went to the office door, instructing a passing office worker, 'Find Bill Gunn and tell him to come to my office immediately.'

Meanwhile, Charles and Jane found her brother leaning over some weather charts.

When questioned about who he may have made comment to about the robbery, he said, 'Bill Gunn asked me to have a drink with him Saturday evening and he raised the subject fleetingly. I only told him what Jane had mentioned during dinner.

'The enquiry was over but there was a possibility the shooting had not been resolved. I didn't think that was important.'

Charles asked, 'Have you read today's issue of the Star?'

Jane's brother replied, 'No, why?'

'I would suggest you be more selective with your drinking partners in future. You may have cost Jane her job.'

He replied to them, 'I hope not. I'm sorry.'

Charles and Jane returned to the barracks where he wrote out a brief report and had a mounted constable deliver it to the chair and George. They had a quick look at it while waiting for Bill Gunn to appear.

Bill Gunn appeared after they had waited for an hour. When he saw he two police officers, he knew immediately he had overstepped the mark. Oblique references were not acceptable; they had to be facts.

Thomas asked, 'Bill, I want to know the name of the police informant.'

Bill hesitated, 'There was no police informant. I received the information second-hand.'

Thomas angrily shouted, 'Are you serious. Second-hand information and you printed it as a headline.'

'Sir, it was good information. Trust me,' he pleaded.

The chair interrupted. 'Thomas, we have just been notified how the leak occurred. There were two people involved. We will handle those two.' He looked at George who nodded in agreement. 'How you handle Mr Gunn is up to you. But as from now, Mr Gunn's police accreditation is cancelled. Please hand me your pass.'

The meeting next morning was centred on how to discover who shot who. The chair asked for a firearms specialist to collect the revolvers from the evidence room and present them at the debrief meeting.

The chair asked, 'Can you examine these revolvers and comment on them.'

'Yes sir. Assuming each revolver had six bullets in the chamber. The first revolver has fired four bullets. The second revolver has fired five bullets. The third revolver has not been fired.'

When asked, 'What is the calibre of the revolvers?'

'The first two are .45 and the third is .36.'

The chairman asked, 'Who owns the .36?'

'I borrowed it from another inspector,' Charles replied.

The Chair said, 'Well that clears up the issue of who shot who, and who fired what!' He then thanked the firearms specialist for his attendance

The debrief was now concluded. George sent a courier to the Star asking Thomas Batty to visit him at his first convenience.

Thomas arrived that afternoon and was advised of their findings. He was delighted when he was invited to write an article giving the facts surrounding the shootings at the attempted bank robbery. The debrief meetings formed the basis for the formal enquiry to be held later. Charles eventually heard Bill Gunn had been posted to a country newspaper, as its editor.

Jane kept her job. She had learned her lesson. She was judged to have been a naïve young lady, rather than an incompetent one. She was eventually promoted to a court clerk.

George approached Charles at the barracks and said excitedly, 'I have a letter for you from the Governor's office.'

Charles opened the letter and was surprised. 'I've been awarded a medal from the Victorian Government for Devotion to Duty.'

George laughed. 'I've been awarded one, too! We have been recognised for our performance during the attempted bank robbery. This calls for a celebratory drink,'

'Let me tell Mary first.' Charles told Mary the good news, who was delighted and kissed him. It appeared the inspector general had approached the Premier to acknowledge their actions in time for the parade. Hence, why the awards had been approved so quickly.

The day advertised for the parade and awards ceremony was a week away. The Stuarts decided to take a coach trip to Ballarat, a large provincial town in the centre of the gold mining area.

They spent a few days sightseeing around the goldfields. The spread of the mines surprised them. The mines were not big but there were pit holes everywhere and the tents the miners lived in dotted the horizon. A local guide related the history of the Eureka Stockade which was a major turning point in the history of Victoria and a low in the public support of the police. They enjoyed the visit, but it was now time to head back to Melbourne.

The day of the Passing Out Parade arrived. There was much excitement in the air. The recruits had all been busy polishing their boots and uniform belts. The mounted policemen had their horses looking spick and span. They had been curry combed to remove any dead skin and dust. Even their hoofs were coloured black.

Charles had prepared one of his mares. She had been used several times for parades and city duty and was quiet by nature. The band's instruments did not faze her, she just stood there unmoved.

Mary had a front row seat next to George's lady friend and they soon began chatting. A bugle sounded and the parade commenced. The participants had assembled outside the barracks. The police band entered first, followed by the inspector general mounted on a white horse.

Following came several senior officers. Then the general recruits marched in accompanied by the applause of the crowd of relatives, friends and other members of the police force. They then formed a line in front of the audience. The mounted recruits looking splendid in their uniforms and with their shiny coated horses, formed a second line. The next to enter, were four policemen led by George. Last, but not least, were Charles and two mounted policemen. The band played the anthem. The entire assembly stood and those in uniform in the front row were at attention.

The proceedings commenced with the recruits being presented with their Certificate of Competence. The Deputy Inspector General then read out the names of the five policemen who had entered the bank with George.

They stepped forward as called. George was first to be acknowledged for his "Leadership during an attempted bank robbery by armed men". Amid applause, the inspector general pinned the medal on his uniform. This was repeated five more times.

Charles and his colleague had dismounted. Charles was the first to be called and have his medal pinned on his uniform for, "His decisive action in foiling an attempted bank robbery by armed men". He then went back to his horse. After his colleagues were each awarded their medal, the inspector general spoke. 'We have a representative from the New South Wales Government here today to present an award to Inspector Charles Stuart of the Victorian Mounted Police Force.'

The NSW Government agent stepped forward and invited Inspector Charles Stuart to come forward. 'I am authorised on behalf of the NSW Government to present to you this medal for Distinguished Service, namely for apprehending the attempted assassination gunman, Gavin Maquire.'

Mary was delighted by the event. She was proud of Charles.

Amid applause, the inspector general thanked everyone and then closed the day's proceedings.

Charles found himself the centre of attention with well-wishers and reporters. It was an hour, before he managed to escape from them and take Mary to the officers' mess for tea and to collect his thoughts. The presentation was over surprisingly quickly, and he wanted to recall the occasion.

George was already in the mess with his lady friend and came over to join the couple. George said, 'Well, you've made your mark, not only in Victoria but also in NSW.'

Charles replied, 'Yes, I've been very lucky in the colonies – my marriage, my career and now these awards. What next?'

The inspector general entered the mess and the policemen all stood. He made a short speech and did the rounds, talking with each table's occupants and congratulating the award recipients.

Charles and Mary returned to Kahuna the following day – Charles to his police duties and Mary to her gardens and orchids.

CHAPTER NINE

The Prodigals Return

The SS Lighting turned north into the Irish Sea. Ian looked at the English coast. He thought, *Did I make the right choice coming back?* Every now and then he recalled his problems in the past. Would he ever see his family and home again? What of Charles – if they should ever meet again? Perhaps the stolen money and his possible business venture would help him turn his life around.

The ship had a smooth trip up to Liverpool with sunshine and moderate winds. The four of them were looking forward to disembarking and being ashore again. After a few handshakes, they each went their separate ways. Hamish said goodbye and headed home to see his family. He and Ian had arranged to meet the next day at the local courthouse, with Hamish's lawyer.

Ian found an inn to stay the night. After signing in, he went to the bar and ordered a drink. He pondered for a short time and then he began to write down a few thoughts. Now he was about to enter the business world, he needed to show he was nobody's fool. Even though Ian could be erratic, irrational and even dangerous in his personal make up, he was not a fool.

He started to list the costs he thought would be the major expenses of his new business venture.

A   Three off X four-horse stagecoaches.

B   Six off X four-horse harness sets.

C   Thirty horses.

D   Lease three corner buildings with stables and a holding paddock.

E   Staff costs - manager (himself), drivers, guards, office clerks and ostlers.

F   Horse care fees (vet and farrier)

G   Fodder.

He would raise this list at the meeting tomorrow and, subject to satisfactory answers, he would sign the agreement.

The day started well with sunshine and no rain. When Ian arrived at the courthouse he was admitted to the office area by a constable. Hamish was waiting in the hall and after greeting him, he took him to the office of the Justice of the Peace, Robert Hill. After introducing him, he introduced his lawyer, John White. The group sat at a round table.

Hamish opened the meeting by confirming the offer he had made to Ian. He then asked Ian if he wished to say anything.

Ian nodded and then went through his list of queries regarding an estimate of set-up costs. Hamish had come prepared for this question and answered each item.

A.	Three stagecoaches	£200
B.	Six off X four-horse harnesses	£180
C.	Thirty horses	£100
D.	Three property leases for 12 months	£60
E.	Staff wages	£100
F.	Horses' care	£50
G.	Fodder	£50

Approx.   £740

Hamish continued, 'Even If there is an error in these estimates it won't exceed ten per cent. We will still have sufficient funds for us to remain buoyant.'

Ian nodded. He was pleased with Hamish's professionalism.

Hamish added, 'If you agree with the figures put before you, and our initial agreement, we could start implementing the project tomorrow.'

John White asked if Ian had a legal representative. Ian answered, 'No I believe Hamish and I will have a good relationship.'

John then passed Ian the contract and asked him to read it and, if he was satisfied with the wording, to sign it. Ian took his time to digest the words and their intent. Satisfied with the wording, he handed over the one thousand pounds and then signed the contract. A copy of the contract was also signed. Hamish then signed both. John then passed them to Robert Hill to formally witness them as a Justice of Peace. Hamish and Ian were then each handed their copy of the contract.

The meeting had only taken thirty minutes. After the signing was completed and the customary handshakes, Hamish produced a bottle of Scotch whisky to celebrate the occasion.

The following morning, Ian went to Hamish's office to plan the implementation. It was agreed that Hamish would do the purchasing, and Ian would locate and lease the buildings needed. Three towns had already been selected by Hamish. Lexon, Brilea and Taran were within twenty miles of each other. They were small towns but in prosperous farming districts. The towns each had a vibrant main street with ample shops and businesses. The partners arranged to meet weekly to advise their progress.

Ian had success in the first two towns and signed two building leases for twelve months for twenty pounds each. The Lexon building even had an upstairs room, which he decided to use as his residence. He purchased a bed, wardrobe, a desk and a table setting for two.

Unfortunately, no suitable property was available in Taran. All the corner sites were owned by well-established businesses. They also had no paddock area for the horses. Ian considered purchasing an acre corner block that was available and erecting a small building with stables and a holding yard for the horses. At the next meeting, he put the idea to Hamish, who agreed if the total cost was no more than one hundred pounds. However, it was necessary for the venture to be up and running for the first service.

Ian purchased the land for fifty pounds and approached a local builder with two plans. The first was the floor plan of the new building. The second plan was the layout of the stables and the paddock fencing.

The builder agreed to do the two jobs for forty pounds and to complete them within three weeks. The company would own the Taran property, and it would be valued at more than the total establishment cost of ninety pounds.

Hamish had completed his negotiations for the three coaches and harnesses. They would be delivered in two weeks, both within the budget estimates.

Normally horses would be a problem to purchase. The majority of horses had been sold to India in the past, but this demand had now ended. Horses were now available at a much reduced cost. The horses were to arrive at Hamish's main paddock in one week, subject to an inspection by a veterinarian.

Hamish then concentrated on hiring the staff needed. He was more skilled than Ian at this task. This left Ian to oversee the builder's progress. The building was completed to Ian's satisfaction, and he paid him thirty pounds.

The next day the builder did not turn up to complete the stables and paddock fences. The following day he was absent again. Ian went looking for him. He found him drunk. He told the builder. 'Be on the job tomorrow or I'll come looking for you and I will not be happy.'

The builder did not arrive at the building site the next day. Ian was now angry. He mounted his horse and found the builder standing talking to several people. When he saw Ian, he tried to explain to him, 'I had other things to do. I'll start tomorrow.'

Ian said, 'No, you can start now.'

The builder replied, 'No, I'll start tomorrow,'

Ian dismounted and stood in front of the builder. 'I said now!' The builder started to turn away from him.

Ian grabbed his arm and said, 'I'm talking to you.' The builder threw a punch at him and hit Ian in the face.

Ian lost his temper and proceeded to punch the builder several times until he fell to the ground. He then began to kick him. His friends grabbed Ian to stop him from hitting him anymore. Ian shoved them away and picked up the builder, shouting, 'I said today.' The builder nodded, mounted his horse and went to the site.

An elderly bystander standing nearby said, 'Be careful with your temper lad, or you'll kill someone one day.' The words stopped him abruptly, making him aware of what he could have done.

The builder completed the stables and fencing to Ian's satisfaction and was paid the ten pound balance of their agreement.

The next weekly meeting was their third. Ian advised a veterinarian and a farrier were available at each town and fodder was plentiful, but he hadn't any costs yet. Hamish was not too concerned. They were not major issues.

Staffing had not been a problem, as there was considerable unemployment in Scotland. Hamish had filled the various positions with staff who were mainly experienced with handling horses and some with office experience.

He had issued bulletins on the three towns' notice boards advising a new stagecoach service would commence the next week. The coaches and horses had been positioned in the three towns and the offices were opened for passenger ticket sales.

The inaugural stagecoach feeder service arrived on time from Lexon. Ian decided to travel as a passenger to see if the maiden service was satisfactory and to identify if there were any problems. Their new driver showed his proficiency. He nursed the horses on hills and galloped them on flat roads.

There were three other passengers on his coach, and he listened to their comments. The coach had six seats inside and four seats outside, with only four onboard, the passengers were able to stretch out.

He listened to their conversations. 'It was about time this service was started.'

'These seats are comfortable.'

'This service is what the town needs.'

'I didn't realise this road was so good. This coach ride is comfortable. The last time I travelled to Glasgow, I could hardly walk the next day.' The passengers laughed.

They soon arrived at Brilea and Ian watched as the horses were changed. The ostler had four horses harnessed and ready to replace the other four. He and the driver completed the task within ten minutes.

The ostler then led the moved horses to the stables where he generally inspected them, paying attention to their hoofs for stone damage and their noses for bleeding. The horses would be curry combed tomorrow. The horses would appreciate a curry brush. Removing dead skin with the curry brush strokes made the horses skin dryer and warmer. Their coat would also be shinier by removing dust and dead hair from their coats.

On the next leg to Taran, the coach had six passengers. Again, Ian listened to the comments from the passengers. They all agreed that this service was long overdue. Hamish had chosen well. This route would be profitable.

At Taran the coach stopped for an hour, which suited

Ian. It gave him a chance to look around the property and check the office efficiency and effectiveness. The young lass behind the counter saw he was returning. She asked him if he would like a cup of tea and a cake while he was waiting. Ian nodded, 'Yes, I'd Like that.' This gave Ian an idea, 'Why not open a small tearoom at each stagecoach office to serve waiting passengers?'

Ian and Hamish met to compare notes and thoughts. Hamish said, 'The figures are good. Passengers are up on the previous route, so it appears the new route is successfully feeding the old route. This is what I was hoping for with my plan. How is your end of the route going. Are there any problems?'

He answered, 'No, the staff are more than capable, and the coaches are leaving on time.' He paused. 'I have an idea. Why not serve tea and cake to waiting passengers? We would not need any extra staff, and it would be appreciated on these routes, particularly when the snow season starts. I suggest we try it at Taron as it's the terminal of the line and see what interest we get from the passengers.'

Hamish replied, 'I like that idea. Yes, give it a try.'

The following month, Ian travelled to Taron and introduced himself to Jenny, the office clerk, and told her of his idea. She said, 'I only hope I don't get too many wanting tea and that it doesn't affect my office duties.'

Ian nodded. 'I'll leave that decision to you.'

As Ian was talking with her, he could see a man with a small leather bag waiting to talk with her. He stepped away and sat down, allowing him to come forward. After he left, Ian asked, 'Who was that man? I think I know him.'

She answered, 'He's the bank manager. He sends his mail with us on the first Friday of the month. James Lynn is his name. We have been carrying the bank's confidential mail since we started.' Ian nodded.

He climbed aboard the coach returning to Lexon. As the coach rolled on through the hills to Brilea, his thoughts were on the confidential mail. What would be the contents? He began to remember the thrill of the robberies he had been involved in back in the colonies.

As the months rolled on, Ian began to become bored. He was standing looking out his bedroom window as the scheduled stagecoach departed, heading out of town. The sun had set behind the hills. The night was dark with cloud covering a waning moon. Ian wondered if he could rob a coach and just collect the confidential mail to see what it was. Just mail or perhaps money?

He had horses available and as he was the route manager, no one would suspect him. He would only rob coaches with women onboard. All he had to do was disarm the guard. He knew the guards had been told "Don't put your life or the passengers lives in danger. If you are held up, just do as you're told."

Ian had made up his mind. He would try one robbery and see what the confidential mail bag contained.

He decided on a Friday night. If the Taron Bank was moving money, he presumed it could be the week's surplus being sent to a larger bank or even the bank's head office.

Ian waited until there were only women's names on the passenger list. He dressed entirely in black, with a cape and a mask. Naturally he selected a black horse. Excited, he headed out into the darkness to try his luck.

Ian placed a wagon wheel in the path of the coach,

on the other side of a crest in the road. He hid behind a large bush adjacent the wheel. He heard the coach approaching and the voice of the driver. When the driver saw the wheel on the road, he stepped heavily on the brake and pulled on the reins to stop the horses.

Unconcerned, the guard handed his shot gun to the driver and said, 'I'll move it.' As he stepped down from the coach, Ian rode from the bushes with his revolver pointed at the driver and said, 'Throw the gun into the bushes.' The driver said nothing but did as he was told. Ian then ordered him, 'Hand me the mail bag.'

After receiving the mail bag, Ian headed into the darkness, in the opposite direction. The guard moved the wheel from the road, collected his shotgun and they continued their trip to Taran. When he reported the robbery to the authorities, they were surprised that the passengers weren't robbed. Why had he only taken the mail bag? They were to find out later.

Ian retired to his bedroom and opened the mail bag. Most of the contents were letters and newspapers, only two items stood out as being different. Both contained bank documents. One contained three hundred pounds. The other item was a property deed. Ian did not keep the mail bag or its other contents. He left it a stable at Brilea for others to find.

Hamish arrived in Lexon worried at the damage this robbery might do to the company's image.

Ian remarked, 'It's only happened once. Don't worry. It could have happened to any coach company.'

Hamish nodded. 'I hope you're right.'

Ian thought about robbing another coach company. He didn't need the money, but he enjoyed the thrill of the deed. Yes, he would rob the Eastern Stagecoach line. He selected the route to Glasgow. There was a small town with a similar rise in the road, leading into the town. This time Ian would lay a large bush in the centre of the road. He aborted the first night when he saw the passengers were all men aboard the coach.

The second Friday night there were only three women passengers. As soon as the coach left the depot, he galloped to the spot he had decided on, and pulled the bush out onto the road.

He was again dressed all in black, complete with black cloak and mask and riding a black horse. He could hear the coach approaching and his pulse began to race. As soon as the driver saw the bush blocking the road, he applied the brake and brought the horses to a halt. Ian rode out of the trees where he had hidden and ordered the guard, 'Throw the shotgun to the side of the road.' The guard hesitated and Ian fired a shot into the air. The guard then threw the shotgun as ordered. 'Hand me the mail bag,' ordered Ian.

When he had been given the mailbag, he turned his horse and rode off in the opposite direction to where the coach was travelling.

When the coach arrived at the next town, the robbery was reported to the authorities. They interviewed the driver and the guard, but their reports were of no value. They did confirm, the robber was dressed in black on a black horse and only asked for the mailbag. He had shown no interest in robbing the passengers.

The authorities did not know where to start their investigation. All they knew were the two robberies were identical. Even the robber's voice had been difficult to identify. It sounded Cockney, but the witnesses were unsure. One driver thought it could have been a Scottish voice. The fact that the women were not robbed puzzled the police. When travelling, women were notorious for wearing or carrying valuable jewellery. The other act of returning the mailbag with its contents had the police scratching their heads.

When Ian opened the second mailbag, he found only one package with money. It was a down payment on a new office block for a lawyer. He kept the one hundred pounds and left the mailbag on the verandah of a bank. The police were puzzled why he would do this.

At their next meeting, Hamish said, 'You were correct. He's robbed another coach company.'

Ian said, 'You worry too much.'

Two weeks after the first robbery, the Taron bank manager was asked by the head office, 'When are you going to forward last month's excess cash?' It was only then that it was realised cash had been stolen. A week later the lawyer, who had sent his deposit to the land seller, reported his one hundred pounds had not been received and was presumed to have been stolen. The robber was only interested in cash.

Charles had been in the colonies for several years and began to think of returning to Scotland to see his parents again. When he visited Melbourne for a conference, he visited George and discussed this with him.

George replied, 'You have asked at the right time. We have been invited to send a senior officer to a multinational meeting in London. I'll run it by the inspector general and see what he thinks. Personally, I think with your experience, you would be the ideal choice. Your city and bush experiences will be of interest, not only to your English peers, but also to other countries such as Canada and New Zealand.'

The two friends dined together and chatted about their lives in the colony. George had been courting a widow and said he may remarry soon. Charles spoke of his happy marriage and the good fortune of having a home overlooking a splendid river. He and Mary were more devoted to each other than ever.

Crime along the river was minimal. A few cases of rustling cattle, some domestic problems. Charles said, 'At times they are unwinnable. Generally, with the male being told to leave or be jailed. Often I've felt the woman had caused the trouble. But it was unthinkable for a woman to be told to leave her home or be jailed.' He said his role as prosecutor had not been too demanding, even with the long time he was away from home and the associated travelling. He finished by saying, 'Meeting you on the ship was a turning point in my life and I will be eternally grateful to you.'

George replied, 'Thank you for those kind words, my friend.' They toasted each other, then retired for the evening.

George sent a constable to Charles requesting him come to the inspector general's office. Sir Giles wished to speak with him.

The constable knocked on the door and an officious voice, replied, 'Come in.' Sir Giles and George were seated at a small table with a teapot, cups and some cakes. Charles saluted and sat down after Sir Giles pointed to a chair.

'Good morning, Stuart. I see you are still getting good reports.' Charles nodded a thank you. 'George tells me you are applying for leave to visit your family. I think it's highly commendable to remember one's heritage. I believe we can spare you for six months. There is a five day conference in London with police representatives worldwide attending. I would like you to attend and prepare a paper on Victorian Policing. What do you think?'

Charles was delighted that he was being asked. 'Yes, sir, it would be an honour.'

Sir Giles stood up. The meeting was over. As he left the room Sir Giles said, 'And don't forget to wear your medals.'

George followed him out. 'Arrange your travel agenda and leave me a copy. I'll send the brochure advising the conference details. Best of luck and enjoy your trip. Regards to Mary.'

After Charles made the voyage bookings for them to Liverpool, he began thinking more of his ancestral home and his parents. Mary had been delighted with the news they were going to visit Scotland. She had grown to accept Victoria as her home, but she had not forgotten her roots. At times she missed the glen and not hearing its unique brogue.

The ship sailed out of Port Phillip Bay and headed east southeast to pass around the tip of New Zealand and then set an eastly course to South America. Mary had bought several books to read to help pass the time.

Charles started to write his presentation. Mainly he gave descriptions of outback crimes in which he had been involved. He emphasised the problem with the distance he needed to travel and the harshness of the inland country. An equivalent city crime could take only a few days to solve. In the outback it could be measured in months. An investigation team needed to be physically fit, have sound horses, be capable of living off the land and finding water.

The ship's other passengers were mainly soldiers returning to England from their tour of duty in the colonies. Even though they looked fit and healthy, they still exercised daily before breakfast.

Mary and Charles dined at the captain's table with two army officers and their wives, who soon became friends. Having a drink after dinner was enjoyable. Sometimes they played cards or just talked of their experiences in the colonies. The officers had seen service in India and spoke highly of the grandeur of the Maharajah's palaces and of their magnificent gardens. But they were critical of the difference of living standards between the very rich upper class and the extremely poor lower class Indians. The difference was extraordinary, almost unbelievable.

They soon reached Cape Horn and Terra del Fuego at the tip of Chile. The convergence of the Pacific and the Atlantic Oceans created large foaming waters. It was the end of summer, and the seas were less turbulent than winter, and with a maximum temperature of around forty-five degrees Fahrenheit.

The ship ploughed on, twisting and plunging into the seas. It wasn't as uncomfortable as their previous voyage, and they were out of the Strait sooner this time.

That evening the captain's table dinner was much appreciated, as they had drinks to celebrate their departure from Cape Horn area after days of hostile seas.

As the ship headed to Rio De Janeiro, the senior army officer, Major Godfrey, had been conducting some military drills, prompting Charles to comment to him, 'You certainly keep your men occupied.'

Major Godfrey answered, 'We are required to perform a parade in Rio for the outgoing British Consul and the Changeover Ceremony with the incoming Consul. You and your wife are invited if you wish to attend.'

Charles nodded, 'Thank you. Yes, we would be delighted.'

Godfrey replied, 'I know you are a Victorian police inspector. You are welcome to wear your uniform.' He then went to speak with his other officer.

Even though the gentle pitching and rolling deck of a sailing ship was not conducive for military drills, the soldiers managed to perform them to a high standard.

At dinner, the ship's captain advised they would reach Rio the next day. He also cautioned, 'Be aware, Rio can be a dangerous place. Remain alert at all times.'

They sailed along the coast for two days enjoying the sight of land after so many days of seeing only sea and birds. They dropped anchor within a few hundred yards from the magnificent golden sands of a long beach. Within minutes a large rowing boat could be seen heading towards their ship, flying the British flag. The ship's crew lowered their stairs.

A smartly dressed Royal Navy officer came up the stairs, turned aft and saluted, asking the captain for, 'Permission to come aboard, sir. I am Commander Spencer of the Royal Navy.'

The ship's captain stepped forward and said, 'Permission granted. Let me introduce you to Major Godfrey of the British Army Fusiliers.' After introducing several other officers, and with greetings completed, the trio went to the captain's quarters.

The next few hours saw a hive of activity on the ship. First the passengers were rowed ashore, next the soldiers and finally a cargo of wool began to be unloaded.

Charles and Mary elected to stay at the British Military Barracks as they believed they would be safer there.

As they rode in a coach to the barracks with the officers wives, they could see coloured bunting adorning the shops and lamp posts. It was everywhere. The coach driver told them there was to be an election next week and the local people were excited.

Charles, Mary and the officers wives only ventured out once, because of the potential riots between political parties. The consul had supplied a very ordinary coach with no marking on it. It was inconspicuous and only used when the locals were excitable during their political protests.

Their coach was manned by two soldiers, not wearing their uniforms. One was the driver and the other an inconspicuous guard. They both had hidden revolvers. The two wives and Mary and Charles were the only passengers. Charles also had a hidden revolver. They drove along the magnificent beach. It was pristine with golden sands that led down to the blue waters of the South Atlantic Ocean. They then drove through the old area with the stately homes of the early European settlers.

The driver decided on a shortcut through a side street. The guard noticed two horsemen looking their way. The horsemen trotted towards them and suddenly reined in alongside them. The first to the coach pulled out a revolver and gestured for the two soldiers to raise their arms.

The driver asked, 'What do you want?' The robber held his hand up and rubbed his fingers with his thumb, indicating money, showing they could not speak English.

Charles quietly asked Mary to ask the driver, 'How many are there?'

The driver whispered, 'Two and the one in the blue shirt is the only one with a revolver.'

Charles withdrew his revolver and leant out of the coach and shot the blue shirted robber in the side of his body at point blank range. The gunman fell from his horse, mortally wounded. The noise from the revolver spooked his horse, and it bolted. The other robber's horse bucked and threw his rider to the ground.

The coach driver quickly had his horses galloping and, unfortunately, the other robber was run over by the coach wheels.

As they galloped down the street, the guard looked back. 'Slow down. No one saw what happened and we don't want to draw attention to ourselves.' The drive back to the barracks was at a nice leisurely trot. At dinner that evening, they were the centre of attention. The soldiers' records noted accordingly of their involvement.

The following day was the date for the handover of the appointments of the consuls. Charles dressed in his uniform, as requested by the major. Mary and he attended the changeover ceremony at the barracks and then they returned to the ship with the other two wives and watched the parade from afar. They were able to hear the band echoing between the buildings.

After the changeover protocols had been observed, the soldiers, who had already been assembled, escorted the departing consul to the ship. The major led the parade followed by two officers. Next were eight rows of three soldiers in front of the official coach. Eight more rows of three soldiers with two N.C.O.s completed the group. Although it had been a small parade, it was impressive with the sunlight shining on the bayonets fixed to their rifles. The Rio-based British regiment provided the buglers and the drummers. The locals watched the parade, some even clapped the spectacle, probably not knowing why. The drumbeats and the bugles military marching tune thrilled their senses.

The wind had been from the west and when the tide turned, the anchored ship swung and faced east.

The captain had the bosun unfurl the mainsail and when it began to fill, he ordered the anchor to be weighed. As the ship began to move, the other sails were unfurled as the they left the harbour northbound for England.

The deck was filled with soldiers, sailors and passengers looking at Rio as it disappeared in the distance. Even with its safety risks, most on board had enjoyed their few hours in the city. The city was quaint and historical, with a coastline as good as any in the world.

While others had been ashore, the ship had been loaded with fresh food and water. At dinner that evening the major said, 'I see you are a man of action.' Charles was unsure what he meant and looked at him, puzzled. The major said, 'I am referring to your medals. I've seen the Colonial Star medal before but not the round one.'

Charles nodded. 'Yes, I've been involved in Victorian police actions and survived. The other medal is from the NSW Government for services rendered over the capture of a high profile villain.'

The major nodded. 'Well done. No doubt you not only deserved them but also earned them. Let's drink to your awards.'

The ship was sailing with a good stern wind, moderate seas and a blue sky. Some soldiers were still enjoying the sea air while standing at the ship's bow. Others had gone aft and were fishing.

They were making good time and expected to arrive in the UK within three weeks. Mary and Charles were becoming excited now the voyage was nearing its end. At dinner, each evening the diners spoke of what they intended to do. Mostly they spoke of meeting their families. Others, who were unattached, intended to find a country or seaside inn and just relax.

Charles and Mary were on deck when the coast of Ireland slowly appeared out of the morning fog. The sight of the high cliffs and the green lowlands between them bought tears to Mary's eyes. Charles gave her a hug. 'It's only a matter of days and we will be back at Belcannon again.' He then kissed her gently.

The Liverpool port authorities quickly processed the passengers and soldiers with their customs clearances.

The major assembled his troops on the dock and had a few words. 'I am proud of having served with you. Best of luck and enjoy your leave.' He paused. 'We will meet again at the London barracks in four weeks. Sergeant, dismiss the men.' The soldiers then collected their kit bags and rifles and went their separate ways.

Charles and Mary said goodbye to the officers and their wives, and then hired a coach to take them to the Liverpool Railway Station. Their destination was to Edinburgh by train and by coaches to Glencairn.

After leaving Liverpool, they sat looking out the window at the towns, villages and countryside as the train passed through. The green of the trees and fields was so different from the Australian colonies' outback foliage. As the sun set and they were the only occupants in the first class compartment, they stretched out on the two long seats and had a brief nap.

A knock on the compartment door was followed by a voice asking, 'Do you require dinner?' had them both quickly awake.

Charles replied, 'Yes, please come in.' They were offered a small plate of vegetables and a slice of ham. The meal and the cup of tea were adequate. They sat quietly, each with their own thoughts of coming home after being away so long. They had no idea what changes they would find.

They first realised they were in Scotland when two men joined them in their compartment wearing kilts. When the train arrived at Edinburgh they decided to stay overnight. The next morning, they walked the main street, looking at the shop windows.

It was obvious the buildings were older and the businesses more entrenched in this city than Melbourne, which was only developing. Although, surprisingly Melbourne, in the space of thirty odd years, had become one of the major cities outside of Europe. The goldrush had triggered its growth.

From Edinburgh, they travelled by three coaches. The final coach to Glencairn was packed. It had eight passengers inside and four in the rear outside seat. Mary and Charles were seated inside.

After leaving the city, they headed north to the highlands. The temperature soon dropped, and the rain started. The passengers outside had come prepared for the weather and wrapped themselves in oilskin blankets. They were cold but they were dry. The scenery was covered in fog, giving a ghostly appearance to the trees and shrubs. They changed horses several times and eventually arrived at Glencairn village.

As soon as Mary alighted, she was recognised by a family friend, a school friend with a good memory. Mary introduced her friend to Charles. She suddenly remembered who he was – the son of the Earl of Belcannon!

They adjourned to an inn for tea, while Charles went to find a coach to drive them to Belcannon. Charles returned with a coach, and the two departed for their final destination.

When they arrived, they stood for a moment or two looking at the manor. A farm hand was the first to see them and welcomed them back. He helped carry their baggage into the main hall and left.

Charles walked into his father's den. His father looked up in surprise at seeing his son. He stood up and hugged him. 'I received your letter advising you were visiting, but not the month or the week. You look well. Where is Mary? Ah! There you are. Welcome to Belcannon, young lady.' He kissed her on her cheek and then hugged her. His father had a servant bring Charles' mother to them. She cried when she saw the two of them and hugged them. It was a happy homecoming.

That evening was a very happy family dinner. Nicola was there with her husband, Gavin McIntosh, who was a wealthy local farmer. She was expecting her first child and looked radiant. Between meal courses, Charles and Mary were asked question after question about the colonies, where they lived and Charles' police career, even though some questions had already been answered in letters sent to the earl and his wife previously. At a very late hour, the family retired for the night.

The next morning Charles rose early and went for a walk. A voice called, 'Good morning, sir.' It was Shamus, the earl's gamekeeper. Charles turned and shook his outstretched hand. 'Hello. It's good to see you again. How are you keeping?'

'Just fine, sir, I'm fine, and you?' he replied and continued, 'I need to tell you something.' They walked to the main barn and lay down on some hay bales.

Charles said, 'I'm listening.'

'I shot Ian, and I think I killed him. I was hunting in The Loch and he fired a bullet at me and I fired an arrow at him. My arrow definitely hit him, and he fell into the water, but I didn't find his body. I've told no one of this incident.'

Charles looked at Shamus in surprise. Charles believed Ian had escaped to the Australian colonies. He nodded to Shamus and said, 'I hope you're correct. I don't think even his mother would miss him. It's best if your secret remains between us.'

Shamus nodded and replied, 'Good. It will. I'm off now to do some tracking of the deer herd to count any new births.' He stood up and walked away. Charles was puzzled. He had been certain Ian had been one of the Highwaymen.

The meeting in London was due to be held next week. He had written his presentation speech during the voyage and had asked Mary for her comments. She felt he had not accentuated his role in some of the example cases he described.

She had written a few extra words in the text with which he agreed. She drove him to the stagecoach office and, after a quick kiss goodbye, they parted, Charles to London and Mary home to Belcannon.

The conference venue was in London at Scotland Yard, the home of the English police hierarchy. This had been chosen because the police commissioners were based there and there was a large meeting room available.

When Charles arrived, he found he was one of forty attendees. He wondered if they were all invited to speak. If so he feared they would be there for over a week. He need not have worried. When he was handed an agenda, only twelve invitees were to speak, including the senior commissioner. Two days were allocated for visits. One to the Old Bailey Court for the day and the other day, for a visit to the London Police Headquarters and facilities.

The opening speech by the senior commissioner had been of interest. It showed a common criminal similarity in all countries. The percentage for murder, burglaries, assaults and domestic violence were alike in all countries. Jail also had proved not to be a deterrent. Rehabilitation was in its infancy and had not shown the results anticipated, but all countries agreed to persist with this initiative and share results.

The commissioner then invited the floor for questions. Most confirmed what had been said. The first speaker was from Canada. He gave examples of major crimes in the frozen northern country and the associated difficulties due to the distance and access to supporting units such as forensic laboratories. Charles noted that some of these problems were akin to his.

The next two days went quickly with speakers from South Africa, New Zealand and the Far East. Charles found the speeches informative and wrote a few aide memoirs for later research in Victoria.

His turn arrived and he stepped to the podium, placing the pages of his speech on the lectern. He was nervous facing his peers, but once he started talking and concentrating on his presentation, he soon felt comfortable. He began with the story of the attempted assassination.

The audience were interested and listened intently. He sensed the feeling. He then told the story of the Highwaymen. Again, he had an interested group of listeners. When he finished, he was clapped loudly. Questions now came quick and fast. After he had answered them and sat down, he realised very few of them were aware of the size of the Australian colonies and the vast distances a police officer had to travel to perform his duties.

That evening at dinner, a police officer from Edinburgh sat alongside him and introduced himself as Robert Scott, Superintendent of the Edinburgh Police Force. He said, 'Your story of the Highwaymen was of interest to me. I have a problem with a Highway bandit operating up in your father's district. He has robbed six coaches to date, and we haven't any idea who he is. He only takes the mail bag and only takes the cash in it. He doesn't rob the passengers. Later the mail bag is dropped somewhere in the local towns.'

Charles replied excitedly, 'He's acting similar to the robbers who operated in Victoria. As I said in my presentation, the bank robbers only took cash and never robbed the customers. We caught one, one vanished and the other, we believe, left the colonies. We haven't heard of either of them since the court case. Your case sounds interesting.'

Robert looked at him and asked, 'Would you consider assisting us? Could you take a look at the reports we have collected from the coach drivers and guards? A fresh view would be welcome. The passengers were unable to help at all. I can approve you as a consultant. That would give you the authority you need to be involved.'

Charles nodded. 'Yes, what you have said interests me. I can stop over in Edinburgh on the way home and we can take it from there, depending on if I find something tangible in your reports.'

Robert nodded. 'Agreed, now let's eat.'

The next two days were of interest, but Charles could not get the coincidences out of his mind. Even as he sat in the gallery of the Old Bailey Court hearing a major crime, he kept thinking about the possibility that this robber might be Ian.

He met with Robert Scott and his reports did interest him. Charles received his written authorisation. They agreed to meet the following week at the Taron Inn dressed in civilian clothes.

The two of them met in one of their hired rooms to make an action plan. They decided to carry out the interviews at the homes of the drivers and guards to ensure their investigations were kept in confidence. They had a list of questions which Charles had drafted. Robert concurred.

1   What time did the coach depart the town?

2   Was it a direct route to the next village?

3   How many male passengers were there and were they local?

4   What caused you to stop?

5   Was there only one robber?

6   What language did his voice sound like?

7   What did he say?

8   Which direction did he take after the robbery?

9   Describe the robber's attire and colour of his horse?

10   Was there anything else out of the ordinary you noticed?

The first team who were robbed, answered as follows:

1   10 p.m.

2   It was a direct route.

3   None, only female passengers.

4   An obstruction across the road.

5   Only one robber.

6   They think he sounded like a Scot?

7   Throw your shotgun to the side of the road and hand me your mail bag and be quick about it.

8   Back and towards the way we came.

9   All black with a cape. The horse was black
     with no markings.

10   No. There was something about his
     manner, but neither could remember.

Both Robert and Charles were pleased with the first interview. The second interview was almost identical, except the route was around the base of a large estate and a large bush was across the road. The third and fourth were identical to the second robbery. The fifth was virtually identical to first robbery. The only significant difference was one guard recalled the robber couldn't reach the mail bag with his right arm and turned his horse and used his left arm to take the mail bag from him.

On the sixth robbery, the guard had a revolver under his seat and as the robber rode away, he fired two shots at the robber. But he was unsure if he hit him.

The sixth driver was talkative. He said, 'When we were robbed, we only had women onboard, same as our other coaches. I felt the robber knew this. I don't know how he knew. Perhaps he watched the stagecoach office or maybe he'd been told by an employee. I told the police this.'

Charles asked, 'How was he dressed?'

'All in black as was his horse.'

'Anything else you noticed out of the ordinary?'

The driver thought for a moment and replied, 'He seemed to have an arm problem. When I offered him the mail bag, he couldn't reach me, and he then turned his horse around to take it with his other hand.'

'Last question. Did he speak and sound English?'

'It wasn't English. I think his accent could have been Welsh, Irish or, like you, Scottish.'

Charles thought, it could be Ian. Especially if he had returned to this district. Robert and Charles sat down to decide what to do next. They had identified:

1 So far, he had robbed six times on two routes.

2 Only taken money from mail bags.

3 Only women passengers.

4 He had only fired his revolver once as a warning, not in anger.

5 He operated alone.

6 Black clothes and horse.

7 Had blocked the road each time and caused the coach to be stopped.

8 He had ridden back the way the coaches had travelled.

9 Normally around two to three week intervals between robberies.

Charles said, 'The last driver has been helpful. Added another positive clue.'

Robert agreed. 'No men aboard. That's a good clue. He must have known before he attempted a robbery. It could be an employee who is giving out this information.'

Charles added, 'Or an employee who is also the robber.'

Robert said, 'I'll contact the owners of both the

Eastern Stagecoach line and the McDonald Stagecoach line and ask them confidentially for a copy of their employees' names and addresses. Hopefully we'll have the information within the week.'

McDonald Coaches had a direct route, and the Eastern Coaches had to go around a very large estate.

Charles wondered if there was a pathway across the estate wide enough for a single horse to travel. If so, this meant the robber could know of the gender of the passengers on board and have sufficient time to take the pathway to his prepared hold up position. The route of McDonald's Coaches was a non-stop route so the robber would have had prior knowledge of the passenger list before the coach left.

When the employees list arrived, they discounted the drivers and guards first. They discretely checked on each employee, their bank accounts, homes and acquaintances. Nothing stood out for any of them.

They met with the owners and told them their findings. Hamish McDonald said, 'I didn't expect you would. My partner and I selected our staff carefully.'

Charles asked, 'I thought you were the owner?'

Hamish shook his head. 'No, I have a silent partner.'

Robert asked, 'Is his name on the list?'

'No, but it won't be him. We are a very profitable company. We can go see him if you wish. Ian lives in a room above our Lexon office and stables.'

When Charles heard the name, his heart started to pump. He asked, 'What is his family name?'

When he heard the name Flint he had to sit down. Robert noticed but said nothing. Charles asked, 'When did these robberies start?'

'A few months after we opened this new route,' was Hamish's reply.

Outside in the street Robert asked, 'What was that all about? Did you recognise the name?'

Charles laughed and replied, 'Ian Flint has been my nemesis for many years. I think he was one of the three Highwaymen in Victoria. I would like to capture him alive, so I can get some answers only he will know.'

Robert said, 'Well let's hope so and don't forget I'm a local policeman; you're not, so it's my call. I will arrest him if he surrenders peacefully.' Charles nodded. Finally, to find Ian so close to Glencairn after all these years.

Ian's room was reached via a stairway in the sales office. When Robert and Charles arrived, the office was closed. The duo found an unlocked widow and accessed the office by climbing in. Robert quietly led the way up the stairs. At Ian's door he called loudly, 'This is the police. Open your door.'

Ian opened the door, and Robert entered the room without being invited. Ian turned and followed Robert, his back to the doorway.

Ian asked, 'What's this all about?'

Robert said, 'We wish to question you in relation to the armed robberies to stagecoaches in this district.'

Ian answered, 'Me? Are you serious? I'm a part owner. I've never robbed anyone in my life.'

Charles then said, 'That's not true, is it, Ian?'

Ian's face went pale when he recognised Charles' voice. He turned and looked at him in astonishment.

After so long, their paths crossed again. Ian walked over to a chair and sat down.

Charles waited for Robert to start questioning him.

When no questions were forthcoming he took his eyes off Ian and looked at Robert. Robert had drawn his revolver and then fired twice at Ian. Charles turned back to Ian, and watched him fall to the floor, dropping a revolver. It was obvious he had intended to shoot Charles.

Robert said, 'I saw him pull the revolver from the side of the chair. I had no choice but to shoot him.'

Charles knelt by Ian who was still alive but mortally wounded from two chest wounds.

'Ian, you are badly wounded. Tell me, were you the robber of the six stagecoaches in Victoria?'

Ian was coughing up blood and bleeding heavily from his chest wounds. He nodded. 'Yes.'

'Were you one of the three Highwaymen in Victoria?'

Again, Ian nodded. 'Yes.' He tried to speak, mumbling, 'Tell Mum I'm sorry.' He then lay there, quietly accepting he was dying.

Robert had heard his words and asked Charles, 'What did he mean by his last words.'

Charles stood up and shrugged his shoulders – Ian was dead.

Charles felt sad and yet relieved that Ian was no more. He and Robert parted company the next day. Robert sent a letter to the Victorian Police Inspector General acknowledging his contribution to ending the career of the notorious stagecoach robber – Ian Flint.

Charles travelled to Mrs Flint's home. He had assumed the uncomfortable task of telling her of Ian's death. She sat quietly as he told her. She was quite stoic at the news and just nodded. She arranged for Ian's body to be returned and a small funeral which Charles and Mary attended. When he told Shamus what had happened,

Shamus nodded. 'As I said, I didn't see his body. I have always wondered if I had killed him.'

That evening Mary asked Charles why he had been so secretive during the last few weeks. He sat down and told her the story of his falling out with Ian and what happened afterwards.

She kissed him and said, 'It's all in the past now.'

Over the next two weeks, the couple visited relatives and friends and just relaxed. It was time to return to Victoria. The earl organised a farewell dinner.

After a short speech and a sumptuous meal, his father asked Charles to come forward. He then presented them with a family heirloom – a gold and jewelled cup. It was over five hundred years old and virtually priceless.

Charles thanked his parents and thought for a moment. He then surprised everyone, when he said, 'I'll leave this treasure here in Scotland. Mary and I will return here one day and then we will take possession of it. The cup belongs here.' The gathering clapped his response, and his mother cried.

The day of departure was overcast and gloomy, as was the mood of the farewelling group. The women cried and even his father looked emotional. After many kisses and handshakes, they entered the gig and headed to the stagecoach office. Charles was pensive, wondering if he would ever see his family again. The couple slept cuddled together during the coach trip. The train trip was at night, and, after a meal, they dozed off again.

They were fortunate to arrive a few hours before a ship destined for Melbourne was due to depart. The ticket clerk commented that a ship bound for the Australian colonies departed nearly every day.

The ship only had passengers, no cargo. Charles

paid for a first class cabin, one of ten on the main deck. The bulk of the passengers were Irish immigrants; many were Government assisted, hopeful of starting a new life in the Australian colonies. The effects of the Irish famine were still being felt in the countryside of Ireland and would be for many more years.

The ship sailed on the tide, heading south through the Irish sea down to enter the Atlantic Ocean. A strong north-westerly wind had the ship clipping along at a good speed. The seas were moderate with some cloud about.

At dinner that evening the captain said, 'We're sailing non-stop to Cape Town. We will stop there to handover some mail and papers and take on fresh food and water and will sail immediately we are loaded. There will be no time for sightseeing. Hopefully with favourable winds, we will be in Sydney by the middle of next month The winds are normally strong westerlies at this time of the year.'

Mary decided to pass the time doing some needlework she had been taught during her ladies college days. They had both spent enough time looking at the sea, although they did daily walks around the deck when the weather permitted. Charles wondered what he could do to pass his time productively.

Mary suggested, 'Why not write a book about your criminal cases?'

He nodded, 'I can, but I probably won't be allowed to publish it for many years. But, yes, you're right. I'll write a book or two. Anything to pass the time.' Fortunately, Charles had purchased two journals, and ink was not a problem. He had a jar of ink, several pens and nibs plus blotting paper.

The voyage south, down the west coast of the African continent, was smooth and fast. They left their cabin when they heard other passengers outside their door talking about seeing Table Mountain for the first time. They had arrived at Cape Town. The mountain loomed high behind the town. It was an impressive mesa shape, three thousand metres high.

As the captain had advised, as soon as the mail was offloaded, the fresh food and water were loaded, they would weigh anchor and sail out of the harbour and head due west. He was correct. There were strong westerly winds as soon as the ship left harbour. The sails soon billowed with the strong wind, and they could feel the ship picking up speed.

Mary had completed one table setting and went on to commence another. Charles had almost finished writing one criminal case.

At times he wandered around on deck trying to collect his thoughts, then put them to paper.

One afternoon, they sat out on deck sheltered from the wind, drinking tea, when Charles said, 'You were right, writing does help to pass the time. I'm happy with what I have written so far. I'll get you to proofread it.'

Mary nodded. 'Yes, it helps the time to pass quickly but I'll be glad when we're home.'

The days passed quickly. The winds remained strong as the ship ploughed through the seas. Every now and then a sudden gust caused a shower of water to spray over the bow and drench anyone on the open main deck. Charles had completed his first book for Mary to proofread.

Her comments surprised Charles. He knew she was well educated but her suggestions were excellent, and he agreed with every recommendation she made. When he reread his amended draft, the story flowed much better.

The ship docked several days earlier than predicted. After a few farewells, they hired a cab to take them to the Melbourne police barracks, where Charles and Mary were given a visitor's room. After settling in, Charles reported to George's office. George was delighted to see him again, both as a friend and a police colleague.

After he briefed George on the meeting, he told him of Ian Flint and his involvement in the Highwaymen saga and his demise.

George nodded. 'Yes, the inspector general has received a complimentary letter of your involvement in the case from Superintendent Robert Scott. The inspector general would like to say hello to you before you head home.'

'Enter,' commanded the voice from within. George walked in with Charles. The inspector general looked up from his desk and said, 'Ah, you're returned. Welcome home. Be seated. I see you not only attended the conference, but you solved the Highwaymen saga. We can close the book on those cases now. Well done. How was your presentation received? I haven't received a report on it yet.'

Charles answered, 'I felt comfortable when I compared it with other speakers' presentations.' The group then chattered about general happenings, while Charles had been overseas.

The next morning, Charles and Mary travelled to Kahuna. As usual Sergeant Crosbie was at the stagecoach office checking for the new arrivals in the district.

He walked over and offered to help carry their luggage. He advised the district had been reasonably quiet for months, only minor crimes had occurred.

'Some minor cattle thefts, an arson case, a suicide and the normal domestic violence case but this time the woman was the offender.'

Charles said, 'I'll be in my office next week. I'm going to have a few days at home.' The sergeant nodded. The couple commandeered the police gig and soon had the horse trotting to their home.

As they came to the top of the hill, Charles stopped the gig. They sat for a few minutes enjoying the view, looking down at their home and the river flowing behind it. He could see Murray feeding their horses.

Before they left for overseas, they had moved the contents of the tack room into the fodder shed and put a bed and straw mattress in it for Murray. He had agreed to tend the horses and the dog while they were away, feeding them and ensuring they had fresh water. He exercised the horses, and curry combed them and often stayed overnight. Isobel had watched over their small orchard and vegetable garden. She took home whatever had ripened, with Murray helping himself as he needed. The couple were pleased with their efforts.

As Charles and Mary approached their home, Murray heard a horse's harness clinking and looked up at them with a cheery smile. 'G'day boss. Horses and dog, dem all good.'

Mary went to the horses and patted them. 'Yes, Murray, you've done very well. Thank you.' Toby, her dog heard them and ran to her, barking and happily bounding around her.

That afternoon they visited Stephen and his family.

They were invited to stay for dinner which they accepted. They were delighted to see they had returned safely and now wanted to be told about their relatives, what they had seen and what they had done during their travels. The evening passed pleasantly and quickly. That night, Charles and Mary slept deeply and peacefully. Home again after so many months.

The weather was changing. Soon the alpine snows would begin to thaw, and the resultant water would pour into the river systems. Charles kept an eye on the rising water. He checked the river depth marker daily. Then the rain came. It rained non-stop for three days. The river was the highest Stephen had seen in twenty years.

The river broke its banks and flooded the low land. Their lagoon became part of the river. Charles moved the livestock to higher land where they were safe. The house was on high land and the water level was of no concern.

After a week the water level peaked and then slowly receded to the river's normal height, leaving behind a few drowned cattle from upstream and plenty of trees in the lagoon. The worst part of the flood was removing the dead cattle from the lagoon.

Charles decided to use an old ship's sail Stephen had. With the sail pulled under a carcass it was towed to the river and dumped. The carcass would disintegrate over time in the flowing water. The trees were removed and chopped into pieces small enough to fit into the kitchen stove.

It took over a month to clear the lagoon. Within a week or two and with plenty of sun, the lagoon was soon back to its best, green grass with wildflowers surrounding it. Even some colourful water lilies were floating.

When Charles returned to his office, he had only one letter of interest. It advised the scheduled magistrate's two monthly visit would occur in around two weeks. He checked the list of cases to be heard. Most were minor and would require little investigation.

One was a domestic violence charge. The woman had been assaulted. The alleged offender had been bailed on his own recognisance. The case notes were vague and did not explain why she been attacked.

The offender had no previous police history. If Charles was going to be the prosecutor, he needed more information on the family's background. He had met the alleged offender, Jake Maloney. He was a timber cutter who Charles had met at a local agricultural show day. He was a big, powerfully built man, polite and quietly spoken. The charge seemed out of character for him.

Charles was aware domestic violence cases were mostly either due to alcohol, bullying, money matters, adultery, denial of conjugal rights or difficult children. It was unclear which applied to this case? The case notes recorded she had a bruise on her left check and a cut on the back of her head. They had been married for twelve years, and this was the first time he had allegedly struck her, so he was not a drinker, a bully or prone to anger. They had no children. This left money matters or adultery.

Charles spoke to the local bank manager for some background on their financial status. He was sympathetic to Jake and knew him as a responsible person. He said Jake came in every Friday afternoon and deposited his week's wages, only keeping a few shillings for himself. His wife came in on the following Monday to take out her housekeeping money. This had been the pattern for many years.

Charles asked, 'Has any change in this pattern occurred recently?'

The manager nodded. 'Yes, for the last three weeks his wife has emptied the account on the following Monday.' That sounded suspicious.

Charles decided to look further. He needed to find out if anyone else was involved. He asked the sergeant if he had heard any rumours.

The sergeant answered, 'Yes, but only vague rumours. She visits the blacksmith frequently. It may be nothing, but I can quietly ask around.'

'Keep it quiet,' requested Charles.

When the magistrate arrived, Charles had not received an answer to his questions. The court was full of interested local people. The magistrate's clerk opened proceedings and then asked Jake Maloney, after he had been sworn in, 'How do you plea to the charge of assault of May Maloney.'

He answered quietly, 'Guilty, Your Honour.'

Charles stepped forward and asked him to relate what had happened on the night in question.

'May and I had an argument, and I struck her in the face. She fell and hit her head on the corner of the fireplace. I then helped her to the bedroom and bandaged her head wound. I waited until she recovered. I then went to stay with my brother.'

'What was the argument about?' continued Charles.

'She has been emptying our bank account each week and wouldn't tell me why.'

'Did she give any reason at all?' asked Charles.

'No, and she said, *Wouldn't you like to know, but I won't be telling you.* She then laughed at me. That's when I hit her with my hand.'

'Have you ever struck your wife before in your twelve years of marriage?' asked Charles.

'No,' replied Jake.

Charles looked to the magistrate and said, 'I have no more questions at this moment, Your Honour.'

The defence lawyer called May Malony to the witness box, and she was sworn in. He asked her to relate what happened on that night.

May said, 'My husband came home angry, and we had an argument, and he hit me and injured my face and head.'

'How did he hit you, with an open hand or a fist?'

'I can't remember,' she replied.

Her lawyer asked, 'Did you give him a reason to strike you?'

She hesitated and then said, 'No.'

The defence lawyer asked, 'Do you love your husband?'

'No, not now,' she answered.

'One incident shouldn't break up a marriage after twelve years,' stated the lawyer.

'Yes, he has tormented me for years. I've had enough.'

He then asked, 'Can you explain the money issue?'

Her reply surprised everyone. 'I loaned it to a friend who is a goldminer. I knew Jake wouldn't give it to me.' The audience gasped and May realised what she had said.

The magistrate asked her, 'Please explain what you have just said.'

May was unsure what to say next and said, 'I've done nothing wrong.'

The defence lawyer asked her, 'Does he intend to pay you back this money?'

'Yes, when he finds gold.' The courtroom laughed at her ignorance of the chances of finding gold.

Charles rose and asked her, 'Are you in a relationship with this goldminer?'

'No, we are just good friends,' she answered.

Charles continued, 'Is he in town now?'

'Yes, we will be leaving when this case is finished.'

Charles asked the magistrate for a side meeting. He agreed and indicated to the defence lawyer to join the two of them.

Charles said, 'I'm uncomfortable with this charge. I would like it downgraded to a lesser charge.' The defence lawyer nodded in agreement.

The magistrate said, 'Yes. I agree.' They returned to their desks.

The magistrate recalled May Maloney to the witness box and said, 'I find this charge is not what it seems.

'I have several character references from respected members of the local community stating that Mr Maloney is a conscientious and law-abiding man. You have admitted to stealing or borrowing from your husband and giving it to another man. If you are more than a friend to this goldminer you mention, it is understandable that Mr Maloney would be angry. Also, he is a big powerful man, if he had punched you, I believe you would have more damage to your face than a small bruise.' He turned to Mr Maloney. 'However, Mr Maloney, I find you guilty of assault with extenuating circumstances. I therefore fine you one pound. You are free to go.' The court clapped the verdict. A judge is responsible for sentencing persons who commit criminal acts, but he is also there to see justice is dispensed as he deems fit and proper.

May immediately left the court and went to the blacksmiths where the goldminer was waiting. He had been in the court and left when he heard the verdict. He saw her coming and asked, 'Are you ready to go?'

'Let's go via the bank and get the rest of this week's money.' When May asked the bank teller for the money, she found that Jake had not deposited the money. The account was empty. When she told the goldminer, he said, 'I'll meet you behind the blacksmiths.' That was the last she ever saw of the goldminer. She now had no money, no husband, and little hope for a future. A tragic lesson.

CHAPTER TEN

The Final Chase

The police office was quiet, only a budget submission request and a monthly report needed to be completed. The cells were empty, although over the weekend they would house a few drunks as guests of the Queen. Charles wondered if the sergeant's act of meeting each coach arrival and saying hello to each passenger kept potential villains moving on to other destinations.

The weekend newspaper headlines were of interest. There had been an escape by four criminals being transferred from Ballarat to Pentridge Jail in Coburg, a Melbourne suburb. The Black Maria Prison Coach had been ambushed at a narrow junction in the ranges. A log had been hauled onto the road and the ambushers had hidden in the roadside trees. The two outside guards were caught unawares and had no choice but to throw away their guns, leaving the guards inside to surrender and exit the prison coach, unarmed. The driver and guard were also ordered off the coach. The six policemen were then told to remove their boots and put them in the coach. With no horses and no boots, they could only wait until someone came along the road.

The ambushers and the prisoners headed back in a northerly direction. The coach was found abandoned forty miles from the ambush site two days later.

The four prisoners were dangerous men. Two were murderers and two had committed robberies with violence. The two ambushers were Yeo brothers, brothers of the murderer, the notorious James Yeo. He killed three people after a gambling game erupted into violence. James had contracted a heavy cold and was now very ill with influenza. The brothers thought it would pass in time, neither of them realised how ill he was.

The six of them travelled to a shack high in the ranges with a clear view on three sides. The other side was dense forest. The two Yeo brothers had stocked up the shack with food sufficient for at least a month and the roof had guttering, collecting rainwater into a large tank. The hut was dry, but very cold and they didn't want to light a fire due to smoke.

A meeting was held at Melbourne Police Headquarters to decide on a plan of action. Inspector George Mason had been selected to head up a taskforce and organise search parties. He presumed the escapees would head north and try to cross the border into the Colony of New South Wales.

He organised teams for a three-pronged movement to the border. Each team consisted of ten men under an inspector. They were to immediately move towards the major river border crossings. The Murray River was in flood, now that the winter snow in the Alps had thawed, so they would need to cross by ferry with their horses. They had no other choice. George was concerned he may be wrong, and they headed for the South Australian border instead. However, he felt confident they would head for the major river ferries. Although, they might hide for a while until they were no longer featured in the newspapers and public interest had waned.

Charles was surprised to see George enter his office. After the introductions to the local constabulary, George asked to talk to them about the escapees. He had received word that James Yeo had relatives living a day's ride from Kahuna.

The sergeant said, 'I know the area but not where they live. They should be easy to find. The locals would know, and he knew a few of them.' George asked if he could borrow the sergeant. Charles agreed and, within the hour, George's team were off to find the Yeo's house.

They asked around town with no luck until they went to the blacksmith's. He had lived his life there and knew the district well. He drew a map for the sergeant to follow to locate their hut.

The police spread out and slowly crept towards the hut. A dog started to bark and alerted the occupants. When they got to within one hundred yards of the house, a man ran out with a rifle and began firing at the party. A policeman returned fire and shot the man, who crumbled to the ground. A woman and a man came to the front door and walked out with their arms up in the air. 'Don't shoot. We're unarmed.'

George asked, 'Where is James?'

The woman answered, 'He's inside, in bed. He's very ill.' The sergeant and two constables cautiously entered the house with their revolvers drawn, ready to shoot.

The woman was right. James Yeo was in bed. His face was ashen, and he was perspiring profusely. He was indeed very ill. George borrowed a horse and cart, loaded James Yeo onto it and then headed back to Kahuna. When they reached the local doctor's residence, they discovered James had died en route. George's team had now accounted for James Yeo, shot his brother dead and had captured the other ambush culprit.

There were still three escapees on the run. The surviving Yeo brother told them the others were heading to a Murray River ferry terminal, but he didn't know which one. George hedged his bets and sent his men to cover the three nearest ports to Kahuna.

The sergeant was at the stagecoach office when he spotted a man leaving by another door. As he approached the man, he began to run. The sergeant drew his revolver and called on him, 'Halt or I'll fire!' The man stopped. Without realising it, he had captured one of the escapees. The escapee had left the other two after an argument. He then sold his horse and was heading for his sister's farm, near the South Australian border.

After in-depth questioning by George, the team learnt that the escaped murderer and the robber were heading to a farm on the Murray River, out past Kahuna. They intended to wait a few weeks and then catch a ferry to cross into New South Wales. He didn't know exactly where the farm was.

George requested the newspapers have a complete blackout on any mention of the escapees. He was hoping they would become complacent. He kept two policemen watching around the clock, at each of the three ferry terminals. Two weeks later his plan paid off.

Two horsemen rode into Echuca after the sun had

set. A plain clothed constable saw the two men talk with each other for a while and then separate. His suspicions raised, he decided to follow one. He saw him heading to the terminal to board the ferry. Soon after he saw the second horseman approach. As the constable rode towards him, they made eye contact. The second horseman immediately turned and galloped away into the night. The constable gave chase, but the other horse was too fast. The horseman already on the ferry was unaware of the incident and when challenged, he immediately surrendered to the constable. The only remaining escapee at large was a notorious murderer.

At the debriefing of the constable, Charles asked if the horse had any distinctive markings.

The constable nodded. 'It had a white tail and mane. It was a smart looking horse and was speedy.'

Charles suggested Murray had a look at the place where the horse was last seen.

George nodded. 'Yes, that's a good idea. Go and do it.'

Charles, Constable John Lane and Murray were shown where the escapee was last seen. The day was mostly cloudy with very little sun shining through. Murray rode in front, looking alternatively right and left. Suddenly he stopped and pointed. 'See der, Boss. Horse he stop and hide long tree.'

Charles said, 'Well done. Which way should we follow?' Murray pointed and trotted over to a track though the grassland. The track led them from the town in a westerly direction.

They followed the telltale signs of the horse for two days to a deserted mining settlement. They dismounted and Charles cautiously moved to a small hill overlooking the settlement.

There were several dilapidated buildings which could provide a hidden shelter for the escapee, and of more concern, it could be an ideal place for an ambush.

Murray pointed to a shrub. After a few seconds Charles could make out the shape of a horse. He was excited and pointed for John Lane to also spot the horse. He nodded. But there was no sign of the escapee.

Charles decided to wait until dark and then move closer.

As twilight fell, the escapee appeared, looking around. This was what they had been hoping. Constable Lane was ready. He aimed and fired. The escapee fell to the ground. The trio mounted their horses and rode to the place he had fallen. The ground was marked where he fell, but he had disappeared. Murray headed to the mine entrance.

The three of them entered the dark tunnel. After they walked fifty yards they were unable to see and thought it safer to leave. When they reappeared, night had fallen, and the escapee's horse was gone.

Little did they know, but the escapee had previously been a miner there and knew the area. Now he had escaped with his horse. Further into the mine was another exit. When the team entered the mine the next day with some brush torches, they found the other exit. Charles was angry with himself for letting him get away.

Murray was stoic as ever. He said, 'We go dis way, Boss.' He mounted his horse and started searching. Charles and Constable Lane followed. They were heading in an almost straight line, which surprised Charles. The escapee obviously did not realise he was being followed by a blacktracker.

The escapee had several hours start on the trio and was riding fast. But the straight course he had taken saved Murray from having to dismount constantly to find the horse's hoof marks. The galloping hooves had left deep horseshoe prints.

Constable Lane said, 'I think I know where he's going. There's another deserted mine on the other side of that hill.'

Charles asked, 'Is here a short cut to it?'

'Yes, but it will be hard on the horses. The surface for several hundred yards is a type of shale and can cut the inside of their hooves.'

Murray was listening and said, 'Us'um saddle cloth on horses. Fix'um good.'

'Let's do it.' The trio cut their saddle cloths into four sections and tied them to their horses' hooves.

Even with cloths on the hooves, they only walked the horses over the shale. When they reached the end of the shale, they removed the remnants of the saddle cloth pieces and examined the horses' hooves. No damage had been done. They now rode fast to the deserted mine to lay in wait for the escapee.

The trio positioned themselves at the entrance to the old mining town. Constable Lane was correct. They had arrived an hour before the escapee, who came trotting along the track, whistling an Irish air. When he was twenty yards away from them, Charles called him to surrender. He was totally surprised and hesitated for a few seconds. He then decided to gallop back the way he had come.

Constable Lane fired his rifle, and the bullet struck him in his left shoulder. The impact sent the escapee falling from his horse to land flat on his back.

Charles walked over to him, looked down and said, 'Well, it's all over for you now. No more escaping!'

George was delighted when he saw the final escapee, laying injured in the wagon, with leg irons fitted at long last. He had been the last of the culprits at large. The two ambushers, the two murderers and the two robbers were all accounted for – some dead, some alive.

Constable Lane's shot at the first mine had hit the escapee's revolver in his shoulder holster and he had only suffered bruising. The second shot was more successful. The escapee was taken to the local doctor who successfully removed the bullet and bandaged the wound. George and his teams returned by train to Melbourne with the escapee in handcuffs and leg irons. There would be no opportunity for him to escape again.

The inspector general welcomed the police contingent back and arranged for the newspaper reporters to receive the full story. Some papers did it in a serial form. Others were content with a full frontpage spread. The Premier was delighted and invited those concerned to an official luncheon. Charles, the sergeant and Constable Lane were invited, as well as Murray, who, when asked to come to Melbourne, went into hiding at the river camp and stayed hidden until Charles returned.

The Premier gave a speech to which George responded. The Premier then stepped forward with suitably embossed certificates, presenting one to each police officer involved in the mission. Charles was given one for Murray.

When he returned home, he had Murray's certificate framed and hung in the tack room. Murray looked at the certificate and walked away, unsure how or what he should say or do.

* * *

Mary and Charles had been married for a few years, so it came as no surprise when she visited the doctor and came home with the good news. She was pregnant. Charles told all and sundry, whenever he met friends in the local streets. The couple prepared the spare room for the coming day.

Charles had been given a new multi-purpose polish to try out, and had been polishing the police gig seat, wearing old clothes. Murray came running up the street and pointed to four camels being led by two Afghan cameleers.

Murray said, 'Boss, what dem fellas like horse and fellas dress like Meri's.'

Charles laughed and replied, 'Those are for sandy deserts, where horses are no good.'

A bystander saw Murray's fear and said, 'They eat blackfellows like you,' and laughed.

Charles responded angrily, 'Leave him alone and piss off.' A few passersby heard his remark and stopped.

The man who laughed, turned to Charles and said, 'It's a free world and I'll say what I want.'

Charles replied, 'You have said enough. Just go.'

He walked up close to Charles and said, 'I don't like being spoken to like that,' and swung a punch at Charles, hitting him in the shoulder. Charles became angry and retaliated. He threw a punch and hit the assailant in the face, breaking his nose. A second punch to the jaw, knocked him to the ground with blood pouring from his nose.

Just then a local man ran up to the assailant and asked, 'What do you think you're doing?' He turned to Charles and said, 'He's my brother-in-law, and a bit of a smart arse. I'm sorry. Don't lock him up. My wife will give me hell.'

His brother-in-law stood up. 'He got me with a lucky punch. Why should I be locked up?'

'He's the local police inspector, you idiot. You're lucky it wasn't the sergeant. If it had been him who hit you, you would be heading to hospital. Now, get your horse and let's go home.' A crowd had gathered and clapped his sensible suggestion.

Charles took Murray to the camels and let him watch them as they padded down the street. When they stopped, he asked a cameleer, who said he was named Ahmed, 'Are they tame enough to ride?'

'Yes, they are female and tame.' Charles asked if he and Murray could have a ride. He nodded and had his camel kneel.

Charles mounted first and had a very reluctant Murray climb up behind him. As the camel started to rise, Murray closed his eyes and hung on tightly to Charles. The cameleer led the camel back into town. Murray soon relaxed with the monotonous plodding feet of the camels calming him. Charles paid the cameleer a shilling for the experience. It was a valuable lesson.

When Charles told Murray he could live in the converted tack room, he made it clear to him, that only he could stay there. The one exception had been, if he were to have Bessie as his meri. Bessie was the daughter of an Aboriginal woman and a local stockman from Windlass Station. It bordered Stephen's property. She had played with the station manager's children and even had some schooling with them. Bessie was articulate and copied the ways of her school friends. She worked as a maid at the homestead.

Murray and Bessie knocked at the front door and Mary answered. 'Hello Murray, what can I do for you?'

'Bessie now my meri. Come to lib long tack room?' Mary knew of Charles' promise to Murray and just nodded.

She asked Bessie, 'Are you still going to work at Windlass?'

'Yes, missus, in morning, that's all,' replied Bessie.

'Perhaps you can work here sometimes. I'll tell Boss when he comes home.' Charles agreed, as he knew of Bessie and her schooling. He and Murray expanded the tack room and Bessie worked three half days a week for Mary.

When Charles arrived home one day, Mary said, 'You need to talk to Murray. He has another of his tribe with him in the tack room.'

Murray had seen him coming and the two aborigines stood up to meet him.

Charles said, 'What's this mean? Murray, you know the rule.'

Murray, embarrassed, replied, 'Boss dis man my brudder from camp long riber. Him have trouble with whiteman boss. He take his meri. He angry.'

'Well, he can't stay here,' Charles replied.

Murray nodded. 'I tellum he go now.'

Charles nodded and walked away.

A fortnight later, a station hand rode into Kahuna and stopped at the police station. Breathless he ran to the front desk and said, 'A blackfellow has just speared the boss and kidnapped a young woman from Billabong Station.'

Charles heard the man shouting. He stood at his office door, listening. The sergeant turned and looked at Charles. 'Do you want to go. I've a subpoena to serve by noon. I can meet you there later.'

Charles answered, 'Yes. Get Murray for me and we'll go now.' Murray was in the stables and the duo left with the station hand.

The station was over two hours riding distance. When they arrived, they found the station boss dead with a spear wound to the chest. The head stockman had taken charge and had cleared everybody away from the crime scene.

Charles asked him, 'What happened?'

The head stockman was hesitant to answer. 'The boss was with the girl in the tack room and Jiji saw them. The boss laughed and Jiji became very angry. When the boss left the girl, Jiji threw a spear at him and killed him. I saw him throw the spear. He then helped the girl mount a horse and they both rode towards the river. Oh, also they stole a new Winchester rifle and some ammunition.'

'Tell me about the girl. How old is she and where is she from?'

'The girl is a white girl named Diana around eighteen years of age, an orphan who works in the laundry. The boss gave her a job two years ago.'

'How does Jiji fit into this incident?' Charles asked.

'Jiji and Diana are very close, if you know what I mean, and the boss did not like a blackfellow messing with a white girl. There was always going to be trouble.'

Murray was listening and said, 'Jiji my brudder.'

Charles asked one last question. 'Were they station horses?'

'Yes, they are both branded with a XOX,' he replied.

Charles thought how best to handle this. *I need Murray as my blacktracker, but can I trust him?* He asked Murray, 'Will you find Jiji for me?'

Murray nodded and said, 'Me police tracker good. I find h'm.'

Charles nodded but thought, *I had better remain alert.*

When the sergeant arrived, he had Constable Lane with him. They decided Charles, Murray and Lane would follow Jiji and the girl. The evidence of a kidnapping did not appear correct. She appeared to have mounted her horse without a threat from Jiji. The sergeant would take the body to the local doctor for a death certificate to be issued and to record the cause of his death.

Charles and his team, with two pack horses, then rode towards the river with Murray leading the way. He soon pointed to a tree line, and they headed in that direction. When they reached the trees, Murray had to dismount and walk to locate their tracks. He soon found them. The horses' tracks had turned abruptly to the right.

Charles dismounted and Murray showed him the hoof prints going to the right. They remounted and continued to follow Murray until dark. The night was cold and windy. The wind rustling noisily through the trees caused them a sleepless night.

At sunup and after a quick meal, they were on their way again. Murray said, 'Dem go long riber.' He pointed in a westly direction and showed them where they had camped the night.

The river was flowing too fast for a man or a beast to swim across. When the river turned and headed in a northerly direction, the duo continued to the west. The foliage began to turn brown and the soil looser.

They eventually reached the border of the Little Desert. Looking into the distance, they could only see sand and stunted vegetation. Shrubs and trees were scattered throughout the sandy desert soil. The duo would be easy to follow but Charles was reluctant to ride into an area he had not experienced. There was no knowing how the horses would handle the soft sand.

He also wondered if there would be water available.

Murray said, 'Plenty water, Boss.' Murray took the lead as before. After two hours he stopped. 'We get water now.' He could see where Jiji had stopped and dug at the base of a large shrub. He had filled in the hole, but the soil was still damp. After thirty minutes digging, they had a sizable pool of brackish water. They filtered the water through their shirts and then drank their fill of water and filled their canteens. When the horses had their turn to drink, they nearly emptied the pool. The hole was then filled in again.

Murray stopped and pointed. In the distance, a small puff of smoke was visible in the scattered shrubs. Jiji was confident he was not being followed. The team kept riding until nightfall. Hopefully they would catch up to them soon and arrest them both until Charles investigated their stories.

When they reach the smoke, much to their surprise, they found the two Afghans and their camels camped there. It was a junction where the meandering river and the desert came together for a short time.

Ahmed explained, 'We're going to Borree to collect some valuable museum freight.' Borree was a small town on the fringe of the desert, where some remains of ancient animals had been discovered.

Constable Lane commented, 'I read an article in the newspaper about that find.'

Charles asked Ahmed, 'Have you seen any other riders during your travels?'

'Yes, two horsemen late yesterday. But they were far away from us, heading west into the sun. They were leading their horses.'

Charles understood why. The police horses were very tired also. He asked, 'Could your camels go faster than horses walk?'

'Yes, they can go faster in sand.'

'Can I hire you to take two of us to catch up to the two horsemen?'

Ahmed nodded. 'Of course. When do you want to go?'

Charles said, 'After we have something to eat and drink.' He turned to Constable Lane. 'I want you to follow the river and met us at the police station in Borree. Keep your eyes open. They may arrive after you. Murray and I will go by camel across the desert in a more direct route and hopefully reach them before they get to Borree.'

Murray was reluctant to ride on a camel, but eventually he agreed and the four of them headed due west, hoping to reach the two fugitives before Borree. Constable Lane rode alongside the riverbank and followed a track worn by previous travellers who had wanted to avoid the desert sands.

Ahmed had his camels moving with long strides and Charles could soon see they moved much faster than a horse could move in the sand. He wondered why Jiji preferred the desert and not the river track, seeing he only had horses. He found out later when Jiji turned north, leaving the desert and joined the river track.

The wind shifted to a northerly direction, increasing in strength and stirring up the loose sand, and, as expected, obliterating the horses' hoof prints. The sand began to sting their eyes. Ahmed loaned a scarf to each of them to wrap around their faces. The sand, not only got into their eyes, but their ears, nose and mouth. They wet their scarfs. It helped a little. The wind howled and continued unabated for the remainder of the day.

At sunset Ahmed decided to stop for the night. He made a windbreak with some poles and material. The evening meal consisted of bread, fruit and water. It was filling but not the best meal to finish such a demanding and uncomfortable day. Fortunately, the wind had eased by daybreak. After a quick breakfast they were on their way again with the camels moving quickly.

When Murray lost their horses' tracks, Charles decided to keep heading for Borree. He felt confident Jiji would head to a town and Borree was the nearest.

Constable Lane, with the horses in tow, was not making good time. He rode from dawn to dusk trying to make up for the lost time. When he reached a small rise in the road, he could see Borree in the distance.

He also noticed some fresh horse dung. The ground was soft and with some grass. He could see there were several hoof marks. He became alert and began to wonder if they could be Jiji's and Diana's. But that would mean they were in front of him.

He expected to reach Borree by nightfall. He assumed they would beat him to town. He kept riding, remaining very alert. About noon he saw two riders. He thought it was them entering the town, but he was too far away to be certain. He continued and entered the town to find the local constable. Charles and the group were making good time and expected to arrive at Borree at sundown.

* * *

The two fugitives arrived in Borree feeling confident they had no pursuers. Little did they know, two pursuing groups would arrive in Borree only a few hours after they had arrived.

Constable Lane located the local constable and related the event of the murder of a station boss by an Aborigine and the kidnap of a white woman. As it was now late evening, the Borree constable suggested they wait until morning and then search the town for any sight of them. Constable Lane agreed, as he knew Charles and Murray would soon arrive. After tending the horses, he retired and slept in a local jail cell.

Charles and Murray left the cameleers and slept outside the town and walked in the next morning. The camels would draw unwanted attention. When they located the police station, the two constables were sitting down to breakfast. After briefing each other, Charles decided to walk around the town and casually look for branded horses XOX. Murray was told to remain in the police station, out of sight, in case Jiji saw him. After a two-hour walk around town, they had no luck.

Murray suggested they check down by the river. This idea was successful. Constable Lane rode down to the river and saw a horse tied to a tree. When he got closer, he saw the horse was branded with a XOX. But the two suspects and the other horse were not in sight.

Jiji saw Constable Lane approaching and hid behind a large shrub. Diana had ridden into town for supplies as Jiji and she intended to leave the town by noon. Constable Lane rode back to town with the horse in tow and reported to Charles. When he told them where he had found the horse, the local constable replied, 'I know the area and there's only one track in and out.'

Charles thought for a while. 'If they only have one horse now, what will they do – stay or go?'

The local constable said, 'They may wait until night and steal a horse. I doubt if they would try in daylight.'

Charles agreed. 'We will go to the river and wait for them to return.'

The team quietly approached the place where Constable Lane had discovered the horse. Murray dismounted a hundred yards from the river and was creeping through the shrubs when he saw Jiji hiding behind a large shrub, looking at the police trio. He crept up behind him and said, 'Lo, Jiji.'

When he heard Murray's voice, Jiji spun around in surprise and stood up.

Charles saw him and drew his revolver. 'You're under arrest, Jiji. Don't move. Lane, handcuff him.'

A female voice said, 'Leave him alone and drop your revolver.' Diane had ridden back from town. She saw the team and had surprised them. She had the Winchester rifle and pointed it at them. Murray had moved stealthily behind Jiji, while Diana was watching the policemen. Murray quietly picked up one of Jiji's spears and threw it at Diana.

It stuck her in the left side and came out the other side of her torso. She cried out and fell from her horse, mortally wounded. They ran to her and took the rifle. Charles saw she was dying. She could not move her legs. He saw her eyes glaze over.

The team were distracted when they ran to Diana. This allowed Jiji to escape unhandcuffed into the river foliage.

Charles was annoyed with himself. They had caught Jiji and let him escape when they went to Diana. He was on foot with no horse or food. He had silently vanished. He could not go far.

Diana's body was taken to the local doctor who also performed the district burials. Charles pondered the disadvantaged life Diana had and now dying in this way. Life was so unfair.

The police team thought that Jiji would not leave town without stealing a horse and food. They were correct. Jiji waited, hiding down by the river. When the sun set, Jiji entered town, hiding as necessary. He crept around looking for the opportunity to steal a horse.

The only stable in town was on the corner of a vacant block. They had six horses that were protected by a large savage dog. While the policemen searched the town, Jiji played cat and mouse with them, evading them each time one of them got close.

Jiji watched the stable to see if anyone was around. When he was satisfied no one was there, he climbed over the fence. As he approached a horse, he awoke a large dog he had not seen.

It ran at him, barking furiously. It knocked him to the ground, grabbing him by the leg and would not release him. The local constable who had been quietly sitting by a tree just across the street from the stable, ran to the screaming Jiji and quickly handcuffed him. At the same time, the dog's owner appeared from the stable and called the dog to heel. Finally, Jiji had been apprehended.

The police team had been away for nearly three weeks. The trio headed back to Kahuna, tired but satisfied with the result. They left Jiji in the local cell for the next magistrate's visit.

They visited Waroo Station on their way home and advised the senior stockman of the result and returned the Winchester rifle. He informed Charles the owners were aware of the murder and were sending a new manager.

Mary saw Charles riding up to the house and happily waved to him. That night as they lay in bed, he told her the story. She agreed Diana did not have a chance to enjoy a normal life. It made them think of the coming birth of their first child.

Charles took a few days off to attend to some small jobs around the farm and to spend some quality time with Mary, walks to the river and visits to Stephen's family. They enjoyed being together.

When Charles returned to the office, he had a few letters in his in-tray. Only one was of interest to him. The other letters were official notices of visits and events due to occur in Melbourne. The letter was from Scotland. It was from his father. He had written to tell him his mother was ill with a severe chest complaint. He was concerned how long she would last. The cold weather had kept her indoor for several months. A continuous fire had been maintained day and night in her room. It helped her tolerate her illness but could not improve or cure her.

Mary still had three months to go before she was due to have their baby. The letter had Charles in a quandary, so he went for a walk around town to decide what he should do. He went to a local hotel for a drink and to think.

Sitting out on the hotel's verandah with a whisky, he tried to balance the two situations – his ill mother and Mary and the imminent birth of their child. He decided to wait until he spoke with Mary before he decided. When he told her, she sat silent for a few minutes.

Mary was blunt but logical with her answer. She replied, 'You probably won't like my answer. We have a very good idea of the date for the birth of our baby, but we don't know how ill your mother is. She may also pass away before we get to Scotland. I think we should stay here until the baby has been born. You asked my opinion. There you have it.' She looked at Charles, waiting for a reaction.

He nodded and replied, 'Yes, I can see your comments make sense. I agree and I think you're right, but let's sleep on it and make a decision at the end of the week.'

The week passed quickly for both of them, each hoping they could make an agreed decision. The two of them sat together holding hands. Charles kissed Mary and said, 'We will stay for the birth of our baby and then go to Scotland.' Mary was delighted Charles had supported her suggestion.

The baby was due in three weeks and Mary had been invited to stay at Stephen's home. His family thought it would be more comforting for her, having women around if or when Charles was away on police business.

Charles had become more attentive towards Mary as the date approached. He had dinner with Stephen's family every night Mary stayed with them. Mary was excited and talked of nothing but the baby. Clare smiled and recalled the births of Isobel and Finlay and her excitement.

Isobel ran into the police station to see Charles. He looked up apprehensively as Isobel breathlessly said, 'Mary's in the doctor's treatment room. Her waters broke and Dad decided to bring her into town. She's feeling well and is calm.' Charles was up out of his chair and leading Isobel out of the police station to the doctor's surgery.

When he entered the surgery, the doctor said, 'The birth might take some time. I suggest you and Stephen go to the hotel and have a drink or two. I'll let you know of any developments.'

Stephen and Charles sat out on the hotel verandah. Stephen said, 'You'll find your life will be different with a child. Their demands change your lifestyle, such as being woken during the night. At first you will be happy getting up at all hours, even while Mary is breastfeeding. But the novelty will soon wear off.

'You'll become short tempered and irritable with your sleep being interrupted. However, on the upside, the enjoyment you'll have when playing with your child will more than make up for the downside.

'Both of you will enjoy watching your child grow from an infant to a mature adult.'

Charles smiled. 'I'm looking forward to our future as a family.'

During their second drink, Stephen saw Isobel running towards them. She shouted, 'It's a boy.' Stephen and Charles walked quickly to the treatment room. Mary was sitting up holding their new son in her arms. Charles kissed her and asked, 'Are you alright?'

'Yes, it was easy. They kept saying push, push again and again and all of a sudden, he just popped out! There was very little pain. Look at him, isn't he beautiful?' The baby was sound asleep.

Stephen asked, 'What have you named him?'

Charles said, 'Keith Charles Cornelius George

Stuart.' The future Earl of Belcannon. Mary just smiled looking at Keith, their son.

The doctor interrupted. 'I think you should all go now and let Mary rest. She's tired but she should be well enough to go home in a few days.' He was right, Mary was rather pale.

Charles kissed her and said, 'I'll see you two tomorrow.' He kissed Mary again and then invited them all to the hotel for a few celebratory drinks.

Mary went home four days later in a police gig. Charles had Bessie wash the floors, dust the furniture and change the linen. She had cleaned the whole house. It was immaculate. She had also walked to the lagoon to pick some flowers for the dining room.

The baby's room had been prepared a month or so earlier. Mary was delighted with Bessie's efforts. She had been a good choice as a trustworthy and capable housemaid.

A week later, during dinner, Mary said, 'I would like to have Keith baptised, so we need to decide on Keith's godparents. Who would you like?'

Charles thought for a moment or two and said, 'George as godfather; he's been instrumental in shaping my career.'

'Good,' replied Mary in agreement. 'I would like Isobel to be godmother. She has been a great help to me. Then we agree?' Charles nodded in the affirmative.

They planned to have the baptism in Kahuna and sent out invitations a month prior. This was to ensure adequate notice for Mary's parents and friends in Sydney time to plan their travel south. George and Isobel were delighted to accept their roles in the future of young Keith. The local Presbyterian church was large enough to accommodate the family group and guests. A get-together and meal was planned to be held in the nearby local hotel immediately after the service.

The special day arrived, sunny with light winds There was happiness in the air.

The previous evening the guests staying at the hotel, enjoyed a social evening, mingling and getting to know each other. Mary met with her Sydney friends to catch up with the gossip. After a late breakfast, they walked to the church only two hundred yards from the hotel. Guests who stayed elsewhere, travelled by the local coach. The coachman enjoyed the extra business.

As the guests arrived, they gathered in small groups chatting in the sunshine, until the minister encouraged them to enter the church. The minister had arrived early at the church to meet and greet the people. The church was soon filled with organ music playing softly in the background. Charles, Mary and baby Keith entered, following the godparents, and sat in the front row. The music increased in volume, as the minster entered the church. He walked up the aisle to the baptismal font and then turned to face the congregation

The minister welcomed the congregation on behalf of the parents of the baby going to be baptised today. 'All please stand.' He read a psalm relating to the bible story of the baptism of Saint John on the River Jordan. Following this, he led the congregation in prayer.

'Would the parents with the child and the godparents please come forward.' It was now time to ask Mary to pass him the baby, who was half asleep. He then asked the godparents, 'Do you accept your responsibilities regarding this baby in his future life?'

They answered together, 'Yes, we do.' The minister then sprinkled some water on the baby's head. 'I baptise you, Keith Cornelius Charles George Stuart. In the name of the Father, the Son and the Holy Ghost and welcome you into the church.' The congregation clapped. The minister thanked everyone for coming. 'Go safely. You are in God's hands.' The service was over.

The parents, godparents and guests all adjourned to the hotel. The meal was typical country style. There was ample food for all. The main meal and the dessert were healthy, plenty of fresh vegetables, fruit and either lamb or pork.

Charles assumed the role of speaker. First, he thanked everyone for coming and then he read a letter from his parents in Scotland. He kept his speech short as he knew others wished to say a few words.

Mary's father was the next speaker, then George followed by Isobel. She surprised them with her eloquence and diction.

The alcohol flowed freely and soon dancing commenced to the music of a fiddle, piano and harmonica. Late afternoon, Mary said she was tired and wanted to go home. Charles made a short final speech to wish their guests a safe trip home.

They were the first to leave. Handshakes and kisses were plentiful. Guests waved to them until they were out of sight. It had been a memorable day.

As they had agreed previously, they now focused their attention on the return trip to Scotland. After examining Mary and the baby, the doctor stepped back and said, 'It's been a month since the birth and you're both hale and healthy. I see no reason why you cannot travel to Scotland. The baby should travel well, as you will still be breast feeding him for a few more months yet. Particularly while you are at sea, as obviously fresh milk will not be available. As for you, Mary, make sure you eat plenty of green vegetables. It will ensure your iron levels are maintained. Well, goodbye for now and have a safe voyage.'

Charles had applied for six months leave. He had been in the colony for ten years and had only been home once in that time. Eventually a letter arrived from George, stating his leave had been granted and wishing them a safe trip. He looked forward to meeting them when they returned.

After a farewell evening with a Scottish theme at Stephen's home with kilts and bagpipes no less, they bid farewell to one and all, not knowing when they would return, if at all.

The six months leave request had really been irrelevant. Charles had not forgotten he was the Earl Apparent and would one day be responsible for the Belcannon Estate and its staff. Not forgetting it was also a business. He realised his father was ageing and would not last forever. He had mentioned his concern to Mary. She shook her shoulders and replied, 'Wait and see what eventuates and we can make that decision when your father passes on.'

The ship was the SS Great Britain. It was a wooden steamship with sails and a one thousand horsepower engine and could carry up to six hundred passengers. The ship departed early morning from Melbourne in time to catch the outgoing high tide to exit Port Phillip Bay. The bay's narrow exit was commonly called The Heads, and its waters were notoriously unforgiving. Several sailing ships had fallen foul when they had been caught in the changing tides and its eddy currents and without sufficient wind to help control the ship's steerage.

They were on deck as the ship sailed out in the swirling sea without any drama. The ship was clear of The Heads in under an hour and entered the calmer waters of Bass Strait.

The giant ship then turned to starboard and headed west into a mild headwind. The voyage would be nonstop to Liverpool. They were travelling first class and had one of ten cabins on the main deck.

The ship was only half full of passengers homeward bound. On its outbound voyages, it was almost always full, with paying passengers and government sponsored immigrants. The sponsored ones were mainly Irish immigrants escaping the horrors of the endless Irish poverty, started by the potato famine.

As first class passengers, they were invited to join the captain's table for dinner. Dinner was served, while a pianist and violinist played the music of the day. The meals were excellent as one would expect on such a grand ship. The days passed quickly. When seas were calm, they strolled the deck of the magnificent ship. Other times they would read.

The doctor had been correct, and Mary was happy to continue breastfeeding until they reached Belcannon. She would wean him there, where fresh milk was available. She often teased Charles by bouncing her bare breasts in front of him, after feeding the baby. Charles sometimes played cards with other passengers, but he did not gamble.

The ship's captain sent a sailor to Charles' cabin inviting him for a chat. The captain knew of his police and legal experience. He had discovered that a passenger on board was wanted by the police for armed robbery in the colonies, and he wanted Charles' advice as to whether he should place him in the brig now or wait until they reached Liverpool and hand him over to the authorities.

Charles replied, 'As captain you have a duty of care responsibility and now that you know, you need to decide if he is going to be a problem to other passengers. Is he a risk or not?'

The captain replied, 'Well, I don't know the risk, so I'll place him in the brig and play safe.' He thanked Charles, who nodded in agreement with his decision.

The remainder of the voyage passed uneventfully. Most passengers were now bored with the same view every day. Water, water everywhere, with only a few birds gliding above the ship to ease the monotony. When the English coast first appeared on the horizon, there was an almighty cheer. Even the captain laughed at the passengers' reaction. Land at last! The cruise up the Irish Sea had more passengers out walking the deck as more ships appeared in this busy waterway. These passing ships were a welcome distraction as passengers waved to each other.

Finally, after fifty-five days at sea, the ship arrived in Liverpool on a sunny summer's day. This was the weather they had been hoping for when they planned their visit in Kahuna.

After clearing customs, they booked into an hotel for the night, just to get used to walking on dry land again. They had an early dinner and retired within the hour.

The next morning Charles went looking for a stagecoach heading north to Scotland. He knew they would have to change coaches several times before reaching home. Their first stop was in Glasgow and then on to Edinburgh, where they stayed for a day to have a sound sleep in a comfortable bed. They could only doze in the coaches due to the rough roads. Next day they went for a walk to see the sights.

Little had changed. A few more shops and more people. It felt good to see people in kilts again. It made them feel proud of their Scottish heritage. The baby was now thirteen weeks old and had travelled comfortably. He was happy enjoying a tickle which made him laugh and wave his arms around.

Mary was content to breastfeed him and intended to for a few more months. Although she had her night sleep interrupted, she accepted this as a mother should and normally had a nap in the afternoon.

A few more coach changes and they were finally in Glencairn, where Mary had spent her youth. They hired a local coachman to drive them to Belcannon. As the manor came into sight, Charles had a tear in his eye. After so many absent years, he was home again.

The coachman helped Mary and the baby alight as Charles collected their luggage. A servant ran out to help them. 'Welcome home, sir. It's good to see you again and now with a bonnie wee laddie. Congratulations, madam.'

They entered the hall as his sister walked towards them. When she saw them, she started to cry. 'Oh, it's so good to see you again.' They greeted each other with kisses and hugs. Nicole continued, 'We were wondering where you were. I'm sorry to tell you, mother died three months ago. We wrote to you, but I presume the letter would not have arrived before you departed from Melbourne. Father has taken it badly. He's having his afternoon nap. We can talk first and then I'll wake him.'

She continued, 'So this is the new laddie. What's his name?'

Mary replied, 'Keith Charles Cornelius George Stuart.'

Nicola laughed. 'I see Cornelius is still with us. You know he was the leader of the Stuarts, fighting a highland war centuries ago and was killed.'

Just then a voice said, 'No, it can't be. The colonials have returned.' It was his father, the earl. Charles walked to his father and hugged him. He was now showing his age.

His hair had greyed, and he was a little stooped. The earl turned to Mary and the baby, kissed Mary on the cheek and looked at the baby who was awake and sitting quietly in Mary's arms. He asked her, 'May I hold him?' Mary handed him the baby and she could see the joy in his face. He said surprisingly, 'I've lost a wife and gained a grandson in exchange.' They all nodded at these sage words. They then went to the drawing room and sat down, while they were served drinks. Nicola gave a rundown on the local scene and events she thought would be of interest to them.

Dinner that evening was a happy event, although it was noticeable that the lady of the manor was no longer with them. Nicola's husband, Gavin, arrived during the meal. He was a busy farmer breeding Highland cattle. They were long haired brown/red cattle. Although they were small, they had very sharp and wide imposing horns. A servant, who was a balladeer, sang for them, accompanied by a violin to complete a very pleasant homecoming. Mary left early to feed the baby and did not return.

Nicola and Gavin then departed to their room. After

a nightcap with his father, Charles went to bed. Mary and the baby were fast asleep. The following morning, Mary and the baby went to visit and have lunch with some old school friends in Glencairn.

The head stockman had two mares ready to be served. Arrangements had been made for a local stallion owner to bring his horse at noon. The head stockman called on Charles to see if he agreed. The mares were restless but were comfortable in their stalls. He had tied oilskin covers over the mares' bodies to protect them from the front hoofs of the stallion if he became hyperactive.

The stallion was six years old and was led in by a horseman, who said, 'Be careful with him, he's a rogue. Maybe he'll settle down after he's done his business, but be careful, don't trust him. He's a kicker.'

Charles arrived and looked at the stallion and was in two minds whether he should let the stallion near the mares. The head stockman said, 'I'll put two head ropes on him, and we can pull opposite each other to keep his head straight, as we pull him quickly forward to the mounting stall. It's worked before.'

Assured by this advice, Charles stood back and watched as the handlers moved the stallion to the first stall. They kept him moving to it and then he went straight to the mare and mounted her.

The oilskin covers were not needed, as the stallion settled down and did not rake his front legs, while he was servicing the first mare. When the mating was over, the stallion was led to the main stables and left there with food and water. He would be required to perform once more later in the afternoon.

The handlers were pleased the stallion had behaved and had not been as dangerous as the horseman had warned. Charles joined the men, enjoying a cup of tea and cakes to celebrate the event. Hopefully, the service was successful, and a new progeny was on the way.

At five p.m. the stallion was led back to the servicing stall. This time he was excited and difficult to handle. Charles had not remained; he was busy going over some accounts with Nicola. Even though Charles had been made the nominal managing director of the Belcannon Estate, she handled the finances.

The stallion was kicking and standing on his hind legs. The handlers still managed to keep him heading to the stall. Unnoticed by the handlers, the earl walked into the stable just as the stallion kicked out. A hind leg hoof struck the earl in the chest. He fell to the ground. The handlers hurriedly got the stallion into the mounting stall, as other staff went to the earl's side.

He was still breathing but in a bad way. One of the staff ran to inform Charles of the accident. Others quickly prepared a light coach to transport the earl to the doctor's surgery. Charles and Nicola ran to the stables. They could see their father was badly injured. They carried him to the coach and immediately headed for Glencairn. It was a thirty-minute road trip. The earl was still unconscious, but his breathing was laboured and uneven. The doctor saw the fast approaching coach through his office window. He recognised the coach as one owned by the Belcannon Estate and went to meet it.

They carried the earl into the surgery. The doctor could see with just a glance that the injury was very serious. He cut the clothes from the earl's chest and then saw the bruising with the hoof print mark. The kick had shattered the sternum and several ribs. His heart had also been damaged.

He looked at Charles. 'I'm sorry, but there is nothing I can do for him. It's just a matter of time for your father to pass on.' The doctor was right. The earl died ten minutes later. Both Charles and Nicola were shocked. The doctor's receptionist made them a strong tea. The doctor explained the damage to the earl and showed them a medical diagram of the chest and internal organs within. The brother and sister then went for a walk.

They said little, each with their own thoughts. Charles had always known that one day he would be required to take his father's place as the Earl of Belcannon. He had not considered it of late, as his father had been in reasonable health for his age and had no physical problems. He had not considered an accident would change his destiny.

The estate was not only a family heritage, it was also a thriving business, employing people from the local village of Glencairn in raising livestock.

Mary had always been aware of this situation arising some day and accepted their lives would change. They would probably not return to Kahuna now. Apart from their friends there, they would miss the warmer weather and river view from their home.

The funeral arrangements were to be organised by Nicola, while Charles attended to the potential mourners. Being an earl meant his father had a wide circle of friends, ranging from politicians to Glencairn villagers who had worked for him. As the family cemetery was at Belcannon, it was natural to hold the memorial service there and not in Glencairn. If the weather was fine, it could be held outside. If not, they could use the ballroom. They had fifty chairs that could be moved as the weather dictated.

The burial day arrived with not a cloud in the sky, even though it was winter. It was cold but fortunately, no rain or snow. God had smiled on them. The first mourners duly arrived. Most women occupied the chairs, as their men preferred to stand. The fifty seats were soon filled, with over a hundred mourners standing behind. The coffin was placed adjacent the plot dug for his burial. The plot was at the end of a line of his ancestors, dating back several hundred years.

The minister opened proceedings with a prayer and then invited Charles to speak on behalf of his family. Mary had helped Charles to prepare his words. He welcomed her help, as he still had trouble coping with his father's sudden death. He spoke clearly with some emotion showing as he related his father's many deeds during his busy life. Nicola did not speak. Several notable businessmen spoke and, finally, an employee.

He surprised everyone with his eloquent words, acknowledging the earl's contribution to the village wellbeing for many years. Few outsiders were aware of the earl's input to the local scene. It varied from him assisting the poor with food or money, to having an additional room added to a single bedroom cottage when the family had children.

The coffin was slowly lowered into the grave, amid bagpipes playing a funeral dirge. The minister recited several prayers, with most mourners joining in. Charles and Mary stepped forward and sprinkled a handful of soil onto the coffin, turned and walked back to the manor without talking, followed by the mourners. Daylight was fading and evening arriving.

Most of the mourners adjourned to the ballroom for refreshments. Scotch flowed freely and soon his friends began telling some stories of the earl's youthful days. He must have been popular with the girls long ago.

A bugle sounded a long G. Charles, and Mary with baby Keith led the mourners to the bank of The Loch. A light breeze ruffled the water with the stars twinkling in the ripples. The view up The Loch was dark with the moonlight showing the outlines of the mountains in the distance. Silence prevailed.

Shamus had resurrected a long forgotten Scottish ritual for the funeral of an earl. Earlier he had a loaded a dinghy with dry branches. He had then towed the dinghy to the centre of The Loch and now he set the branches on fire.

As the dinghy burned, a lone piper, high up in the lookout, played several sombre tunes in keeping with the occasion and surprisingly *Garryowen*, the earl's favourite tune, finishing with *Auld Lang Syne*. The remaining mourners then joined in singing this stirring song. The music and singing were eerie, almost surreal as it echoed over the rippling loch waters. When the piper finished, a drum roll started and continued for ten seconds and abruptly stopped. Silence reigned throughout The Loch.

The people on the shore had tears in their eyes following this dramatic finish. The fire slowly extinguished, as the dinghy vanished beneath the dark waters of The Loch. The new earl carried baby Keith and held Mary's hand as they walked to their future – The Belcannon Manor Estate.

THE EARL IS DEAD. LONG LIVE THE EARL.

EPILOGUE

Charles and Mary did not return to Victoria. The demands and the responsibilities of the estate were paramount. They missed the colony, but Scotland had been the land of their births. They could not leave now. Their lives now had a new focus as they had two more children, both girls.

George eventually married his lady friend. He and his wife visited them in Scotland when he retired. He left Melbourne and settled in a Victorian seaside town to write his memoirs. It was published and helped replenish his retirement funds.

Stephen Stuart and his family eventually purchased their own cattle station in New South Wales. Isobel became a nurse, married a local shearer and had two children. Finlay entered Parliament and married a banker's daughter. They had a son who became a military officer and served in the Boer War.

Mary's parents, Thomas and Stella, became successful in business. Their mare dropped several valuable colts and fillies. Two were gymkhana champions. Charles had donated his horses to the Victorian Mounted Police, and they stayed in Melbourne. Regarding Mary's three hunter horses and Charles two walers, they gave the hunter horses to Stephen and the walers to the Kahuna police.

Murray remained the Kahuna police blacktracker. He was successful in the apprehension of many offenders and was often loaned to help other police stations. Unfortunately, he was shot and killed by a drunken drover. Bessie became a domestic servant for Stephen's family and went with them to their new station.

NOTES

Billy	Australian bushmen's name for a for tea kettle.
Carbine	Short barrelled rifle made for a saddle holster.
Duffer	Cattle duffer. Cattle thief.
Garryowen	Irish jig tune associated with horse riders.
Heads	The name for the narrow opening for sea water at the entrance to Port Phillp Bay in Victoria.
Heel	Master's order given to cattle/sheep dog to get behind them.
Holy Ghost	Christian term changed to Holy Spirit in the 1960's.
Loch	Scottish term for highland lake.
Reef	Sails have canvas strips (reef) on the front. When a sail is lowered, sailors tie the strips. This reduces the effective sail area to collect the wind. This is done to remove a sail, to stop or slow the ship.

Remand	Alleged offender jailed, pending a court hearing.
Sea legs	After being on a ship, a person walks 'Softly, feeling for the moving deck'. Hence the sailors' roll. It takes a day or so to walk normally again when ashore.
Shanks pony	Walking. Not riding a horse.
Sundowner	Australian term for a traveller who arrives at a cattle/sheep station at sundown looking for shelter and food for the night or having a drink at the end of the working day.
Tack room	Storage area for horse saddles, bridles and reins etc.
Waler	A horse bred in New South Wales. Stocky but rugged. Made their reputation during First World War in the Light Horse Regiments in the Sinai Desert.
Waning moon	The time the moon is becoming smaller during the moon phase of a full moon, to a half-moon.

THE AUTHOR

John P F Lynch was educated at St Bernards CBC in Moonee Ponds in Victoria.

He is the great, great, grandson of a Kyneton pioneer, Joseph Hall, who established Windmill Farm in the district in 1849. He built two other nearby farms in the 1850's – Sunbury Lodge and Pine Lodge. He also had land at Phillip Island named Ventnor and at Essendon which became part of the site of Essendon Airport.

The books he has written are primarily based on Australian colonial events in the mid 1800's and WW1. He has travelled several times to the UK and Ireland to discover his family origins and spent his sixty-year aviation career working around the world.

John is an ex-Navy veteran and was President of Romsey R.S.L. for just on ten years and is a Life Member. He joined Macedon Ranges Legacy and served a term as Chairman and was Sergeant of Arms for six years. He is also a Life Member of the Romsey Football/ Netball Club after twelve years as President, Secretary and Committee Member.

Currently, he is Technical Advisor to the Craigieburn War Memorial Remembrance Committee after serving several years as Vice President and is a Life Member.

He has been awarded the Order of Australia, is a Knight of the Order of St John of Jerusalem and is a Fellow of the Royal Victorian Honorary Justice Association.

He has now retired and lives with his wife in the Highlands Retirement Village in Craigieburn Victoria.

OTHER BOOKS

By John P. F. Lynch

The Convict and the Soldier
The Aborigine and the Drover
The Constable and the Miner
The Shearer and the Magistrate
Twice Wounded
Another Australian Eagle.

LOCAL HISTORY BOOKS

St Mary's Parish Lancefield – 1858 to 2006
The Romsey/Lancefield R.S.L. – 1933 TO 2008
The Romsey Football/Netball Club – 1878 to 2009
Joseph Hall. Kyneton Pioneer – 1804 to 1872

AUTOBIOGRAPHY

A Lifetime's Journey